NIGHT OF THE RADISHES

Also by Sandra Benítez

A Place Where the Sea Remembers

Bitter Grounds

The Weight of All Things

NIGHT OF THE RADISHES

Sandra Benítez

AN IMPRINT OF HYPERION
NEW YORK

Library of Congress Cataloging-in-Publication Data

Benítez, Sandra
    Night of the radishes / Sandra Benítez.—1st. ed.
      p. cm.
    ISBN 0-7868-6400-1
    1. Hispanic American women—Fiction. 2. Americans—Mexico—
Fiction. 3. Depression in women—Fiction. 4. Minnesota—Fiction.
5. Mexico—Fiction. I. Title.

    PS3552.E5443 N54 2003
    813'.54—dc21

                                                    2002032830

Hyperion books are available for special promotions and premiums. For details contact Michael Rentas, Manager, Inventory and Premium Sales, Hyperion, 77 West 66th Street, 11th floor, New York, New York 10023, or call 212-456-0133.

FIRST EDITION

10 9 8 7 6 5 4 3 2 1

In loving memory

SUSANA BENITEZ ABLES

my identical twin sister

. . . oh, how much brighter my life,

had you been there to share it . . .

ACKNOWLEDGMENTS

As ever, I'm indebted to Jim Kondrick, beloved husband and first reader, who gives me wise counsel and prompts me to write the best stories I can. Deep gratitude to Ellen Levine for always telling me the truth and for saying the right words through thick and thin. Thank you to Leslie Wells for her keen eye and steadfast support, and to Adrian James for carefully going over every single word. And again, thank you to Bob Miller for keeping a place for me at the table.

I am obliged to the Jerome Foundation for two generous Travel and Study Grants, which made possible long stays in Oaxaca. While there, I was fortunate to meet and be helped by some extraordinary people. Jane and Thorny Robison, owners and operators of La Casa Colonial, a delightful inn where I spent some wonderful days. Thanks to Henry Wangeman and Rosa Blum, owners of Amate Books and Corazón del Pueblo, for providing a place to nourish the soul and please the senses. Thank you to the staff of the American Lending Library, who were so helpful in pointing me in the right direction.

I am blessed with friends who support and inspire me: Mickey Pearlman, my www's: Mary Francois Rockcastle, Patricia Weaver Francisco, Wang Ping, Kate Di Camillo, Faith Sullivan, Alison McGhee, Lorna Landvik, Judith Guest, and Julie Schumacher. Blessings and thanks go to all of you.

Thank-yous as well to dear friends and professionals Ed Bock, Pamela Holt and Lyle Chastain for their help with the little radish-man photo, for library research and for advice with the realities of depression.

Eternal gratitude to the Spirit, without whom my stories would not come.

And finally, thank you, Daddy, for being at my side while I wrote this book, even though you were way up there in heaven. Before you passed you said, "Don't worry, honey, you'll get it done." And now I say to you, "Look, Daddy. I did it."

Night of the Radishes

PROLOGUE

It happens all the time. Women snared by depression. That tight clump of despair that sits on our chests weighing us down, gathering strength, until it spills over, sliding down our cheeks, pooling in our ears if we're in bed, the opportune time for it to show itself. Dark of night. Maybe the winter wind howling outside. Maybe not. Maybe our man breathing noisily beside us. Maybe the kids down the hall, all snugly under their quilts. Maybe the world stopped on its axis the better to hear us moan as helplessness gives way to anger, anger to fury, and fury to the hot flame of rage that makes us throw a hand over our mouths to stifle ourselves, to hold back the murderous impulse to do harm to something or somebody. Ourselves topping the list, of course. We creep cat-like out of bed, hoping to leave despair behind, under the blankets and beside the pillow bunched on the far edge of the bed. But no. Dejection follows as we steal down the cold stairs, the dog trailing sleepily and perplexed after us, the pale moon a crescent framed in the windowpane of the front door, the house ghostly with all our familiar, impassive possessions.

In the living room, the drawn drapes, the plump sofa, the comfy chairs, the tables and their lamps are dark stains against a deeper black. In the dining room, the slice of moon casts a yellow pall over the sturdy rustic table, over the centerpiece fashioned by piling fruit and vegetables upon a French-bread baking tray. In the kitchen, the counters are a dull long smudge, and the Mixmaster, the coffee machine, the blender, rise up against a Talavera-tiled wall. Is all the world, are all the things the world contains, chiding us, saying: Still that long face? Still those tears? Enough already. Enough.

Outside, the incomplete moon casts a milky sheen on the snow heaped so high it will be weeks, months even, before it disappears. Is it this gloom that fuels our unhappiness? The bone-chill of winter? The never-ending snow, first bright and hopeful, then sullied into something unrecognizable? If we wanted, we could fling wide the back door, meet the shocking blast of air, stride across the porch, down the steps and out across the walk. If we wanted, we could fall backward into the snow, the heat in us melting all that our bodies press down upon. As if we were branding irons, we'd hear the hiss our impressions make, watch our sadness rising up like steam around us.

Yes, it's true. It happens all the time, though it's also true we don't usually quit our beds. Most times we muffle sobs with our pillows, asking, What is happening to me? What in heaven's name is wrong? And if we do slip down the stairs, we might tiptoe to the kitchen, look out the window, gaze at the dappled shadows on the lawn if it's not winter, but a kinder season. In the night, the velvety dark lawns roll and dip away from us. Flower beds and shrubs and those glorious trees are lookouts casting shadows. The houses, grand and varied in their presentations, sit mutely by, observing. See that? we might whisper, noting such a peaceful panorama. See how all is well? And then depression turns a small corner. The blues takes a breather, collects itself. But not for long. Not for long.

 Early March in Minneapolis. A cold, raw time, colder and rawer for being the dead of night. Ma is downstairs, dying, and I'm up here, curled like a wounded cat on Hub's bed. Despite the weather, I'm not cold. We've cranked the thermostat up high to keep Ma warm. Besides, there's that hot coal of anger burning in my brain. I wish that, once and for all, I could let loose and open my mouth and send emotion spewing. But no. I'm a good girl. I'm a good girl who keeps her grief, her discontent, trapped inside her, secured in a box, which is locked inside another box, the key tossed long ago into that tangled, impenetrable wilderness that is my psyche. I know all these things about myself because I'm studious and have a career that demands I keep up on such subjects. And so I lie on Hub's bed, a chenille throw wrapped around my stockinged feet, my ear trained to any unusual sounds that might filter up from downstairs. I'm still in the jeans and bulky sweater I put on days ago, when we brought Ma home from the hospital and delivered her into hospice care.

Ma has emphysema. For the past five years, it's been a steady, downhill slide. It's those god-awful cigarettes, of course. Since Maggie's death when we were nine, it seems a cigarette has either dangled from Ma's lips or glowed between two fingers, yellowed with nicotine. The doctor says her lungs are cottage cheese. Listening to her labored breathing is torture, so I've left her with Nikki, the hospice worker, and stolen up here to have a little talk with God. I say, Listen, God, this is Annie Rush. I know Ma's only fifty-eight, but I think she's had enough. So, please God, end Flo Hart's suffering and take her soon. This is what I say, but I don't think I really mean it. I'm only thirty-three, much too young to lose a mother.

The desk lamp casts soft light about the room Ma's never touched since Hub vanished from our lives. On the floor, the same rag rug. On the bed, the bucking bronco spread. On the oak desk, still tucked under the window, my brother's carved initials: HHH, for Hubert Henry Hart. Tacked to the wall, his favorite pennants: the West High Cowboys, the Vikings, the Twins. Adventure stories and travel accounts still crowd the bookshelves, as do manuals on car repair and pamphlets on painting: *How to Paint Hands. How to Paint Torsos. Painting Landscapes. The Magic of Color.* A few of his creations catch dust on the wall: the red barn and the Guernseys standing in the lot, the pond and the cattails surrounding it, the oak tree in full leaf in the backyard of our Saint Peter, Minnesota, farm.

I wish Hub would saunter through the door, pull a book from the shelf—maybe *A Tale of Two Cities*—and hunker down and read to me. "It was the best of times, it was the worst of times." Hub was seventeen when he willfully took off and disappeared. He's been gone long enough. If he walked in this moment, I might consider forgiveness. If my sister, Maggie, were alive, we'd be sticking together like glue. After all, it's the nature of twins to cleave to each other.

I rub my eyes, gritty from lack of sleep. In a week, I've been home once, home being Hopkins, just a quick drive across town, twenty minutes away. When I went back, I hugged the boys maybe too long for Jack's comfort, but never long enough for Will's. After the kids were asleep, Sam and I made love. On my part, a fierce, desperate kind of love, starting in the kitchen and proceeding up the stairs and down the hallway before we tumbled into bed. Afterward, I slept like the dead. Given the situation, no lack of respect intended.

The clock down on the mantel chimes the hour. Five delicate bongs. When we settled Ma into the hospital bed we'd rolled into the front room, I attempted to remove the clock for fear it would disturb her, but Ma wouldn't have it. That thing's all right, she said between wheezes. It reminds me I'm still ticking.

Though it's god-awful early, I want to call Sam. I need to hear his voice. I lie still for a moment, trying to talk myself out of waking him, but then I think, what the heck, and untangle my feet from the blanket and get up. I dig through my purse for my cell phone.

Sam answers on the first ring. "What?" he says, that one word filled with alarm.

"It's okay. She's still struggling. I just needed to hear you. Sorry to wake you."

"Don't be silly." A stifled yawn. "How's she doing?"

"I'm up in Hub's room. Listening to her try to breathe is agonizing."

"I'm so sorry, babe."

"I know." What more is there to say? First, it was Maggie. Next, Pa. Then Hub, performing his own kind of leaving. Now, it's Ma. My world is one giant train wreck, and as ever, I'm the one left standing, the one who cleans up the mess. Damn Hub. Damn Ma, if I want to really tell the truth.

"Babe, you still there?"

"Yeah, it's just that I'm so sad."

After we hang up, I trudge into the bathroom and splash warm water on my face. I wouldn't think of peering into the mirror. I've pulled my hair into a ponytail, but it's still snarled. I smooth it back with a hand. Give the scrunchy holding it up another turn.

Nikki wiggles her fingers in greeting when I walk into the room. She's sitting up, bunched like a sack of grain in the corner of the sofa. The room has an orange glow created by the low-wattage bulbs I've placed in all the lamps. The room smells of exhaustion and effort and of the lavender oil heating in an aromatherapy pot on the built-in hutch that's a part of the dining room. The heady vapor helps to allay the reek of a million cigarettes encrusted into the walls of the house.

The head of Ma's bed is upright; she's propped against pillows. She appears to be sleeping, though her breathing is raspy, an in-and-out effort that vies in volume with the rhythmic whirr and puff of the oxygen tank delivering purified air through the tube clamped at her nostrils. I slip onto the sofa, next to Nikki. "What's happening?"

"She woke up drenched a while ago. Even the bed had to be changed."

I nod. I can hear the lulling sound of the dryer tumbling away in the utility room beyond the kitchen.

"Did you sleep?" Nikki asks.

"No. I don't think I'll ever sleep again."

Now it's Nikki who nods. "There's coffee in the pot." She bends her head toward the hutch.

I pour myself a cup. It warms my hands as I step slowly around the room, watching my shadow cast tall smudges against the wall.

From the bed comes Ma's raspy voice: "You're pacing." She pants as she speaks.

I set the cup down and go to her side. "How you feeling, Ma?"

"Punk."

I lay a hand on my mother's warm brow. I run a hand through her hair, short and thick and swirling with yellow curls. I massage her scalp just the way she likes it.

"You know what?" I murmur, as I had done when each of my babies was at my breast and I rocked and rocked and lost myself in those earnest, innocent gazes. "You're beautiful, Ma."

Ma blinks as if to comprehend, and then comprehending, to object, but then she allows an "Ahhhh."

I take her hands and hold them between my own. I set my lips to them, my mind hurdling over the brown odor of nicotine embedded in her flesh. No amount of scrubbing, of lotion, of perfume, will dispel it. Tonight, I pay it no mind, my thoughts settling instead on the memory of my mother at the stove, at the table, at the washing machine, at the ironing board. My mother in the yard, out in the field, in the barn. My mother busily working, her hands sometimes a blur of activity, some-times moving slowly and methodically; her hands rarely resting as she went about the day, doing the things that needed to be done. "Think, Ma," I say, "think of all you've accomplished with these hands of yours. When we were on the farm, there was the gardening and the cooking and the canning. You did it all, Ma." I blink back tears at the memory of such a place, of the joys and the grief that it contained.

"I did the wash," she whispers.

"And yes, the washing, too. And don't forget the ironing. Tons and tons of it, don't you think? Remember how much Maggie liked her dresses? She was so particular. She liked her dresses . . ."

". . . starched," Ma mutters, "so the skirts would stand out." She lifts her arms to demonstrate, and that might be a smile playing at the corners of her mouth. Soon, she drops her arms, exhausted. She closes her eyes, maybe to the memories.

"Your brother," Ma says, after a moment.

"Hub?"

"Hub didn't like starch."

I chuckle. "Neither did I. It felt too scratchy."

"Your pa didn't, either."

"Yes," I say, but I hadn't known.

"Remember what I told you. About my important papers."

"I know, Ma. They're upstairs in the folder in your desk. Top drawer on the right."

Ma nods. "Don't forget."

"Don't worry. I won't." I had opened the folder once, taken out the living will that both the hospital and the hospice had required. No extraordinary measures, no resuscitation. But the rest of the papers I had not gone through. I simply could not. Somehow, holding these back was like holding Ma back from the abyss over which she teetered. I bring her hand to my lips. "I love you, Ma."

Ma smiles, and mouths the same thing back.

The clock chimes again. When the reverberations die away, she asks, "Is it night or morning?" Each word, each syllable, is surrounded by a gasp.

"It's morning, but don't talk. It takes too much out of you."

"I need to. I need to tell you about Hub."

"What about him, Ma?"

Ma pulls herself up, away from the pillows. "Go up to my closet. Look on the shelf, at the very back."

"Ma, you're wearing yourself out."

"No, listen. There's a cigar box up there. Get it." She collapses against the pillows.

Some minutes later, I say, "Is this what you mean?" I hold the box out toward her. I know this box. It's Hub's old cigar box. On the lid is printed "Winecke & Doerr, since 1873." A wide rubber band stretches around it.

"Open it."

I slip off the band and lift up the lid. Just as I remember, scrawled in black oil pencil on the inside lid are the words "I yam what I yam," then "Hubert Henry Hart, born 1962." There is a drawing of a bent arm with a bulging muscle.

"I yam what I yam." I whisper the words as if they were a mantra.

"It's from Popeye. Remember what you'd say when Hub said that?" She takes little breaths between words.

"What did I say?"

"He'd say, 'I am what I am,' and you'd say, 'You're a can of Spam.' " Ma attempts a chuckle.

"Oh, yes." A surge of feeling fills me, a combination of love for my brother, of longing for his return, of anger that he has left. Left me to cope with Ma without Maggie. With Ma without Pa. Left me to cope with Ma and all that now entails.

Ma points a finger at the box. "Take out the stuff."

There isn't much inside. One marble, an aggie, a Boy Scout neckerchief ring and a Hank Aaron baseball card. There are nuts and bolts and some screws. There are a few postcards, one with a photograph of the Corn Palace in South Dakota.

"There's more." She makes a feeble motion.

I slip the cards out and shuffle through the pictures: a pine forest, a herd of pretty horses, an Indian mound, a lake, a country lane, two cards featuring palm trees and a final one, a resplendent hotel called the Coronado.

"Turn 'em over."

I stare, incredulous. On every one is written: "I yam what I yam." Under the phrase, the little drawing. There is no signature; none is needed. Each card is addressed to Mrs. Florence Hart, here, to this house on Holmes Avenue South, in Minneapolis.

"They're from Hub," Ma says.

"When? When did you get them?" And before Ma can answer, I'm reading the postmarks: 1982, 1985, 1989, and on up to 1997, two years ago. The last card was sent from San Diego, California. The others are from Oregon, Montana, North Dakota, Michigan, Rhode Island, and two from Florida. Miami, to be exact.

"The boy's been traveling," Ma mutters.

I'm stunned. I picture the wide spiral Hub's travel has made: out from Minnesota and then in a clockwise loop around the country. Twenty years gone and only eight cards and his favorite expression to substantiate his absence and his existence. Why did he even bother? And what of Ma's silence about this? "Why didn't you tell me, Ma? You should have told me."

Ma closes her eyes.

I wait for an explanation, but none comes. "Is there more? A letter maybe?"

Ma rolls her head back and forth across the pillow. "That's all there is."

My mother is gravely ill. My mother is dying. These undeniable facts make me hesitate for a moment before I blurt, "You should have told me, Ma. It's not fair you didn't tell me. All those years, don't you think I deserved to know about Hub, too?"

Ma's face is a stone. There is no cracking her. For years and years it has been so.

I lay the cards in the box again, hold it against the place in my chest now guilt-stricken for opening my mouth and letting her know that she has wronged me. I go back to the sofa, to Nikki, who sits, trying to appear as if she hasn't heard a thing.

Across the room, Ma begins to cough. Nikki jumps up. Hurriedly, she gathers supplies and then props Ma up, steadying her. Ma's face turns dark, the cough deep and phlegmy. I can't watch. It's all my fault. Everything's my fault. I go into the kitchen and run water in the sink to drown out what's happening. I gaze out the window. Over the row of salt and pepper shakers Ma liked to collect. Beyond the window frame, the world is an impassive lunar landscape. Rigid. Desolate. A lot like me, I think.

Nikki brings in the refuse. "Your mother's asking for you."

"That was a bad spell, wasn't it?"

"It was bad." Nikki stuffs the trash into the bin. She scrubs her hands in the sink, then comes over and lays an arm across my shoulders. "Sweetie, I think it's getting to be time for the morphine."

My stomach twists. I puff out a breath. I know what morphine means: the real beginning to the real end.

"You know she'll be more comfortable that way."

"I know. It's just that . . ."

Nikki enfolds me in her plump arms. "Listen. Why don't you go up and get some sleep. It'll do you a world of good. I'll be here till eleven."

For a moment, I lay my head on her shoulder. She smells of lotion. Jergens lotion with that almond scent. "When would you start the morphine?" I ask.

"I tell you what. You go up and get some rest and leave everything to me. Okay?"

"Okay." I try to smile, but it's useless. Instead, I give Nikki a hug and go out to my mother, who is calling me.

I pull the chair up close. "What is it, Ma?"

"Promise me."

"What, Ma? Anything."

"Promise you'll find your brother." With great effort, she sits and tries to narrow the distance between us. "After I'm gone, promise me you'll find him."

I hesitate. Again, it's left to me. Always me.

Ma's deep green eyes burrow into mine. "Promise me."

"I promise, Ma. I promise."

Ma falls back against the pillows. "Yes," she says, in one long and lonely breath.

I lie on Hub's bed again, cocooned in the blanket. Bone-tired, I allow myself to drift. I float into a dream. Or maybe it's a memory, a memory as real as a dream. As real as a motion picture I am watching.

Maggie and me on the farm. A hot summer day. The summer we were eight.

Maggie was in the tree house. I climbed up toward her, using the three rungs nailed solidly into the thick trunk of the oak, going up toward the tree house that Pa, along with Hub's help, had built at the start of summer. Maggie and I had clamored for such an extravagance since the summer before, when we had spied one in Ma's *Midwest Magazine.* That one was built in a chestnut whose branches had been pruned and cut back for the purpose of allowing a little gabled house to exist inside its green canopy. When I brought up the subject at the supper table, using the glossy photo for what I thought would be the deal clincher, Ma had glanced at the picture and shaken her head. "Look how they just ruined a perfectly good tree," she said.

"Aw, Ma, it's not ruined," I said. "See all the green leaves."

"No, Ma, it's not," Maggie said right after. "See the thick branches."

Ma continued to pass the food around. The bowl of heaping mashed potatoes. The green beans with onions. The platter of fried Spam, a family favorite. "Besides, a tree house is dangerous," Ma said. "That's all I need. For my girls to fall out of a tree and go landing on their heads."

"Their heads can take it," Hub said. "Pass the babies' butts." He was referring to the basket of steaming Parker House rolls with that crease right down the middle.

Pa said nothing after Hub's remark; he only smiled around a mouthful of Spam.

It had taken us the whole of that summer, the winter and spring as well, to whine and complain and beg our way into winning Ma's approval. The following summer, the year we were eight, maybe in order to hear the last of it, she said, "Well, if the men are willing to build it, and they don't set it up too high, I guess it's okay."

The tree house was more than okay. It was not as fancy as the one in the magazine, but it was our tree house, and as such, it was perfect. It consisted of a wide platform and slanted walls that formed an enclosure that looked like a teepee. There was a wall at the back, but the front was open, and we could look across the yard to the flower beds and out over the eastern field and its green expanse of tall, blond-tasseled corn, to the thick copse of oaks and poplars that bordered the far side of it. Beyond that, if you squinted hard and used a bit of imagination, you might make out the spire of Gustavus Adolphus College, the seat of education that sits on the hill and is the pride of Saint Peter, Minnesota.

That afternoon was hot and sticky and the cicadas were humming their whirring songs somewhere in the bushes and the trees. Cosmo, our black Labrador, stood at the base of the tree, looking up. His tongue hung sideways out of his mouth and he was panting. "Go away now," I said over my shoulder to him. I didn't want him whining to climb up or barking for us to get down. I was in my blue shorts and my red spaghetti-strapped tank top, my favorite outfit that year. My hair was gathered up into ponytails that seemed to spring out of the sides of my head. My scalp was perspiring as I scaled the tree, and sweat slipped down my forehead and stung my eyes. I got to the top and climbed in next to Maggie, whose thick, taffy-colored hair was also pulled into two ponytails. She wore the same outfit as me. The only difference between us was that Maggie's Keds had red laces, while mine had green ones. I looked down at Cosmo, who was still at the base of the tree, his tail a metronome. "You lie down, boy. You'll get heatstroke if you don't calm down." I swiped my forehead with the back of a hand. "It's too hot. That's what it is."

Maggie was digging into a plastic bag she'd brought up. "I got cookies," she said. "Oatmeals and some peanut butters." She dipped her head in the direction of two cans of Coca-Cola setting in the corner. "I got sodas, too, but they're probably hot by now."

"Well, I got something much better," I said. I had strapped my backpack on, and now I pulled it off and unzipped the top. "Guess what I got in here."

Maggie craned her neck to get a look before voicing an opinion, but I wouldn't allow even as much as a peek. "You guess."

"Okay. It's a new Chevy car, like the one we saw in town yesterday." We had gone into Saint Peter with Ma to pick up some rickrack at the five-and-dime. The red Chevy with the gleaming trim had been parked there, nose first, up to the curb, when we pulled up in front of

the store. "I wish we had a car like that," Maggie had said to Ma. What
we had for vehicles was an old Ford truck with major rust and an even
older panel truck the color of overcooked asparagus. "We could use
something new. Something in a fashionable color." Maggie had learned
the word "fashionable" the week before at school, and she was pepper-
ing a great number of her sentences with it. She did that with many
new words, the ones that caught her fancy. This week it was "fashionable," last week it was "incorrigible." Who knew what next week would
bring.

"No, silly," I said, "guess again."

"Okay. Then how about a wardrobe filled with summer dresses."

"Nope. You lose," I said. "Close your eyes."

Maggie craned her neck again.

"I said close your eyes."

Maggie obeyed me this time, something she usually did. "Okay.
But you better hurry up."

I reached into the bag and pulled out a square cigar box. On the lid
it said "Winecke & Doerr, since 1873." Under that, "Longfellows." A
wide rubber band was stretched around the box to keep it shut. "You
can look now."

Maggie opened her eyes and gasped. "That's Hub's!"

"I know," I said, "I crawled under his bed to get it. What a stupid
hiding place. It's a mess under there." I used a hand to brush off my
tank top. "Very very dusty."

"Hub's going to kill us."

"He's not going to know," I said, slipping off the rubber band and
lifting up the lid. Scrawled in black oil pencil on the inside of it were
the words "I yam what I yam," then, "Hubert Henry Hart, born 1962,"
like he was some famous historical person, and then, "Keep Out! And

That Means YOU!" For proof of power, there was a drawing of a bent arm and a bulging muscle.

Though he was eleven, Hub didn't scare me. I poked a bold finger through his treasures. There were three silver dollars, four large marbles, aggies from the looks of them, a Boy Scout neckerchief ring and a square-sided carpenter's pencil. There were baseball cards of Hank Aaron, Mickey Mantle and Roberto Clemente. Postcards with pictures of Mount Rushmore, the Empire State Building and the Corn Palace in South Dakota. There were nuts and bolts and some screws, all loose so that they rattled around. A partially smoked cigarette with a blackened stubby end and a book of Hy-Vee matches, half of them struck. I lifted the cigarette as if it were a bug I had hold of. "Pretty good blackmail material, don't you think?"

Maggie nodded. "Ma'd kill Hub if she knew."

I laid the evidence back in the box. I continued rummaging through it, coming to a slender cylinder with a lens on the end that brought a kaleidoscope to mind. I raised it to one eye and squeezed shut the other. I peered into the barrel and adjusted the lens: a half-naked woman popped into view. She was doing the hula upon a stage and she had big boobs and they jiggled as she danced. "Oh boy!" I said. "A naked lady." I twirled the ring that held the lens in place, which caused the girl to dance even more provocatively.

"Let's see. Let me see," Maggie said.

I handed the instrument over and watched Maggie peer into the thing. Maggie's mouth was hanging open. As she turned the lens, her mouth grew even wider.

"It's a lady from Hawaii," I said. "In Hawaii they go around naked." I knew they did the hula in Hawaii, this I had learned in social studies class. But the "naked lady" part was just something I supposed. While

Maggie was occupied with the kaleidoscope, I came upon an envelope in Hub's cigar box. The envelope was fat and cushiony. I lifted the flap and extracted a length of cotton that had been doubled to form a pouch. Lying upon the cotton was a perfectly formed sea horse. "Oh!" I exclaimed. "Look how pretty." The sea horse was as delicate as lace. It had a curlicue for a tail and its mouth looked like the end of a miniature horn. Maggie and I took turns holding it in our palms. "I got a notion to keep it," I said.

"You better not," Maggie replied. "It's Hub's."

"Maybe you're right." I laid the sea horse back upon its cotton bed. I covered it up as if drawing a blanket over someone sleeping. I slipped the pouch back into the envelope.

"But look at this," Maggie said. Her eyes were wide as she held something up. It was a key ring with a very small key.

"My diary key!" I exclaimed. "Let me have it." For weeks and weeks the little key had been missing. I had looked for it all over the house, asked everyone about it, but they all denied having it or seeing it. I had even begun to doubt Maggie. Now here the key was. Hub had been the culprit. Maggie handed it over. "The big ole rat," I said.

"You must've suspected all along that the key was in there," Maggie said. "That's why you took Hub's treasure box from under his bed, right?" Her face was a study in earnestness. Those green ingenuous eyes. Those brown freckles marching across the peachy bridge of her nose. That tawny hair shot through with gold.

Looking at Maggie, it was as if I were looking into my own face. I lowered my head and mumbled a "yes," although it wasn't true. I had gone after the box out of mere curiosity, maybe even spite. I had seen the way Hub protected it. Had caught him once, as I passed the open door of his room, lying halfway off his bed, his arm tucked beneath, as if concealing something there. Luckily, he had not seen me. Luckily, today he had gone off with Pa to the feed store and I knew I had a few hours to satisfy my curiosity.

"Since he took my key, I'm keeping his sea horse," I said, figuring in this way I'd even things out. After all, because of him, I'd been kept from writing in my diary for weeks because it was locked and I didn't want to break the clasp. Still, despite all this, I felt guilty. Guilty, because I was taking something on the sly, something that did not belong to me. Guilty, because now I was as bad as Hub.

I am shaken awake, and for the briefest of moments, I think it's Hub standing over me, calling, Hurry, hurry, it's Ma. But no one is there. Only stillness in Hub's room and an urging presence. Is that you, Maggie? I ask, silently.

I fly down the stairs to find Ma's face, purple as eggplant. How can flesh be such? Ma claws at her throat, fighting for air. Nikki clamps the oxygen mask over Ma's face and she claws at that, too.

I clamber into Ma's bed. I scoot behind her, legs spread wide, draw the wisp of my mother's body against myself. "I'm here, Ma. I'm here."

Ma is a board.

"Let go, Ma, let go."

Unbending.

"You've done enough, Ma."

Rigid.

"You've been a good ma. The best."

A slight easing.

"I'm sorry, Ma. I love you."

A sudden collapse, like a dam breaking.

"Tell Maggie I love her."

The head rolls back onto my shoulder.

"Tell her I miss her."

One last exhalation . . .

"Ask Maggie to forgive me" . . . before it is over.

 We hold Ma's wake in Saint Peter, Minnesota, at Winston's Funeral Home, in the very same parlor that had once held Maggie's casket, and later, Pa's. The room is filled with flowers: bouquets in wicker baskets as well as two sprays of blossoms wired to tall frames and in glass vases. Inside and out, the air is chill. Sam is beside me; we both stand alongside Ma's open casket, looking away. I can't bear to lay eyes on my mother's body. She is thin as fence wire, her face leathery and mapped with wrinkles. No amount of cream or powder can erase the devastation cigarettes can exact.

People line up and approach me. I am truly grateful for the effort some have made to attend a funeral fifty miles from home. Old Saint Peter neighbors are few in attendance; after all, it's been twenty-three years since Ma and Pa sold the farm and moved to the Twin Cities. But some have remembered, and they have come. It takes so much effort to be gracious. I accept the words being offered. I am touched by the quick and clumsy embraces. Mercifully, only one person asks about Hub, and I make up a lie to excuse his absence.

The line wanes and Sam and I are a raft on open water. Despite my cowl-necked sweater and my blazer, I can't keep from shivering. "Here," Sam says, noticing. He takes my hand and warms it in his own. "I want to get out of here," I whisper.

"I know." He circles an arm around my waist.

Across the room, on a green leather couch, my boys sit with Milly Innes, our next-door neighbor and the kids' self-appointed aunt. The boys are in their new suits with the little ties, and they look so sweet and fine. At nine, Jack's face, like Sam's, is all angles and planes. He has Sam's dark hair and dark eyes and those incredible lashes. Jack sits ramrod straight, soberly taking all this in. A year younger than his brother, Will slumps against Milly, as though to be shored up. He's my little pudding boy. He still giggles when I call him this. Seeing him there, it's as if I'm gazing at my own self, sitting on the same couch years and years before.

Back then, at Maggie's funeral, I kept by Pa's side. He sat on the couch like a cricket, his long bony legs crooked, the knobs of his knees jutting through the fabric of his blue shiny suit. I had worn the pink fuzzy sweater set given me for my ninth birthday on April 24, a month earlier. Red hearts were embroidered along the neck of the pullover; the cardigan featured tiny, pearlized heart buttons. I wore raspberry corduroy slacks with the stitched hearts along the pocket edges and new pink ankle socks with winged hearts. My shoes were the same old Mary Janes I'd had since forever. I remember I kept my feet poked back against the bottom of the couch for fear Ma would notice them. Ma had said to shine them, but I didn't do it. The shoes looked dull, as dull as I felt. Part of the reason I felt dull, part of the reason my mouth was cottony, was because when Doc Nygren drove out to the farm, he took one look at me and shook some pills onto Ma's palm. "Cut some in half. Give one of those to Annie. You, dear Florence, take a whole one." All in all, I'd had three halves: one the day Maggie died, then one the next day, then one just before the funeral. That morning, Ma had set the blue jagged-edged pill next to my juice glass. She hadn't turned toward the stove until I washed it down.

At Maggie's funeral, sitting next to Pa, I kept my hands bunched in my lap, my fingers curled under, lest someone notice my fingernails, which four days before, I had painted turquoise. It was a new color Maggie and I had found at Richert's Dime Store. It was called "Sea Breeze." I snuck a peek at my fingers. The nails were short and ragged. The polish was flaking off. I poked my fingers back into a ball again. I glanced up and looked across the room, at Maggie's coffin, resting on a platform against the wall. The coffin was sealed. A spray of yellow and white roses lay like an aromatic blanket upon it. A wide satin ribbon trailed toward the floor. The words "Beloved Daughter, Beloved Sister. In Our Hearts Forever" were etched on the ribbon with gold glitter. When I dressed, I had carefully counted the number of hearts I was wearing. There were fifty-three, fifty-four if you included my own beating heart. These were all the hearts that I possessed. Enough, I prayed, to hold Maggie forever.

"I need some coffee," Pa said, and I nodded. "I'll get you some, Pa." I welcomed the occasion to go across the room, away from the sight of the coffin, to the cart that held the big silver coffee urn and the hot-cups, the containers of cream and sugar. Pa shifted in his seat as I stood. He started to say something and I read his mind: "I know, you want it black."

Pa tried to smile in gratitude, but his lips remained in the grim, straight line in which he'd set them three days ago. He kneaded the back of one hand with the other. Over and over, this slow pitiful movement.

I went to get Pa's coffee, making my way around the people. I kept my head down, avoiding eye contact to deny any opportunity for someone to engage me. When I got to the coffee cart, Hub was there, pouring himself a cup. He was tall, like Pa, but not quite as cricketlike. He was wearing his dark corduroys, a white shirt and a very narrow tie.

"You can't drink coffee," I said.

"Why not?"

"You're only twelve."

"So? What does that have to do with it?" Hub dumped three tea-spoons of sugar into his cup and stirred and stirred with a plastic stick. "Besides, I'm almost thirteen."

I shrugged, because if I stopped to think of it, being twelve, being almost thirteen, drinking coffee, stirring sugar into coffee with a stick, it all held no meaning. Not after what had happened out in the field three days ago.

"Take a cup to Pa," I said. "He wants it black. I'm going to the bathroom."

"Again?" Hub said. "You've made three trips already."

"So?" I said. "What does that have to do with anything?"

In the bathroom, I went to the farthest stall, closed the door and threw the lock. I sat on the toilet. Luckily these had lids and were not the open kind, so I could sit cross-legged so that no one would find me. If someone tried to enter and then rattled the lock, I would say nothing. If they went on to look under the door, and the stall appeared empty, and if they went back to rattling, I'd say nothing some more.

I bent my head over my lap. My hair was long to my shoulders and I had not gathered it back and so it hung like a curtain on each side of my face. It felt good to be hidden like this behind a screen of thick blond hair. I worked on my fingernails, picking away at the polish. Little turquoise chips peeled away, collecting on the pink field of my trousers.

Now, so many years later, Sam gives me a little shake. "Annie? Are you okay?"

"Oh," I say, taking in a quick breath. The memory of Maggie's wake has been so real, I have to turn to this current coffin to regain my bearings, to see my mother in it. Her hands are entwined. So clean and so still.

I lean into Sam, feeling like the small girl I once was. I take his hand and squeeze it, not only for support, but to keep myself anchored. To keep myself from flying off across the room and into the bathroom, into the last stall, where I would lock myself in and pull my legs up. Bend my head over my broken heart.

 After the funeral, I'm a much-used paper towel, the generic, flimsy kind. I want to squeeze myself out, toss myself into the trash can. Ma's gone and now there's no one in this world who's known me from the start. No one who can take the questions that, until this time, it never occurred to me to ask: Did you know you'd have twins? What did Pa think about it? Was Hub jealous when we came? Did you breast-feed Maggie and me? Did we suck our thumbs? Were we colicky, fretful babies? To be sure, not big questions, but ponderable ones, now that they'll go unanswered. I believe I can begin to understand what people mean when they say not to wait until it's too late to open yourself up and be honest with your loved ones. Ma and I, we were always so closed up with each other. So closed up to our own feelings as well. Shame, remorse, guilt, regret. The big four of my emotional pain. Add anger to that, follow it up by the shame that expressed anger always brings, and you have my own special vicious cycle. All of it boiling down to one big huge thing: depression.

After the funeral, I push myself to rise early to see Sam off to work and the boys off to school. I plod about the kitchen in my furry moose-head slippers, in pajamas and Sam's flannel shirt for a robe. I have been away so much during Ma's final days that I try making up for it with hearty breakfasts: eggs, bacon or fried Spam, stacks of buttered toast. Sometimes, I add a pan of hash browns. Sometimes, I make waffles. I pour coffee into Sam's cup and juice into Jack's and Will's glasses, refreshing them as if I were a waitress. I ignore Sam's protestations: For heaven's sake, Annie, stay in bed. I'll take care of it. Or, Cereal and toast would be just fine. Or, Here, have some of this yourself. But no. I can't help myself. Mea culpa, mea culpa, I think, smiling lamely and poking with the spatula through the eggs I'm scrambling in the pan. I don't care to eat. It's been weeks since I've had an appetite. These days, all I can muster is to sip black coffee while at the stove, or while I'm perched on a kitchen chair, feeling that at any moment I might totally lose my mind.

This morning I watch the three of them at the table. Sam in his dark suit that will see him through a day of work at his downtown bro-kerage. He's tall, his flesh firm and deliciously meaty; this is what I've always thought. I love the taste of him. I love his dark hair, short and spiky and thick. I love the feel of his hair between my fingers. But all that was then, weeks ago, before the sky fell in. Now, it takes all my strength not to pretend to be asleep when he reaches for me in bed. Sometimes, I have to bite my lip not to lash out at him. Sometimes, I lash out no matter what.

A few days ago, he was fixing a leaky toilet. He asked me to hold up the float ball, so he could see to install the tank ball. Standing there, pulling up the contraption, I could feel the anger rise in me as Sam took his sweet, methodical time. When his fingers fumbled for the third time with the tiny, slippery screws, I pushed him aside and yelled,

"Here! Stand back! Let me do it!" And I was just as mean to Jack the day he came home from school and tossed his coat down on the couch. I pointed to the hall closet. "Yeah, yeah," he said, and I swear I heard a snarl in his voice, saw a sneer in his eyes that made me hiss and spit at him, too. I don't know. These days, ugliness swirls inside my head, threatening to spill like some major industrial accident.

Now, the boys bend their heads over their breakfasts. They wear bright-colored pullovers. Jack's is blue. Will's is green. In contrast to past times, my men eat carefully and quietly, looking up periodically from their plates to cast concerned glances at me, seemingly taking measure of my mercurial moods. Can't say that I blame them. I'm smiling bravely one minute, my eyes tearing up the next. Even Elvis, our old Australian herder, points his head cautiously in my direction from his place next to the side of the refrigerator, the spot where the warm air seeps onto the floor.

After breakfast, and when homework and backpacks have been gathered, I kiss the boys at the back door and watch them rush down the walk toward Sam's Subaru. It is he who drops them off at school each morning and I who pick them up in the afternoon. Elvis lumbers out after them, sniffing the bracing air and looking for a good place to do his post-breakfast business. The back porch light is on, but the morning itself is still shadowy. The yews lining the walk are dusted with fresh snow. So are the pines, the thick branches of the oaks, elms and poplars growing so abundantly in the neighborhood. The small hills and valleys that make up the yard are iced like a cake.

"See you this afternoon," I call out, as the boys wave behind them and then clamber into the car. Today, it was Will's turn to use the remote on the key ring set to open up the car.

At the back door, Sam sidles up behind me. For a moment, I lean against him, but then I turn in the circle of his arms and lay my face against his chest. He smells of the musky aftershave he habitually uses. He is solid and real and true. For these things I am profoundly grateful, but lately, expressing this gratefulness, demonstrating it, seems almost impossible.

"Will you be okay today?" he mumbles against the top of my head.

All I can do in response is nod.

He steps back from me. He takes my face in his hands and looks into my eyes. "I love you, cutie. I love you forever. This is one guy who'll never leave you. You can count on it, okay?"

I hear the little sound I make, like a hurt animal being stroked. I lower my head onto his chest again. The knot in my throat is almost painful.

Out on the driveway, Jack calls from the car. "Daaaaaaaad!"

I lift my head. "Go, go."

"You'll be okay?"

"I'll be okay."

Waving all the while, I watch the car back down the driveway. When it rolls down the road, I whistle for Elvis and we both climb the stairs and trudge into the bedroom. I fall back into the warm nest of my bed. Elvis collapses at the foot of it, as though his world, too, had caved in on him. I've kept the drapes pulled. In the corner, the humidifier provides a white noise that for days has not soothed me. I burrow under the covers, forcing my mind to picture a wide black slate that I try to wipe clean of the terrifying images that rise up to overtake me: Maggie on the tractor. Pa down in the basement with the rifle. Ma choking to death a week ago. The image of Hub, as well. Hub somewhere in the world, free of family cares and obligations. The thought of my lost brother so blissfully disconnected further darkens my mood. I

curl up into a ball, closing out both memories and realities. Despite trying to hold her back, my sister comes to me.

Me and Maggie and the mirror game.

Me and Maggie facing each other, both standing straight, shoulders back, heads up. "I'm a mirror," we say simultaneously.

We hold each other's gaze. The same sea-green eyes and caramel-
colored hair. Same round faces. Same pale freckles over the wide bridges
of our identical noses.

We lift our arms, bend our elbows, palms exposed to one another.
Now we are trees. I move right, Maggie left, our images swaying in
unison.

Now we are birds, our undulating arms flying us anywhere.

To the land of Nod. To the land of Gitche Gumee. To the land over
the rainbow.

I am Maggie, I say.

I am Annie, Maggie says.

We are we forever.

Tears flow over, running down my cheeks and pooling in my ears.
I need my sister. I want what, in a spring morning's moment, was cruelly wrenched from me: a sister for comfort and consolation. A sister to
share my new orphan-ness. I use the edge of the sheet to stanch my
tears. At the window, the light now spills earnestly around the drapes.
The blue-flowered boudoir chair is more than a dark bundle in the corner, the dresser more than a long slash against the wall. In the mirror
above it are reflected the family photos hanging over the bed. Framed
faces emerge, like spirits showing themselves: Jack and Will in the
canoe up at the lake last year. Sam and me lying in the hammock under
the trees. Eons ago, Ma and Pa sitting at the kitchen table, their eyes on
each other. Hub pitching hay in the barn loft. Me and Maggie in the
tree house.

I heave a sigh. To the air in the room, to Maggie, who veils herself in it, I say, "Let's pack up and go to Gitche Gumee." I picture myself far away, in some foreign land, where I can . . . Where I can do, what? Truth is, I don't know. Truth is, I don't know what to do with myself.

The phone rings on the bedside table. I grope for the receiver. "Hello."

"It's me," Milly Innes says from next door. "How you doing?"

"I'm whale shit at the bottom of the ocean."

"That bad?"

"That bad."

"Want me to walk over?"

"That's okay." I yawn. "I have to get up. I need to get over to Ma's house. I have a million things to do over there."

"I could help you with that, you know."

"Thanks, but today is paperwork day. Actually, it's read-the-will day." Since Ma's death, I've resisted opening the folder that contains a copy of her will. It frightens me to do it. I fear what I might find there. I hope to God that her house has not been compromised. Five years ago, when Sam and I found our house in Hopkins, Ma surprised us with $50,000 for a down payment. We both were flabbergasted at the amount. Where could the money have come from but from a second mortgage? we thought. Fearing Ma would rescind the gift if we inquired directly, I offered mild protestations, but Ma had insisted. "There's plenty where that came from," she said, and greedily I believed my mother's white lie and gave in, the lust for my dream house driving my decision. What had I been thinking? It shames me to know I had taken such clear advantage of my mother.

I say into the phone, "I'm getting up. Getting any sleep is impossible." I throw off the blankets and pull myself up to sit on the edge of the bed. "There. I'm up."

Milly says, "Are you sure you don't want company?"

"No. It's okay. One thing, though. If I get deep into things over at Ma's, could you pick the kids up at school?"

"Of course. Stay as long as you want over there. I'll tend to the boys here."

"I don't know what I'd do without you, Mil." Milly is in her late sixties. Age-wise she could be my mother. In a sense, she has been, will ever be. Truth is, I'd be lost without her. When Sam and I moved into the house, it was Milly who knocked on the door and thrust a basket of goodies into my arms. Milly who walked me around the neighborhood, pointing out each house and its occupants. Milly who hosted a back-yard get-together so Sam and I could meet them all. "Mil," I add, before ringing off, "you're the best."

"Ah, get out'a here," Milly says. And even over the phone I can hear her smiling.

A long, hot shower helps lift my spirits. I catch my hair up in a ponytail and pull on jeans, a long-sleeved T-shirt, plus my favorite big sweater. I head downstairs, to the study. I love my room. I love the books, the framed photos, the art objects. I love the large painting hanging on the north wall. I bought it fourteen years ago, in Cuernavaca, Mexico, when I lived with the Lopez Mela family for a semester of my junior year at the university. The painting shows a cobalt sky sprinkled with silvery stars. Sometimes, when I'm at work here, I like to gaze at the painting and let my eyes go soft. I imagine myself soaring off into that vast serene blueness. If I could, I'd take off into it right now, but no, work looms. To procrastinate, I straighten my desk, which needs no straightening. I open my daily planner to the crossed-out squares with the NOT WORKING scrawled across them. Last week, this week, next week and the one after that. I am a freelance corporate trainer who works from my home office when not traveling around the country. I have given myself plenty of time: a month free from boarding airplanes, from conducting workshops, from attending meetings, from writing reports. I plan to spend the time going through Ma's things, settling her affairs.

Top on my list of priorities is readying Ma's house for sale. Located in the desirable Uptown area, the house will fetch a handsome price. The money will certainly pay off Ma's second mortgage. Also, difficult as it may be, I'll start the search for Hub. No matter how angry I am at what he did and did not do, the fact is, Hub is now my only living relative. Because of it, I'm going to work on allowing myself to throw a small token of love his way. I'll try, but I won't make any promises.

Elvis shuffles in. He nudges my thigh with his graying muzzle. I close my agenda and give him a pat. "You want to take a ride, boy? You want to go in the car?" At the sound of the word "car," Elvis peels his lips back and smiles, an expression you could easily mistake for a snarl. He snorts and heads for the kitchen and the back door. I trail him through the living room with its river-stone fireplace, with the plump and colorful furniture, the tables and the lamps. I go through the dining room, catching the bright light of morning spilling from the window onto the sturdy rustic table.

In the kitchen, the room gleams with cheerfulness and the reflection of the sun off the snow outside. I pause at the big bulletin board attached to the side of the refrigerator. On it are posted the kids' activities, the who, the what, the where. On the space allowed for notes, I scribble, "I'm at Ma's," not because anyone will find the message before I get home, but simply because there is solace in writing the word "Ma."

 Ma's house was built in the 1930s. It's a dove-gray two-storied stuccoed bungalow with a wide front porch. The porch is not enclosed; it holds a slat-backed wooden swing that over the years and in the areas that catch the sun has turned from hunter green to a shier hue of it. I park myself on the swing, resting my feet on the lip of the short wall that serves as a railing, my feet on the spot where I've always placed them, whether booted, as they are now, or shoeless. With time and usage, the spot has grown scuffed, and there is even a slight depression that serves for a place marker. It has secretly pleased me that Ma never went after the spot with touch-up paint, that she never was irked by my habit of sitting here. Being here now, my feet set upon such a prescient place, I imagine all the girls I have been while sitting here: daughter, sister, wife, mother. Each phase like a different lifetime.

I'm still in my coat, but I should slip out of it. The day has turned glorious. The sun is high and the sky is brilliant blue with not a cloud in sight. It has snowed overnight, just a dusting, but enough to frost the old slushy stuff with glittering hopefulness. Still, the snow is melting rapidly. I have stopped at Dunn Bros. Coffee, a block over, and bought a tall latte and a cranberry scone. It's almost noon, so this is either a late breakfast or lunch. As I eat, I keep an eye on Elvis, who sits back on his haunches at the top of the path that leads to the sidewalk. He makes a comic figure, like one of those bobble-head dolls, the way he follows the traffic hissing up and down the street. I take my time, putting off the inevitable fact that soon I'll let myself into the house, pick up the mail that might have accumulated under the slot in the front door, go up the stairs and into Ma's bedroom, to the desk under the window where, in the top drawer on the left, Ma's important papers are kept.

Lillian Kissell, the next-door neighbor, ambles up the sidewalk. She's a spry old woman, in her late seventies perhaps. She has a round, doughy face, accented by the triangle of scarf she wears like a babushka. Her small eyes, the color of faded denim, hold a gaze as intense as a wren's. Elvis sashays over to greet her, his back end swaying, the very reason for his name. The two are not strangers to each other, for Mrs. Kissell has been a frequent visitor to the house. During Ma's illness, she brought over casseroles and salads and pies. "Here, my dear, Flo," she always said, "here's a bit of sustenance."

"Morning, Mrs. Kissell," I call, giving a little wave. I sit up straight, lower my feet to the porch floor.

The neighbor comes to stand at the bottom of the stoop. "How's my girl?" she asks, using her old familiar appellation. Mrs. Kissell has lived next door for all the time Ma has owned the house. Mrs. Kissell has known me since I was eleven. It was to Mrs. Kissell's house that I bolted the evening the rifle shot down in the basement blasted apart what was left of my family.

"I could be better," I reply.

"And you will. No doubt about it. Just give it some time."

I nod and lift my paper cup. "I got coffee at Dunns."

"I see that." Mrs. Kissell bends to rub Elvis behind the ears. "What do you think you'll do with your mother's house?" she asks after a moment.

I set the paper cup on the porch railing. I brush crumbs from my coat. "I'm going to sell it."

"I'm not surprised. You'll get a good price. There isn't a year goes by that people don't knock on my door, saying they want to buy. Not long ago, one young couple said they'd give me two hundred and fifty thousand dollars. Cash, they said." She shakes her head as if in disbelief. "Imagine that. I bought my place in the fifties. The husband and me, we paid fifteen thousand for it." She laughs when she states the figure.

I chuckle, too. "Ma and Pa paid twenty-five for this one, I think. That was in the early seventies."

"My girl, we're sitting on gold mines, that's what we are." Lillian Kissell turns to look up the street, as if taking stock of all the other gold mines lined up, one after the other, down the block. "Well, I'm off," she says. "You know where I am, if you need anything."

"You're an angel," I say, watching her go.

In reply, Mrs. Kissell bats the air dismissively behind her.

Well, I think, the time has arrived. I haul myself up off the swing. I pat the side of my leg. "Come on, boy," I call to Elvis. "Time to face the music."

I slide open my mother's top desk drawer. I expect to see a row of fat Pendaflex files inside, and these *are* there, but now I note that they've been pushed back to accommodate what looks like a large black notebook, the kind with a sturdy, dimpled cover. It's lying on its side. How has this gotten here? I've never seen it before. It certainly wasn't here when I riffled through the files for Ma's living will. Did Ma climb out of her hospital bed, scale the stairs and come lurching down the hall to place this here herself? For Ma, the trip might as well have been to the top of Mount Everest. I set the notebook on the desk. I open it.

On the inside cover is written: *"For my children, Hubert Henry and Ann Margaret. To be read after my death."* Ma's signature is below. It's been made by a shaky hand.

My heart knocks against my chest. I fan the edges of the pages with a thumb. The notebook is thick. All its pages are plumped by the impression a sharp pencil point has made as it crossed them. I try to swallow, but my mouth has gone as dry as a boxful of nails. I turn to the first page. There is a date there: June 5, 1997. Ma's writing follows. This writing is in my mother's familiar hand: the small, tight letters, all slanting to the left.

I have enfasema. I found out today. This is not a surprise. Whats a surprise is the doc says my lungs look like cottage cheese. I dont want to picture that, but I guess he should know. He did some kind of test and looked in there himself. It doesnt matter. Whenever the end comes, I guess Im ready to go.

I pass a hand over my mother's writing. That old habit of hers of never bothering with apostrophes has always been irksome, but now circumstance has turned the quirk into something intimate and endearing. Bittersweet. I read on.

But before I go, I want to write things down to set the record straight. For myself. Maybe even for Hub and Annie. Lord knows

they both could use some explanations. All these years I kept silent.
Its not my style to talk things out. When trouble comes, I think its
best to bite your lip and go on.

The page ends and I'm totally perplexed. What did Ma mean about
"setting the record straight," about keeping "silent"? Keeping silent
about what? Reading Ma's words is like hearing her talk. Downstairs,
on the mantel, the clock reverberates the half hour. "Ma?" I say. "Is that
you, Ma?"

Elvis is stretched like a warm rug beside the chair. When I speak, he
lifts his head and looks up at me. "It's okay, boy," I say. In response, he
thumps his tail against the side of the desk, stretches his lips back and
smiles. He lays his head down again.

I turn around in the chair to peruse the room. "I know you're here,
Ma," I say.

Ma's everlasting reserve is in the tightly furled buds of the pink
roses blooming perpetually on the room's wallpaper. Her scent stop-
pered in the perfume bottle resting on the mirrored oval on the dresser.
Her footsteps traced upon the nap of the rug that lies alongside her bed.
And even in her absence, she is most present on the expanse of the old
bed with the short, turned posts at both ends. The bed that has felt the
heft and ardor of two sweethearts when twice they conceived, at all the
other times as well. The bed that in time became weighted by despair,
salted with tears.

I tuck all these things under the wings of my heart and gather
them to me. I go back to my mother's notebook but find I can't turn
the page. Whatever truth these pages might contain, this I cannot face.
Not today. Not here. Not in this empty, lonesome house echoing with
ghosts and memories.

I close the notebook. I slip it into the tote bag I've carried up and set on the desk. I'll take the notebook home. One of these evenings when I'm ready, with the boys in bed and with Sam close by, with all my comforting possessions surrounding me, I'll sit in the easy chair beside the fireplace and open myself to my mother's explanations.

For now, there is a job yet to be done. I take a calming breath and extract the file marked "Last Will and Testament."

The first page is filled with the usual legalese. "I, Florence Agnes Hart, being of sound mind and body . . ." and "on this day, June 15, 1997 . . ."

The will had been drawn up just days after my mother's diagnosis. I turn the page. The words leap up and assail me.

"I bequeath my house, at 2204 Holmes Avenue South, Minneapolis, Minnesota, as well as all the contents in it, to my son, Hubert Henry Hart . . ."

I let out a scream so highly pitched that it startles me and sends Elvis scrambling, his nails scuttling against the oak floor. I scrape back the chair and stand, meeting the shock of disappointment that rolls over me like thunder. "Oh, Ma," I yell out. "How could you, how could you, how could you"—the words an incantation that fuels my dismay and heats up my neck, my cheeks. Bitterness rises at the back of my throat and I think I will be sick. I pass a hand over my face, breathe into my cupped palms. Elvis stands by the door, looking both afraid and perplexed. I pat my thigh and call him over. "It's okay, boy," I say, and soon he draws near and I squat and lay my head against his side. I run a slow hand over his big head. Back and forth, back and forth, pulling calmness from him.

After a time, I feel composed enough to take up the will again. I page through it quickly, searching for my own name, for my own inheritance.

On the fourth page, I find what I'm looking for. "To my daughter,

Ann Margaret Hart Rush, I bequeath the total monies in my checking account at Norwest Bank. In addition, I bequeath her all the holdings in my portfolio at Merrill Lynch, including all stocks, bonds and cash."

The paragraph amazes me. What stocks, bonds and cash? My mother had never mentioned an account with Merrill Lynch. Sam is a financial officer at a brokerage firm, yet Ma had not once discussed any financial dealings with him.

I sort through the files and extract two bulging ones: Norwest Bank Account and Norwest Investment Account.

I open the bank folder first. On the very first statement, I find the bank balance: $6,746.24. "Aw, Ma."

Hands trembling, I look in the second folder. I flip through the quarterly report lying atop the others. It's dated December 1998, only three months earlier. I run my finger down the column of numbers until it rests on the final balance. The shock I feel when I read the figure is jolting and electric. I take a wild breath for it seems that all the air has gone out of the room. I glance out the window rising at the top of the desk. Surely the world is now upside down, but no, the world is immutably the same. The day still bright. The snow still thawing splendidly. The traffic still making its slow progress up and down the street.

I turn back to the figure on the page, certain that I'd read it wrong the first time. But no, the figure has not changed.

Shaking, I pull my cell phone from my tote bag and punch out Sam's office number. It seems like forever before he comes on the line. "Sam, it's me."

"Annie? What's wrong? You sound funny."

"I'm at Ma's. I . . ." I choke the words out.

"Tell me what's wrong."

"I read Ma's will, Sam."

"And . . . ?"

"Ma, Sam. Ma left me almost a million dollars."

There is a long silence at both ends of the line. Then I say, "It's all here. In a Norwest Investment Account report. A quarterly report."

"How much?" Sam asks.

"$927,215.25."

"Good Lord."

"It was Microsoft, Sam. Ma made the money with Microsoft."

 Im not one to write much so I dont know how Ill get this done. Maybe the best way is just start putting things down. Whatever comes thats what Ill write. Even if I ramble. Sometimes when Im over at Annie's visiting my grandbabys I watch Annie working in her study. Shes always reading books and writing things down. Books on sicology and getting along with others. Thats what she teaches. How to get along with others in a business situation like a teller in a bank or an insurance salesman trying to get a policy sold. I recall the salesman that sold me my life insurance. He maybe was somebody that took Annies course. He was mild and helpful not pushy like they can be. A problem solver is what Annie would call it. I should of asked him if hed taken Annies course. Its called managing interpersonal relations. Another one is called counselor selling. Thats a grand title for basic things. So I should of asked, but I didnt. I was just anxious to get that policy bought. It

was soon after Elmer died and after what happened with him and his insurance I couldnt buy mine fast enough. I bought two hundered thousand dollars. Whole life, not terminal. Wait a minute that doesn't look right. Ha. I mean term insurance, not terminal. Actually, when you think about it all life insurance is terminal. Anyway, when the insurance salesman came calling, no way was I going to pass on without leaving my loved ones something. When I first got the policy I put down Hub and Annie for beneficiaries. But then a few years ago I changed it and left it half and half for my grandbabys. Theyll need it for college. College is a fortune and theres two of them.

I think of Annie and what she teaches. Its all sicological. I dont really understand it. But my Annies always been good at getting along with others. Shes always been the one to make peace. She never gets mad or angry. I get mad and angry but I try to never show it. But the truth is that ever since Maggie died, I never stopped being angry. I think of myself like a teapot simmering away on the stove. I just dont allow myself to boil over. Now what good would that do. I did it once with Hub and look what that got us. So never again. Id rather just keep my trap shut. But Annies always been a steady girl. Ever since she was a little girl she was like that. Maybe that wasnt good. Sometimes a person needs time off from being good. Sometimes a person needs a vacation from it. I recall when she pitched the old green tent out in the yard. She set it up under the oak tree and lived there all summer as I recall. It was right after Maggie died. After the nights turned warm. I was taking a load of laundry out to hang and there she was hammering those tent poles into the ground. I went over and asked her what she was doing and she said she was moving out of the house. Why you want to do that I ask her, but she didnt say anything just kept hammering away. Lord knows I understood what she was doing. Lord knows the way the air in the house was thick with grief I would of liked to pitch a tent myself. But not in the yard and not even down the road. Maybe on the moon might have been far enough.

 This year, uncharacteristically, winter slides directly into summer with hardly a spring between. In the St. Bart's neighborhood in Hopkins, trees burst headlong into greenery without a heralding pale shoot. Dormant lawns revivified, stretching lushly beside asphalted drives and around both grand and modest homes. Birdsong punctuates the warming hum of mornings, bees lighting upon fragrant blossoms in the heated afternoons.

Surrounded by such optimism, I languish nonetheless. The boon of my inheritance, which even after estate taxes remains considerable, does not boost my spirits, though for a time I use abundance to try to break my gloom. Because I can now afford it, I take an extended leave from work—I can't stomach the thought of teaching others how to be pleasant and problem solvers when I myself find it troublesome just to get out of bed. I close up my mother's house. I'll wait until I find Hub, and then he can do what he will with it. I have phone and cable ser-

vices disconnected, trash removal and newspaper delivery discontinued. Water, electric and gas service I keep. Whatever mail might come,
I have forwarded to my house.

While the boys are still in school, I take to haunting the malls. Calhoun Square. Southdale. The Galleria. The Mall of America. Torpidly, I
trudge in and out of department stores, decor and kitchen shops, dress
and shoe shops. I eye the surroundings, finger the merchandise, but do
not transfer items from rack or shelf to the checkout line. In book-
stores, I lift self-help books from display tables and stare at the titles, as
if by title alone I might mend my ailing life. I actually buy a book about
sorrow, placing it on my night table beside a stack of unread novels,
close to Ma's black-dimpled notebook, which I still can't bring myself
to read.

When mall-crawling fails to dent my glumness, and the boys'
school year ends, I begin to search for Hub. I start out on the Internet,
feeling torn by the hunt for him. On the one hand, there is elation at
the thought of finding him. Being my only living relative, he's the only
one who shares my childhood memories. And yet the fact that he
walked away so long ago stirs the anger I try so hard to tame. I don't
know what I'll do when I finally face him. And I'm certain that one day
we will stand face-to-face. "I yam what I yam," he's always said. When
I find him, I'll have something of my own to say back: I know what you
are, all right. You're a coward and a quitter.

Despite ambivalent feelings, I press on. Aided by meager, yet perti-
nent information—my brother's name, date and location of birth, his
Social Security number (thankfully, this has turned up in Ma's papers),
last known complete address (the house on Holmes Avenue itself), as
well as the trail his eight postcards have left—I charge the fees to my
credit card and log on to two lost-person locators: US Search and

OnlineDetective. I use the data the one provides for gathering additional information on the next. Amazingly, a mere day after starting the search, after scouring for Hub's name under criminal records, judgment and tax liens, military records, divorce records, bankruptcies and property records, sex offender lists, workers' compensation and voter registrations, up pops an address for Hub in the San Diego area. My pulse races as I see it on the screen. My breath catches as I learn that Hub has served in the United States Army from 1981 to 1984, when he was honorably discharged with the rank of Corporal/Specialist Fourth Class. I learn that no tax liens have been placed against him. No small claims civil judgments, nor, thank goodness, any sex offenses. In addition, no real estate property is listed to him.

Using his address, I turn to the Internet White Pages to find a corresponding telephone listing in San Diego. The result—"Sorry, no matches found"—is disheartening. I try again, using various name combinations: Hub Hart, Henry Hart. H. H. Hart, even "Popeye" Hart; I employ the "Wide Metro" option, which searches outlying areas, but all leads provide the same result. It looks like Hub is not now in San Diego. If he is, he has an unlisted telephone number. Perhaps no telephone at all.

But when I click on to Department of Motor Vehicle records, I find a cache of information that makes my brother real to me: Hub owns a car. A Volkswagen Beetle. The vehicle's registration number is provided, as is the fact that it's insured by State Farm. I picture Hub behind the wheel of an old (blue? black? white?) VW, and I feel something akin to love for him again.

Spurred on, I use all the data I've accumulated and make phone calls to San Diego. To State Farm, to the power company and the gas company as well. I explain that I'm Hub's sister. That our mother has died. That Hub has been estranged from the family. That I'm trying to reach him to relay the sad news. In each case, the person taking the call is patient, kind and understanding. In each case, the person informs me that on July 17, 1997, Hubert Henry Hart had his service discontinued. In each case, no forwarding address has been provided.

The news is crushing. It's obvious that, two years ago, Hub left the San Diego area and moved on. After two years, he could be anywhere.

This morning, I'm awakened by the god-awful racket of Canada geese. They are St. Bart's personal geese, all four adults and thirteen goslings. The two pairs arrive each year and spend the summer waddling around the neighborhood, having babies, pulling up the grass, and pooping on everything ("They're a hard act to follow," Sam likes to say). Most of the time, they honk and hiss as they go about the day. They're doing this now. Down on the lawn, beneath the window. I glance past Sam, who slumbers beside me. The display on the clock on his night table reads 6:14. Already light haloes around the drapes and defines the room. The geese continue clamoring. Sam does not stir. He can sleep through anything. Not me. Since Ma's death, I've been plagued by insomnia. I roll onto my side and softly punch the pillow.

Before the stupid geese, I'd been dreaming about something. No dream images remain, only that vague sense that in the few hours that I'd slept, I'd been somewhere, doing something. I lie very still, trying to remember. The tent when I was nine. I'd been dreaming about that. The mustiness of green canvas floats through my mind. My skinny tanned legs (like a colt's, Ma always said) rub against the nubby pilled flannel lining the sleeping bag. Hub's sleeping bag. The brown one with the bucking broncos inside. The same bucking broncos repeated on his bedspread. I had dragged the small cardboard dresser—only two drawers and stamped with little pink roses—down from my room and set it in the tent. In one shallow drawer, panties, socks, shorts, T-shirts. In the other, books, comics, pencils, crayons, a notebook. In my mind, the light from the battery lantern shoots a brilliant coin against the peaked roof.

The alarm clock goes off. Six-thirty sends it ringing. The bed bobbles and I know Sam has hit the snooze button. I keep my eyes sealed, trying to hold on to the memory. The tent and its warm and cozy closeness, like a nest or a cave. Wet or dry, the funky, earthy smell of Cosmo, our black Lab, sleeping just beyond the tent's zippered opening. Sometimes Cosmo snored. Sometimes I had to hush him. Sometimes I couldn't sleep anyway, and I would look through the net screen and across the yard to the house and the back stoop. Sometimes, late at night, Ma sat on the stoop, her knees pulled up against her chest, her dress tucked tightly around her. Always, the glowing ember of her cigarette punctuated everything.

The alarm buzzes again but is quickly turned off. Sam yawns loudly. The bed bobbles again as he rolls over and draws near. "You awake?" he mumbles. He lays an arm over my side. He yawns again.

"Um."

"Did you sleep?"

"A bit." I had slept in the tent all summer. Not once had I gone into my room. Sometimes Hub snuck up and tattooed the side of the canvas to rattle me. "You're a nut cake," Hub said.

Sam says, "You should go to the doctor. Get some pills."

"Um." Tiny blue pills. Ma had laid one in my palm, an itsy robin's egg.

"Baby?" Sam's hand slips under the edge of my nightshirt. He cups my breast, strokes the nipple with a thumb.

"Um." Why had I moved into that tent?

Sam snuggles against me. I feel the solid length of him, his hardness against my buttocks. "Oh," I say, in a long breath as the tent, its seductiveness, starts to evanesce. "Oh," I whisper, thinking, Stay. Stay.

Sam nuzzles my neck. His hand travels across my belly. His fingers slip into me.

I roll on my back, dislodging his chaffing intrusion.

"Oh, baby, it's been so long," he murmurs. He pulls himself over me. He's a warm weight that pins me. He kisses my eyes, my cheeks. Eagerly he nibbles my lips, parting them with his tongue.

I turn my face away when I remember. Remember, Why the tent? To get away from the mirror in my room. The mirror that, when I peered into it, reflected Maggie's image. Your fault, the image said. It's all your fault.

Sam lifts himself and I squint at the sight of him rising above me. His knees are poked into the mattress and he is still and silent, as if figuring things out. After a moment, he says, "You're not even here, are you?"

Before I can protest, he swings over the bed's edge, hits the floor and heads for the bathroom. Before he goes in, I scream out, "Where are you going! Get back here!" Anger thickens my blood. My voice ratchets up into a screech. "Get back here now! I don't care if the kids are down the hall. I don't care if Milly's next door! I don't care if the whole neighborhood can hear me!"

Sam shuts the bathroom door. Soon, the shower starts to gush and at the sound, I hurl myself from bed, rush over and turn the knob. The door is locked and the fact is infuriating. I rattle the knob, pound the wood for good measure. "Open up! Open up!"

The water continues to cascade. I pound and pound and pound.

My palm burns. My ears buzz. My throat feels raw. "Goddamn it, Sam! Open it! Open it!"

When the water turns off, in a startling moment of new silence, I sink down to my knees, my head against the door. Muffled sounds rise beyond it. Sam tugging the towel off the towel bar. Sam vigorously drying himself. I can't hear it, but I picture it. The door opens and from it rolls a blanket of warm steam. I lift my face to it. To Sam. But Sam takes a wide step over me. "You know what?" he says over his shoulder. "I think you might want to consider seeing a therapist." He goes to his closet. He dresses. He leaves the room and not soon after, I hear the little roar as the Subaru starts up. As he pulls down the drive. Away from me.

Soon after, Jack and Will are at the bedroom door, in their pajamas, their eyes wide with the same unspoken question, What is happening, Mom?

Sometimes it's impossible to live, set apart, in the canvas tent of my emotions. I promise Sam I'll do as he suggests and I find a therapist with an office in downtown Hopkins. After a session, I might stop at Tait's, the supermarket, or the library, which is just across the street. Sometimes, to help dispel the disturbing feelings of a difficult meeting, I walk over to Pekoe and Java and sit in one of their plush chairs and sip a café latte and gaze out their big window at the people strolling past, most of them on their way to a matinee at the movie house next door. They all seem so normal, so carefree. These days, I find it impossible to believe that I might someday be so blissfully unpreoccupied.

At the moment, I've just returned home from another visit feeling drained, yet strangely energized. Today, I allowed myself to rant about how sick and tired I am of being angry and sad, both emotions balled up and tangled into one, the weight of it like an elephant parked on my chest. I went on to rave about how pissed I am at the unfairness of a brother taking off, of a mother who kept news of him to herself. Given my energy level, I decide to take a peek in my mother's notebook. It's been four months since I lifted it from her file drawer, and nothing I read in it can make me feel lousier than I'm already feeling. That's what I'm thinking, anyway.

I carry the notebook out to the back patio. It's a sultry summer afternoon. One of those sticky Minnesota days that we Minnesotans clamor for in winter and complain about in summer. The kind of day that out-of-staters don't believe exists in Minnesota. Will and Jack and a handful of other boys have spent the morning at the Raspberry Festival taking place on Main Street and now they are at the house next door to Milly's, jumping in and out of that neighbor's aboveground pool. Cooling themselves down before setting off again to enjoy the town's yearly festivities. The boys make a rowdy gang, shouting and splashing and carrying on. Even the dogs have convened at the pool, and they add yips and yaps to the merriment. I can keep an eye on them from here. I set the notebook on the patio table. I stare at the notebook, wishing I could make a detour around its sorrowful contents. Can I really do this? I ask myself.

One of the families of geese toddle by on the lawn beyond the patio. The goslings have grown so fast that it's difficult to distinguish them from their parents. I watch the long line of them go up the short incline at the end of the yard. I watch until they disappear over the berm. I wish they would turn back so I could watch them again. After a moment, I open the notebook at a random page and peek at what my mother's written there:

I miss Elmers touch. After all these years after all the anger I miss Elmers big calloused hands on my body. On the farm when the kids

were young and in there beds Elmer and me wed stroll down toward
the pond. The crikets would be making their sawing sounds and as
we stepped across the grass they would stop sawing when we
passed. Back then the summer sky was a big blue quilt and all
Elmer and me needed was each other lying down and looking up
the pond frogs singing their songs as Elmer laid his hands on me

I look up from the words, the pain in them, the pain in reading them so exquisite, I have to close the book. I can't do this I can't do this, these are the words whirling through my mind. I lay my head down, fold my arms over my head. Sometime after, I feel a hand against my back and I jerk up, both embarrassed and surprised. It's Milly here beside me. "Honey, what is it? I saw you from my kitchen." She lifts a chair and sets it close.

"Oh, God, Milly. I think I'm going to die. I'm trying to read Ma's notebook again."

Milly lays an arm around my shoulders. "You know what, you don't have to read that notebook."

"But I want to."

"I know you do, but you'll do it when you're ready. There isn't a deadline to any of this, Annie. You just do what you can, when you can."

"I just can't do it right now, Milly. I just can't." I look into my friend's eyes. "Do you think I'm being awful?"

"Oh, honey, of course you're not awful. What a thought, my God." Milly rests a hand on my cheek. "I'll tell you what you are. You're one of the bravest, truest people I know. I think that all your life, you've held your feelings in for fear of upsetting your mother. Now that your mother's gone, there's no reason to hold back. Now you can allow yourself to feel whatever emotion comes up."

"That's what the therapist said. He said that long ago, after Maggie died, I had divorced my body and moved my emotions to my head, where they could be justified, or worse, denied."

"Makes perfect sense."

"Yeah, well," I say and look across the yard, toward the pool where the boys are. Will is on the diving board, pumping it up and down. His pudgy arms are straight out and he flaps them like a big bird. Will's hair is wet. It stands straight up in clumps around his head. He looks like one of those punkers that frequent Calhoun Square. "You know what I did once?" I ask the question, but keep my eyes on Will. I see him fly off the board. I see the spray of water he sends up with the dive.

"What?"

"Soon after Maggie died, I set up my brother's tent under a tree in the yard. It was when we lived on the farm near Saint Peter. I slept in the tent all summer. I chopped my hair off, too. I know it's a cliché. You see it in the movies; people go crazy and take scissors to their hair. I wasn't crazy, but I did it for good reason. I stole Ma's pinking shears out of her sewing basket and kept them under my pillow, between the sleeping bag and the top of the army cot. It felt good knowing they were there. That when I was ready, I could start whacking away." Will has climbed onto the board again. He takes another dive. "I did it one night, in the dark. I sat up on the cot, lifting one strand of hair after another. After it was over, I lay down again and went to sleep. I felt lighter somehow. In the morning, I gathered up all the hair. It was easy. There were thick long clumps of it on the sleeping bag and on the tent floor. I stuffed all of it into a plastic bag." I am silent for a moment, remembering. Then I go on, "I did something else a few days later. I colored my hair with black shoe polish. The wax kind. I must have looked a fright. Short waxy hair sticking out all over the place. My fingers, too. They were stained black for days."

"My goodness," Milly says. "Why would you want to mutilate your sunny-looking hair?"

"Because I didn't want to look the way I did. Because I thought if I cut my hair off and waxed it black, then when I looked in the mirror, someone else would stare back at me. Someone else who wasn't Maggie."

"Oh, dear girl," Milly says. She shakes her head sadly.

"It's all so hard, Mil, all this grief. It hurts so much."

"Well, of course it does, honey." She lifts a strand of hair from my face and brushes it aside. "That's why it's called grief and not an avocado."

I throw my head back. "Oh, Milly, thank God for you. You always make me laugh."

 *I hated Elmer when he did what he did. Because he killed himself, we couldnt collect on his life insurance. Right then I promised myself I would take care of things and build up a nest egg. I called Merrill Lynch. I was so backward that first time. I asked to talk to Mr. Merrill. When they said he wasnt available, I said I wanted Mr. Lynch. Later my broker and I had a good laugh about that. I guess even when things are godawful theres always something you can laugh about. Still, I hated Elmer for being such a coward. Killing yourself is taking the cowards way. And he could of done it somewhere else and not down in the basement with me at the sink doing the supper dishes, my hands soapy and slick. Hub wasn't even home, he never was home. He was off somewhere with his buddys. I could never keep a rein on that boy. Elmer didnt even try. Annie was up in her room doing her homework. I remember she was in junior high and she was studying the*

stars. Thats what she told me. I said that wasnt a proper subject for school and she said why not. I said because it seems to me that you get enough of stars at the movies and on tv. Annie laughed and said no ma not those kind of stars. Were studying the stars in the sky. Oh I said. I think I was embarrased.

Elmer killing himself was embarrasing too. You couldnt keep something like that a secret, even if you tried. People didnt know what to say. Theyd come up to you and start to speak then theyd mumble something and turn away.

I hated Elmer even though I couldnt help loving him. And I hated Hub too because of what he said about his Pa killing himself. Hubs words were a dagger in my heart. Still are even tho I know more than anyone how you can say awful things when your mad.

 They call him Enrique, un norteamericano who stands out among the people. He is married to Luli, whom he met in San Diego, California, where he worked as a house painter and she at cleaning houses. Hub and Luli moved to Oaxaca two years ago, when Uberto was two. Here they erected a modest house on a small parcel of land belonging to the Huertas, Luli's family.

Today, Enrique and Uberto ride in Enrique's orange Beetle. In the backseat, their mutt, Popeye (in Mexico they say "Popay"), pokes his head out the window and periodically snaps at the wind. Four-year-old Uberto stands against the front seat, strapped in a restraint his father has rigged up with a long leather belt that he's wrapped around the seat and Uberto's waist. Father and son have just been to Oaxaca City to drop Luli off at her job as a salesclerk at Los Tules Gifts and Art Gallery. Usually she takes the bus, but this morning they've made the trip by car because Enrique had three new paintings of his to deliver to the gallery. While in town, he also made a stop at the main post office. Today, he finally sent off the postcard that had been burning a hole in his pocket for almost a week.

As the two go along, they sing a little tune: Soy carpintero y vengo de la sierra, sí señor. Yes, sir, I'm a carpenter who comes from the sierra. Enrique's Spanish is not as good as his son's, but still, he holds his own. After all, he conducts his life in Spanish now, and singing songs with his son is one way to improve it. Uberto speaks less and less English. But he still uses some of the phrases he learned when he lived across the border: "How are you? I am hungry. Give me some. I like that. Get away." All these words hold meaning for him. But there is one phrase he often uses, not because he understands it, but because of its musicality: Minneapolis, Minnesota. Minnesota, Minneapolis. The words rolling like smooth pebbles over his tongue.

Enrique, who was once known as Hub, soon passes the fork that leads to the airport or to Coyotepec. When he nears San Antonino, he does not head for home but continues on, toward the rancho of Luli's parents. Today, don Efrain Huerta, his father-in-law, will, at the opportune time, sow his prized radish seeds in the special plot at the back of the yard. Uberto will help him do it. For almost one hundred years, the seeds have been handed down from one yearly harvest to another, and down through the generations. Don Efrain is convinced his radishes are the best in the land for carving. His harvests produce thick, two-foot-long roots, radishes that grow twisted into esses and figure eights. They have firm white flesh and colorful skins, from bright magenta, to pale pink, to pearly white. The radishes are not edible. They are grown solely to create the raw material for the tableaux for the radish-carving contest that takes place each December 23. Placing first at the contest brings the talented and lucky win-ner a handsome prize. Ten thousand pesos. For some, double a year's salary.

Hub drives down the dusty main street, past the humble church and the bakery, past the eating place that today featured manitas de cerdo, little pigs' feet. Hub takes a right at the cantina, and shortly, he pulls up beside a fence and a gate strung together by wire and branches of copalillo.

A young boy stands out in the road. When the car stops, he unhitches the gate. Uberto quickly unstraps himself from the seat. He and Popeye clatter down onto the road.

"Buenos días, Mansuelo," Hub says to the boy. "You keep a good eye on the car." Hub takes in the morning air, perfumed by the warming sun and by hundreds of tortillas roasting on dozens of comales about the village.

The boy grins and lifts his straw hat, then settles it back on his head again. He closes the gate and posts himself there. The others start down the sinuous, foot-worn path, slippery with loose stones and bordered by patches of prickly vegetation. They make their way carefully down the wide ravine and across the treeless hillocks toward don Efrain Huerta's purple house, rising in the distance like a bruised thumb. The house is made of concrete block and is commodious compared to others dotting the ridge. It features a wide porch, a front room large enough to accommodate a dining table, two bedrooms and, thanks to Luli's efforts in San Diego, an indoor toilet. The kitchen is at the rear of the house, in the lean-to that juts out into the backyard, the place where don Efrain conducts his wood carving business.

Hub and Uberto follow Popeye, who keeps his nose to the path as they go along. Twice the mutt lifts his back leg to mark his way on the trail. As they near don Efrain's, his three dogs catch wind of their visit.

The animals rush down to welcome them, barking and yelping as they go along.

When they reach the house, doña Fausta, Uberto's grandmother, appears on the porch, her fists poked into her waist. "Ey," she calls in greeting.

Uberto rushes to meet her, distracted for a step or two by the remains of the yellow marigold petals his grandmother had strewn on the ground a few days before, on el Día de los Muertos, the Day of the Dead. The bright trail led the spirits of the dead ancestors toward the house and up the steps and into the front room still holding the ofrenda, the altar the family had festooned with spiritual tokens and mementos.

Doña Fausta clunks down the steps and gathers Uberto into her arms. "¿Como 'sta mi ojitos verdes?" How's my green-eyed boy?

Uberto giggles and wriggles out of his grandmother's embrace. He runs around the house and disappears from view. The four mutts gallop after him.

"I took Luli to work today," Hub says. "I'll pick her up this afternoon."

"The girl works too much." Doña Fausta is a lean, dry woman who, when she speaks these words, twists her mouth as if she's ingested a limón.

Hub says nothing; he feels a pang and wishes he himself could be the sugar cube to melt his mother-in-law's perennial disapproval. It isn't just about Luli's working. Heaven knows, to make ends meet, everyone in the family who can, works. He certainly does. He creates paintings for sale at the gallery. In addition, and because art sales cannot be guaranteed, he paints interiors and exteriors. Over the last year, he's landed a few jobs entailing the increasingly popular art of faux finishing. When he can find construction work, he takes that as well. But it isn't easy being a gringo and being passed over for jobs because of it. Though she has not voiced it directly, Hub is certain it's this that doña Fausta can't stomach: that Luli's taken up with a gringo with long arms and legs. A gringo who wears khaki shorts and sandals almost as a uniform. A gringo with yellow hair, in a place where most people's is thick and blunt and as black as well bottoms. A poor gringo to boot. To top off the list, that Luli had a child so far away across the border that a mother could not be in attendance. Luli is pregnant again, this baby due the day after Christmas. Hub fervently wishes for a girl. He hopes that when the baby is born, when doña Fausta finally holds her first granddaughter in her arms, she might begin to see things differently.

"¿Y don Efrain?" Hub asks, though the question is merely rhetorical.

"Allá tras." Doña Fausta tips her head to the right. Her salt-and-pepper hair is piled into braids atop her head. When she motions, the colored ribbons tying off the braids quiver like tiny birds.

Hub nods and says, "Con permiso, Señora." He goes eagerly off, toward his father-in-law and the amity that thankfully exists between them. Rounding the house, Hub steps into the backyard. The main site of don Efrain's carving business is the mud-walled shed that sits in the shade of two guayamuche trees. Piles of wood are stacked beside the shed: sompantle, parota and white copal. This last proves the best wood for carving, for it is soft when green, and because its branches are slender, it does not easily split when worked on. This morning, a few rusty hens peck around the wood stacks in search of powderpost beetles, the bane of the copal. A ginger-colored cat sits atop a stack of parota and watches the chickens with disinterest.

Hub steps into the shed and is enveloped in the smell of fresh paint and newly hewn wood, sharp and aromatic. The room is lighted by a single bulb dangling from a beam that crosses the ceiling, a mere span of tin sheeting. Ramshackle shelves built along the wall hold finished carvings: animals, angels, mermaids, devils. Some hold human figures engaged in various occupations: flower sellers, musicians, farmers, bullfighters, tortilla makers. Even besotted tequila tipplers. Doña Fausta herself is in charge of paint and decoration. All the carvings feature her psychedelic colors with names like sun-kissed orange and jungle blue and electric green. She paints the figures with fanciful dots and spirals and lines using common brushes but also cactus spines, the hair from donkey manes and the bristles from the backs of hogs.

"Buenos días," Hub says, tipping his head to his father-in-law and to Mauricio and Rogelio, his brothers-in law. Luis Eugenio, don Efrain's youngest son, is missing. One afternoon, three years ago, he developed a bad headache while carving in this very shed. By supper, his neck was stiff and he had a raging fever. By midnight, he was gone. A fulminating case of septic meningitis was what the doctor had said.

"Ey, Enrique," the men say in greeting. The three sit at the table in the middle of the room. The table is cluttered with tools: knives of all shapes and sizes, picks, brushes, whetting stones.

Don Efrain is as spare as his wife, but despite the sorrows that life has presented him, his spirits are juicy and humor sparks in his eyes, even as they are clouding over with cataracts. Given his profession, this malady is inopportune, to say the least. A week before, while carving a gazelle, his hand slipped and he deeply cut the middle finger of his left hand. Luckily, Hub had been at the rancho helping with the painting.

When his father-in-law cried out and bent over, clutching his hand to stanch the bleeding, his sons sprang to him. Doña Fausta wound her husband's finger with a clean cloth, then Hub rushed don

Efrain in the VW to the clinic in Oaxaca. Don Efrain protested all the way to town. In his life, there had been many cuts, he said. All they took was a thorough cleaning, a poultice of cempasuchil flowers and a good, tight bandage.

At the clinic, the doctor cleaned the wound, laid his own kind of poultice on it and swaddled the finger in a roll of gauze and flesh-colored tape. "Didn't I tell you," don Efrain said to Hub when they were heading back. "Same remedio as at home." Hub had made no apologies for his caution. "It doesn't matter," he said. "Look, your finger's good as new. Besides, thanks to going, you found out about your eyes." In explaining to the doctor how the accident had come about, the doctor examined don Efrain and informed him that cataract surgery could easily restore his failing eyesight.

Now, don Efrain's finger looks like a wrapped chorizo, but that does not encumber him. He is carving a female centaur, a figure with the back end of a horse and the torso and head of a woman. The work presents a special challenge, for it has to be created in such a way that it will stand without toppling. Mauricio is carving a mermaid; Rogelio, a large rooster; these figures a specialty of each.

Uberto has already been put to work. He sits in the corner, directly on the earth-packed floor, sanding a barrel-chested armadillo. His three cousins, two of them Mauricio's sons, the other, Rogelio's, are hard at work, sanding, too.

Hub pulls a stool out from under the table and joins the men there. He lines up the pots of paint doña Fausta has selected for the mermaid: turquoise, black, aqua, blue.

Soon, the shed fills with banter and with outrageous stories. It practically hums with good humor. With wholehearted industriousness.

.   .   .

When the sun reaches the perfect position in the firmament, don Efrain goes into the house and fetches his prized radish seeds. Hub and Uberto, the uncles and cousins, wait beside the plot at the back corner of the yard where the seeds will be sown. The beds hold soil fortified by don Efrain's secret blend of fertilizers. The soil is dark and moist and well tilled. Beneath its surface, the land itself has blessed the spot with rocks and small boulders, a necessity if radishes are to grow into long and twisted shapes. Yes. Length and root distortion transform the best radishes into the most detailed of tableaux.

Don Efrain soon walks out of the house with the hammered-tin box in which his seeds are stored. Like a priest with a chalice, he holds the box soberly.

They all post themselves around the radish bed. Don Efrain lifts the box lid and intones his yearly prayer.

"Dear Father, bless these radish seeds. May they grow mightily. May they provide the radishes that this year will finally win us the first prize." Don Efrain places a pinch of radish seeds upon each upturned palm.

And so, one by one, and starting with Uberto because he is the youngest, the men of the Huerta family poke the little black seeds into the earth and hope for the miracle that will place ten thousand pesos into the family pocketbook.

 Sam and I snuggle in bed. We lie in the heat of our own making, legs and arms entangled. I rest my head on Sam's shoulder, my face tucked into the hollow beneath his chin. The stalled train that was our sex life, my very life in fact, is now moving, albeit slowly, down the track again. And I'm so thankful. The boys are more thankful. Sam is most thankful of all.

"I haven't even left, and I'm missing you already," I say. I run a slow hand over Sam's chest, springy with dark hair, past the tautness of his belly. His sex is warm and pleasantly flaccid against my palm.

Sam gives my breast a soft squeeze. "Don't go."

"You know I have to." This afternoon I will board a plane and head for Mexico. Two weeks ago, a postcard addressed to Ma and then forwarded to me arrived in the mailbox. NOCHE DE RÁBANOS, Night of the Radishes, was printed in block letters along the bottom of the card. It featured a curious photograph of a tableau of what appeared to be the

Magi, all three carved out of . . . radishes? I turned the card over. "I yam what I yam," the message on the reverse. Beneath, the sketched flexed arm with bulging muscle. The postmark read 4 Noviembre 1999. Along the lower edge and looking like a long smile, Oaxaca, Mexico. I noted all of this in an instant. I remember laying a hand over my heart. It remained there all the way back into the house.

Sam lays his lips against my forehead. "You know what? You're going to find your brother."

"God, I hope so."

We are silent for a time, Sam lost in his own thoughts, me in the secret pleasure I feel to soon be flying off. Flying off into wild blueness like the one depicted in the painting hanging in my study. Since getting Hub's postcard and making plans for the trip, I've realized how perfect the timing is. I would never admit it to my family, but I really need to slip away. Slip away for a time from everything familiar.

Elvis's big head materializes at the edge of Sam's side of the bed. "Morning, boy," I say. Elvis sleeps at the foot of our bed. He is a considerate beast, for he usually allows Sam and me some time before he hauls himself up and asks to be let out.

Sam yawns loudly. "Well, morning has broken," he says, the comment he makes each day when he gets up.

"I'm going to make us all a fabulous breakfast." I stretch out into a long line. Give a yawn myself. "How about chocolate waffles? How about sausages and blueberries with cream? How does that all sound?"

"Sounds like your special I'm-going-away-so-don't-hate-me breakfast. But, hey, I'll take it."

.   .   .

After a quick shower, I dress in jeans and a turtleneck. I will add a blazer this afternoon for traveling. While Sam gets dressed, I start breakfast. Before finishing, I climb the stairs to wake the boys.

Jack's room is clothed in early morning shadows. I step toward his bed, pausing in the dimness to pluck up a pair of underwear, one sock and a sweatshirt along the way. Jack rests on his back, an arm flung over his head. As a prelude to whispering him awake, I gently jostle the bed. His eyes spring open. "Good morning, sweetie." His eyes slam shut again.

"Scoot over." I jiggle the bed once more.

"Geez, Ma," Jack says, but he scoots over anyway.

I lie atop the blanket, next to him. "I'm making chocolate waffles today."

Jack's eyes spring open again. "With maple syrup? With powdered sugar?"

"That's right." I stretch the words out, speaking them in a singsongy way.

"What about Spam? Can we have that?"

"I was going to do sausage, but I can fry up some Spam." This family of mine is a Spam-eating family, just as we had been on the farm.

Jack lays his arm back over his face. "When's your plane, Ma?"

"Not till two. There's plenty of time."

"I have a hockey game this afternoon."

"I know. It's on the board." In the space for phone numbers and whereabouts, I have added "I'm at Casa Amapolas in Oaxaca (Wa-Ha-Ka), Mexico." This is followed by the casa's telephone and fax numbers, and the e-mail address as well.

"You'll miss my game, Ma."

"I know, I'm sorry. But Dad'll be there. Will, too." Since the hockey game and my departure time disappointingly coincided, the plan is that all three of them will head for the game, while Milly will drop me off at the airport. I lean closer to Jack. "You know what? Use the e-mail to let me know how you do. But one thing, it won't be up and running until sometime tomorrow."

"I know. It'll be real late when you get to Mexico."

"I'm going to miss you, Jack."

"I know. You'll e-mail us to tell us about Uncle Hub, right?"

"Of course."

Jack turns his head and looks at me. I can make out his eyes, deep-set and dark, just like Sam's. "Are you really going to find him, Ma?"

"I sure hope so. That's why I'm going."

"What if you don't find him?"

I stare up at the ceiling. At the constellation of stick-on planets and stars Jack has carefully arranged. "I'll find him."

"But you looked all over the Internet and he didn't turn up."

"I know."

"Maybe you should have gotten a detective. Like the woman in those books you read. The ones with the letters of the alphabet. That would have been awesome."

"Maybe."

"So what if you don't find him? What'll you do then?"

I turn back to Jack's earnest eyes. "Well, sweetie, if I don't find him, then I'll just come back home."

Will, on the other hand, is a cheery awakener. He makes no protestations when I curl up beside him and Cooper, his big raggedy-looking bear.

"Did you have a good sleep?" I ask.

"Uh-huh."

"Any good dreams?" Will, like me, often has vivid dreams. He likes to recount them, frequently in never-ending detail. I don't mind the telling, although Jack, if he is within earshot, usually rolls his eyes and bobs his head in silent irritation. When he does this, I snap my fingers for him to stop.

"I dreamed I was swimming."

"Were you an otter?" I ask. "Were you a seal? A fish?"

Will giggles. "Noooooo. I was Will and I was swimming."

"Did you have a good swim? Did Cooper swim, too?"

"Mooooooom! Cooper can't swim. He's a bear."

"Bears swim. Polar bears do."

Will hesitates for a moment. "Oh, yeah, that's right."

"I'm making waffles for breakfast."

"Great! Chocolate ones? Like you always do when you go on your trips?"

I laugh at the transparency of my never-ending guilt. Because I teach workshops to out-of-town bank and insurance company employees, I travel fairly often. In fact, I've made two trips to Mexico City, to teach English-speaking bank employees. For the most part, though, when I go away, it's for only three days at the most. This trip to Mexico will be much longer than that.

"You'll be home for Christmas, won't you, Mom?"

"Of course I'll be home for Christmas." Christmas is almost two weeks away. Still, just to be safe, I've done all the holiday shopping, wrapping and labeling. The whole of it is stashed at Milly's. Even the Christmas cards, all two hundred of them, are on my desk, ready for Sam to mail.

"I'm going to miss you when you're in Mexico," Will says. I can see his lower lip turning under.

"Milly'll be here every day after school. Milly'll take good care of you. Dad, too."

"I know. But I'm still going to miss you, Mom."

I gather him in my arms, giving him and Cooper a squeeze. "Aw, honey, I'll be back before you know it."

 It's almost midnight, but I'm too wound up to go to bed. I'm finally in Oaxaca, at Casa Amapolas, trying to relax on the veranda, on a cowhide bucket chair just outside my room. I've brought a pillow from the bed and tucked it behind the small of my back to ease the dull ache from almost twelve hours on the move. Breakfast this morning with Sam and the boys seems like a dream. Since then I've trudged through airports, Dallas/Fort Worth, Mexico City and then Oaxaca, the strap of my carry-on bag digging a furrow into my shoulder, my arm muscles burning from pulling my huge rolling suitcase along. Since breakfast, I've sat stiffly straight in three different aircraft; I've confronted the tedium of two mind-numbing layovers.

I arrived at the casa about an hour ago. Despite the late arrival, don Gustavo, the night watchman, greeted me cheerfully at the front door. He escorted me to my room, which is across the garden patio, past the large Nativity scene set up under a tree and beneath a small thatched lean-to. In addition to the manger scene (with as yet no baby Jesus), there is a pottery village: little houses, huts, a pebbled road meandering between them, and lots of pottery animals. Conveniently, check-in with Ginny Powers, the innkeeper, was postponed until the morning, but don Gustavo offered a nightcap of hot chocolate, which I accepted gratefully. I watched him hurry off down the veranda, watched him hurry back with a froth-topped mug. He then informed me that breakfast would be in the dining room. At las ocho he'd be ringing the bell, he said, pointing in the direction I'd seen him vanish before. Muy bien, don Gustavo, I replied. Muchas gracias. We bid each other good night.

And so, here I am in Gitche Gumee, just as I secretly wished. Being three thousand miles from home, I feel suddenly self-aware, and for once, this is a good thing. I feel untethered and light, like maybe all things are possible. I sip my hot chocolate—it's deliciously thick—and take in my new circumstances. At home, snow might be flying, but here, even with the scant light coming from the lampposts in the garden, I can see that the world is verdant and lush. The night air is fresh and warm and carries the scent of something beautiful and sweet flowering all around. The house is quiet. No lights come from the rooms set around the veranda. From the guidebook, I know that fifteen guest rooms circle the patio. Though the surroundings are not clearly visible, I'm pleased with what I can observe. These sprawling old houses so prevalent in Mexico have always entranced me. I love how airy and open they are to the elements. How abundantly nature flourishes only steps away.

I set my empty mug down. I stand and stretch, then step onto the patio, springy with lawn. On a whim, I pull off my shoes and socks. Amazing, I think, wiggling my toes in the cool grass. Lights set around the patio softly illuminate tall trees, plump shrubs and bushes. What seem to be birdcages hang from the low branches of some trees. Draped with white cloths, the cages look like specters. I stroll around the inside of the patio, staying away from the veranda so as not to disturb slumbering guests. Above me, an indigo sky shimmers with stars. I cross over the walkway that leads from the front entrance across the garden to the veranda. Flowering vines canopy the walkway. Beyond it, in what appears to be a back section of the garden, looms a small building. I can't see it distinctly, only that it's there and dark and silent. I decide to investigate. As I draw near, I realize the building is probably another guest room, this one tucked away and set apart from the others. I can see a door, a row of small-paned windows, a little patio on the side. I'm about to turn away, when a voice says, "There's someone here."

"Oh!" My hand flies to my mouth as I quickly make out a person sitting in the patio, in the dark.

"I'm sorry. I knew when I spoke that you'd be startled." The person stands, a man from the sound of the voice.

"It's me who's sorry. I shouldn't be lurking around."

"Is that what you're doing? Lurking?"

I give a nervous laugh. "Well, not lurking exactly. It's just that I got in late, and I thought if I got some fresh air . . ." I let the sentence hang there.

"This is my room. I always ask for it. I like the privacy. I also like this little patio, because it's right out under the trees. I watched don Gustavo let you in."

"Well, I'm afraid I've come crashing in on your privacy. I'm sorry about that."

"No need for apologies. I'm Joe, by the way. Joe Cruz."

"Is that 'Cruise,' as in 'Tom Cruise'?"

"No. It's 'Cruz,' as in the Spanish 'cross.' Do you speak Spanish?"

"Un poquito," I say, "but I'm glad you speak English. Right now my brain is fried. Oh, I'm Annie Rush. I'm staying in number eight. I'm from Minnesota."

"Ah," Joe says, "the frozen tundra, ice fishing, Babe, the big blue ox."

"Well, you have us pegged. How about you? Where are you from?" It seems odd to be speaking to someone who is just a long bundle in the dark. But the man has a pleasant voice. And he has a sense of humor. That counts for a lot.

"California. San Francisco, to be exact."

"Well, let's see. That's surfin' dudes and hippies and flowers in your hair."

"Touché. I had that coming. Hey, would you like to sit down? There's another chair here. I wouldn't mind the company."

"That's nice of you, but you know what? I've been on the go for almost twelve hours. I'm exhausted. But I'll take a rain check, if that's okay."

"It's okay, and I'll hold you to that."

 Unfamiliar sounds awaken me: *Swish, swish,* a pause. *Swish, swish,* again. Other sounds I recognize: birds chirping in the cages I'd seen the night before. I roll on my side, head resting on a bent arm. The pillows are plump and hard as salami. I'll have to ask for softer ones, or else do without. The travel clock on the night table reads almost seven. The room is already flooded with light. Walls faux-painted a dusty sage. A canvas of red poppies. A shelf displaying a carved trio of musicians. Animal musicians in polka-dotted bras. Across the room, a long dresser. Above it, a mirror framed in punched tin and little tiles. In the corner, a massive armoire. Rough-hewn wood the color of caramels.

Swish, swish. What *is* that? Then it comes to me. Outside the door, a broom sweeping across floor tiles. Soon the sound lessens as the broom makes its way down the veranda.

I should get up. Last night, I'd started to unpack but hadn't gotten far. Items from my suitcase are stacked on the bed across from me.

Clothing. A few novels. Hub's old cigar box. I've brought it as a strange
conciliatory gift. An album chock-full of family photos the boys and I
put together. Beside it, Ma's notebook, still unread. But maybe now,
when I find Hub . . .

I try to picture us, heads bent over Ma's words. Me leaning into Hub,
he leaning into me. Both of us propping each other up. I have worked at
conjuring up kind thoughts about Hub, because it's struck me that now I
need my brother. I need him to help me keep alive a past I'm terrified
might fade and disappear. If it does, then I, too, might disappear. I might
slowly evanesce, like the smoke from one of Ma's cigarettes.

I'm slipping bare feet into toeless platforms when the breakfast bell starts
to clang. The last meal I had was yesterday's pathetic airline food. Now
I'm starving. I leave the room with still-damp hair. I'm in a sleeveless cotton shift and a light cardigan I probably won't need for long. On the
veranda, the world is sunny and bright. Red and yellow poppies spill
from pots and their glorious faces poke out from the greenery in the garden's flower beds. Casa Amapolas. No wonder the place is named after
them. A hammock is stretched between two catalpa trees. The birdcages
are now uncovered. Small songbirds, canaries, mostly, trill on their
perches.

"Well, good morning," someone says.

I turn toward the sound and the man walking up behind me. He's in
his early forties, maybe. About my height. He's in walking shorts and
Birkenstocks. A navy T-shirt with a knit collar rolls like a petal out from
his neck.

"I'm Joe Cruz. We met in the middle of the night."

"Oh, hi. It's good to actually *see* you." I wait for him to draw near.

"I'm Annie Rush." We shake hands. His grip is firm. His face friendly, open, deeply tanned. He smells of good soap. "Are you going in to breakfast?"

"Absolutely. Today and every day, I can hardly wait for the bell."

I grin. "How long have you been here?"

"A little over a month, with a month to go."

"Goodness. That's a long time."

"I know. That's why I look forward to new people and new company. Most of the guests don't stay long, so there's a constant turnover. This past weekend, the last of the friends I'd made packed up and went home."

We walk together into the dining room. It radiates sunshiny cheer. The walls are mottled amber, the ceiling edged with tiles featuring spirals the color of marigolds, each like a miniature sun. An imposing sideboard, painted the color of robins' eggs, takes up most of the far wall. The long dining table is decorated with spatters of turquoise paint. Deep blue place mats and lemon-yellow napkins make for a striking contrast. The room buzzes with conversation.

"There's Ginny Powers," Joe says. "She owns the casa. She's our own mother hen."

Ginny looks up and waves to Joe. "Come sit. There's two chairs here." Ginny is a plump, middle-aged woman with a welcoming face. Her sharply pressed blouse is the color of persimmons.

"I'm glad you two met," Ginny says, after Joe has made the introductions. When we are settled, Ginny turns to the others at the table: "For those of you who don't know, this is Joe Cruz. He's from San Francisco. He's an anthropology professor at Berkeley. He's been here over a month. Next to me, he knows all there is to know about Oaxaca. Right, Joe?"

Joe smiles and rolls his eyes.

"And this is Annie Rush. She arrived last night. She's from Minnesota."

"Brrr," someone says.

Ginny continues, "This is Harry and his wife, Ingrid, they're from South Carolina. And this is Paul and his partner, David, from Chicago. And over there is Carmen, she's from New Mexico, and that's Miriam, from Houston, and at the end of the table are Chris and Karen, they're from upstate New York. They're here on their honeymoon."

"Hello everybody," I say. "By the way, Ginny, thanks for e-mailing home for me to let them know I made it in safe."

A young girl waltzes in with a pot and pours our coffee, then takes our order. Joe speaks his in perfect Spanish; I screw up my courage and parrot him. Soon, our breakfast is on the table. Huevos rancheros. Bacon. Freshly squeezed orange juice. A basket of hot rolls and tortillas. The eggs are delicious. Creamy yellow and spicy with onions and peppers. The bacon is crisp and shatters in my mouth. "God, I was hungry," I say to Joe. "All I had yesterday was airplane food."

"That's not food," Joe says.

"You've got that right." I take a long swallow of juice. I can taste the Mexican sun in it. I set the glass down. "So, you're a professor."

"I'm on sabbatical. I'm down here doing research for a paper I'm writing. What about you?"

"I guess you could say I'm on sabbatical, too. I'm a freelance corporate trainer. I'm taking time off."

"You're the guys who make the money teaching."

"Maybe. But you're the guys with the prestige."

Joe asks, "Are you staying long?"

"Not even two weeks. I need to be home by Christmas."

"You should stay for the Night of the Radishes. That's on the twenty-third."

"I read something about that, but it was not much information."

Joe says, "I've been here a few times for it. It's pretty amazing the way the artisans take radishes and carve them into figurines and scenes. They're special radishes, you know. You can't eat them. They're hard and woody. Good for carving."

"What exactly do they carve?"

"Oh, they do religious scenes, like the Nativity or the Last Supper or the Virgin Mary. But other things, too. One year, there was a whole orchestra. Musicians with trumpets and drums and flutes. All with so much detail. And there were dancers with headdresses and with lacy skirts swaying to the music. All of this is carved from radish skins or radish flesh or from their green leafy tops."

"Sounds incredible."

"I know. I'm looking forward to this year's competition."

"It's a contest?"

"Yes. All the scenes are set up in booths built around the square. You can't imagine the line that forms to see them. Three prizes are given. Top radish scene wins ten thousand pesos. That's a lot of money here."

"Sounds wonderful. I wish I could stay."

"You know, this season is probably the best for visiting Oaxaca. From the Day of the Dead on November first to New Year's, you can't find a better time. And this year, it's the millennium. That's like icing on the cake."

"You're staying for that?"

Joe nods. "It'll be fantastic. The whole town'll be one giant fireworks display."

I pour myself more coffee. "Tell me something. Is it true what Ginny said, that you know all there is to know about Oaxaca?"

"To put it mildly, Ginny was exaggerating. But I'll say this, I am researching the area, so I've learned a lot. Why? Do you need to know something? Go somewhere? I have a car, if you need to go someplace in particular."

I sip my coffee. I hesitate telling this man, practically a stranger, what I want. But then, he has a car and he speaks Spanish. Besides, if I don't open up to someone, how will I find Hub? I dab my lips with the napkin. "You know what, Joe? I do need some help."

Joe's eyes are light brown and guileless. "Okay. Just tell me what you need."

The patio beside Joe's room affords an ideal place for strategizing. Both patio and room are surrounded by flowering vines and shrubs. A confluence of trees canopy the space. Joe's room is, in fact, a small building set apart from the casa itself. Joe tells me that long ago, before the house became an inn, the room had been a spacious garden shed. He has turned the place into his own personal haven. A row of votive candles line the window ledge. Under the ledge, a battered old table sits on the patio. Upon the table rests a boom box, a Lucite case of CDs, bottles of red wine and bubble-glass wineglasses with bright blue rims. There are coffee cups and saucers, as well as a compact Krups espresso maker. Books, notebooks and reams of paper are stacked on the shelf spanning the table's legs. At the edge of the patio, a padded lounge chair rests in the only spot that's in the sun.

"You've made this so homey," I say. We are sitting at the cowhide-topped table next to a jasmine bush. I pick one tiny, creamy blossom. I twirl it round and round in my fingers.

"It was easy. I drove down from California, so it was easy to bring stuff. I don't think I could make it without my espresso maker."

"Your very own Starbucks," I say.

"Yeah, but let's keep this our secret, okay?"

"My lips are sealed." I pierce the skin of the jasmine blossom with a fingernail and release its heady aroma. After a moment, I say, "So. Let me tell you what I'm after."

"Shoot."

I sketch out the general story: Hub's disappearance twenty years ago, when he was seventeen. The postcards he sent. Ma's death. The last postcard mailed, the one from Oaxaca, dated November 4. I recount my thorough search on the Internet, listing the places I've contacted and the results. "I've studied a few guidebooks to help familiarize myself with Oaxaca," I say to cap off my explanation, "but I have no real idea about how to start a search. I know the city's pretty big, so it's not a matter of going from door to door, or putting flyers up."

"That's right," Joe replies. "There's some three hundred thousand people in Oaxaca, maybe more. As you know from the guidebooks and your trip in from the airport, this is not one of those sleepy little Mexican towns you see in the movies, though Oaxaca's charm is that for centuries it's retained its pre-colonial spirit. Also, a large percentage of the population is pure Indian, mostly Mixtec or Zapotec, and they still speak their native tongues. You'll hear it in the markets. Some speak no Spanish at all. In fact, there are some sixteen different ethnic groups living in the state."

"I read that, and I think it's fascinating. So, I guess the best thing is to start with the basics, like the telephone directory. Then electric and gas. I did find out that Hub drives a VW, and I have the license plate number. So we could inquire at motor vehicle registration."

"Seguro Social would be another place," Joe says. "That's social security, and you sign up there for medical assistance. Remember, Mexico has socialized medicine."

"Oh, Joe, this is all great."

Joe stands. "Let me get my cell phone. We don't want to tie up the casa's phone, and besides, we have privacy here."

I spend the greater part of the morning with Joe as he makes phone calls for me. We start with the phone company. When this proves fruitless, Joe goes on to the electric and gas companies. These draw blanks. He then calls the office of motor vehicles, providing the clerk with the make and year of Hub's car, as well as his California license plate number. After all the explanation, all the waiting, all the answering of more questions, we still come up with nothing. He nets the same result when he inquires at Seguro Social.

"This is frustrating," I say. "By the way, I owe you for those calls."

"It's no big deal." Joe flips the phone closed.

I lean back into my chair. "Listen, I don't want to keep you from your work." I point to the table and the stacks of books and papers. "Looks like you have plenty to do."

"Actually, I've done quite a bit already. It was time for a break. Besides, while in Mexico, I like to go with the flow. This search of yours intrigues me."

"You're sure?"

"I'm sure."

"Well, okay. In that case, I have an idea. I suppose there's a newspaper. I could run a personal in the newspaper."

"There's *El Tiempo*. We can walk down to the office. It's only a few blocks from here. It'll give you a chance to see the city."

"Good idea."

Oaxaca is a city to awaken the senses. Its streets bustle with cars and buses, taxis and foot traffic. The air carries the very scent of Mexico, an aromatic mixture of leather and charcoal, of copal incense and exhaust fumes, of thousands of corn tortillas roasting on hundreds of comales. The cacophony of living fills the day: vendors hawking, beggars clamoring, animals yipping and chirping.

Joe and I wind our way down Avenida Independencia, Joe leading the way, a stream of conversation passing back and forth between us. We pass la Basilica de la Soledad, an ancient colonial church towering at the top of a long flight of steps. "On our way back," Joe says, "I'll take you inside to visit la Virgen de la Soledad. They say she's miraculous. You can light a candle to help find your brother."

"That would be good. 'Soledad,' doesn't that mean 'loneliness'?"

"Actually, it means 'solitude.' But it can mean 'loneliness,' too. Whichever you want."

I stop in my tracks. "Look at that." I peer inside a store window protected by iron bars. Behind the glass is a huge pottery mermaid. Joe steps over and looks, too. "Now, that's something," he says. "I hadn't seen that before."

The mermaid is about four feet high and half as much wide. She is intricately fashioned from unpainted clay. She holds a large dove with widespread wings against herself. Clay fish, some pointing up, some down, form a backdrop against the mermaid, who leans out as if to speak. "I know what she is saying," I tell Joe.

"What's that?"

" 'Take me home to Minnesota.' " I stand back and crane my neck, looking for the name of the store. I find it above the door. "Los Tules Gifts and Art Gallery. I'll remember that."

When we reach the newspaper office, I follow Joe into the building, which like so many others in Oaxaca, appears to have been a former residence. We cross a long shadowy quarry-stone entryway that merges with a spacious interior patio. The patio has a cement floor with an impressive tiled fountain gurgling with waterspouts at its center. Surrounding the patio is a wide gallery, breached at regular intervals by the doors to many businesses. One of these opens to the offices of *El Tiempo*. A broad counter spans the width of the anteroom. Standing behind it, flipping through the pages of a magazine, is a young woman with hair so severely pulled back in a bun that it stretches the corners of her eyes. And painfully so, from the looks of it. The woman does not glance up when we enter. There are no others in the room.

"Is this the newspaper?" I ask in Spanish.

The woman nods.

"I'd like to place an ad."

The woman reaches under the counter and brings out a clipboard with a form attached. She hands it to me. "Llénelo," she says, then goes back to her magazine.

I walk over to where Joe sits, thinking that the woman behind the counter could use one of my workshops. The one on developing people skills. I fill out the form with the usual: name, address, telephone number. I use the casa's information. There is a large space for the text of the ad. Here, I write: "Hubert Henry Hart. I YAM WHAT I YAM. Hub, we got your postcard. I'm here to see you. I leave December 21st. Call me at Casa Amapolas." I add the phone number. I sign the ad, "Your sister, Annie Hart Rush." I look the whole thing over, then hand it to Joe to check.

"Looks good," he says, and then I take the ad to the counter. The woman studies the filled-out form. "You want it in English?" she asks in Spanish.

"Sí, en Inglés."

"And you want this in capital letters, just like you wrote it down?"

"Sí, en capitales, por favor."

"Muy bien."

She asks me how long I want the ad to run, and I tell her until the twenty-first. "¿Y cuánto va costar?" I add.

The woman totals up the words, using a small calculator to figure the cost.

Joe comes up to the counter. "When will the ad start?"

"Thanks, I forgot to ask," I say.

"Today is Monday, so it'll start on Wednesday," says the clerk.

I nod and pay. A sense of satisfaction fills me. I have put into motion what I've come all this way to do.

"You okay?" Joe asks as we step back onto the sidewalk.

"I'm okay, but I'm scared. I'm scared I won't find my brother. I'm also scared I will."

Joe says, "I know that feeling. In that case, there's only one thing to do."

"What?"

"Surrender to the cosmic will of Mexico."

"What does that mean?"

"I'll explain it to you later," Joe says. "When we're sitting down somewhere and not standing in the street."

 Late that evening, after supper and a heated game of Scrabble with other guests in the casa's big sala, I bring my laptop out to the table on the veranda. Earlier, Joe had acquainted me with the casa's system for using e-mail. A telephone jack is conveniently located in the wall right next to the door of my room. Tonight, I'm dressed for comfort: fleece sweatpants and a T-shirt topped by one of Sam's shirts. The night is pleasantly mild, but cool enough to warrant slipping on a pair of socks.

I open up my file cabinet to reread the e-mails I'd stored earlier. I start with one from Will:

Dear Mom Are you having a good time? We had macaroni and cheese for dinner but Dad put in too much chilly pepers and we all had to drink a lot of water. But don't worry. Aunt Milly is taking good care of us. I am missing you Mom. Your kid Willis Hart Rush (Will). P.S. Jack has something to tell you and I want to tell you first but he says if I do he will tear my arm off and wack me on the head with it. P.S. Jack said that Mom not me.

I shake my head and smile, then click on Jack's message:

Hi Ma. I know you made it allright because Dad said so. Guess what? We won our hockey game. I scored two goals! I was the hero. We won 2-1. Everybodys calling me Jack the Jock. I think I like it. Dad put hot sauce in the mac and cheese. I like it better the way you do it. Well I have to go. Dad says lights out. I hate lights out. I wish I could stay up all night. You guys get to do it. Your son, Jack the Jock. P.S. Did you find Uncle Hub yet? Where is he?

I save Sam's letter for last.

Hola, cutie, how's it going? The house is a pretty sorry place without you, but we're doing all right. You only left a day ago, so there's nothing much to report. It started snowing like crazy again. See what happens? You leave and the sky falls in. Hey, but don't let that put any pressure on you. We'll be okay! Write soon, I miss you, and Elvis misses you. He's my new sleeping companion. His paws are much warmer than yours. But hey, I mean that in a good way. I love you, kid. Come back soon. S.

I write a communal letter in reply. I tell Jack I'm thrilled he's a hero. I praise Will for holding back on Jack's news. I suggest to Sam that he stash the Tabasco away. I ask them all to tell Milly I think she is an angel. I tell them about the newspaper ad. Also about Joe Cruz. I tell them I plan to visit the American Lending Library. A guest at dinner happened to mention it, and I say I think it might be a place where Hub might go. I tell them I went to a church and lighted a candle to la Virgen de la Soledad. I tell them "Soledad" means "loneliness." I say, that's what I am, just plain lonely without the three of you.

 *I couldnt believe it when Hub left. He left me a note. I never showed it to anyone. He propped it against my pillow. I didnt see it until it was time to go to bed. I thought it was from Annie. She always bought me cards. Sometimes she made them herself. I love you, Ma. Your the best Ma. When I saw that card by the pillow in that yellow envelope I suppose I had a smile on my face. I suppose I kept on smiling all the while I opened it up. Course it didnt last for long when I saw what Hub had wrote. Now that graduations over, your finally getting your wish Ma. So dont look for me because Im gone. Ill never forget that.*

Ill take those words to my grave. The card I think I threw it out. A person cant keep something so hurtful.

Its a hard thing to contemplate your son taking off like that and you never seeing him again. You get in a fowl snit and you tell your boy to get out of the house. You tell him you never want to see him again and then you get your wish. Of course at the time I figure I was right in saying what I did. Just look what Hub said to me but now I ask God for forgiveness. I guess maybe its good my lungs are cottage cheese. With lungs like that I guess I cant last long. So its good that Im making the effort to write these things down.

I ask God to forgive me. Elmer asked my forgiveness. He wrote it in a note but I didnt see it until later. I was washing the supper dishes when the shotgun went off. Or maybe I was wiping up the kitchen table. It had a linoleum cloth with decorations. The shotgun went off in the basement right under my feet. I think I felt the shock through the soles of my shoes. Annie came flying down the stairs. Get on over to Lillian Kissels I said. Get on over there right now. I just knew what was down there. How I wished I was wrong. It took a while to see Elmers note. I think it was the officer that found it. It was sitting on the washer. It wasnt in an envelope or anything. The words on that paper Ill take to my grave. I cant take it no more. Everythings my fault. I pray you can forgive me. I pray that God forgives me. Also don't bury me next to Maggie. I dont deserve the company.

It pains me to remember these things. Why do I insist on remembering. Maybe its the way when you know you will die soon. When Maggie died there was no note. No explanations. No goodbyes. Sometimes on the farm late at night I sat out on the back stoop smoking my cigarettes and making up goodbye notes from my beloved Maggie, my darling little girl. Dont worry Ma. Im in a garden full of flowers. Ill see you later aligator. And dont you worry Ma it didnt hurt.

 The next morning, after breakfast, as I head down Avenida Independencia toward Macedonio Alcalá Street and the American Lending Library, it occurs to me that I have no idea what Hub might look like now. When he was twelve, he was tall and bony. Goofy-looking, like boys can be at that age. He had stringy arms, hands like baseball mitts. Lank, dishwater blond hair, dark brown eyes, just like Pa's. An intelligent curiosity shone in Hub's eyes when he was twelve. After Maggie died, the shine faded, as it faded from the eyes of us all, from all of our lives. It's why we sold the farm, auctioned off all the farm equipment and moved to the cities, into the house on Holmes Avenue South. What brightness we found there vanished three years later, when Pa figured life would never be worth living.

By the time he was seventeen, Hub's arms and chest had filled out, a consequence of the punching bag he'd set up in the basement, almost in the same spot where Pa had squeezed the trigger. Back then, after supper, after the dishes were put away and the kitchen lights were dimmed, Ma would plop herself down on the easy chair she'd pulled up before the bay window in the front room. Ma'd sit, smoking her cigarettes, the only light cast by the little lamp on the dining room hutch. Ruminating, she'd gaze out the window, across the porch, toward the street where the traffic crawled by intermittently. I used to think that what Ma was contemplating, all by her lonesome, there in the shadows, was how one night she might run out into the street, stop a car, climb in and head off to wherever it was going. Away from Hub and me. Away from our sorry life. The thought of Ma leaving terrified me, and while it was true that Ma was taciturn and morose, that try as I might I could rarely make her smile, she was the only Ma I had and I wanted her close to me. So while Ma sat and mulled, I'd be upstairs, almost directly above her, my ear trained for her opening the door, for her slamming it shut and striking off on her own. I'd be propped up against the head of the bed, doing my homework, catching the stench of yet another cigarette, my head reverberating with the vibrating punches Hub was throwing at the bag down in the basement. Despite the racket, neither Ma nor I ever stopped him. God knows we were each enraged by Pa's selfishness, but it was Hub who delivered the furious, revengeful blows for the three of us. Hub who one day opened the door and walked out, never once looking back.

But that was then. Nine postcards and almost twenty years later, Hub might have grown weary of his tumbleweed life. Now, Hub might wish to come home. As far as his looks, he could be fat and sloppy. He could be missing teeth, the hair on his head, who knows? For now, I'll picture him looking like Pa. If I see a man who looks like Pa, I know I'll have found Hub.

I almost miss the entrance to the library. I had assumed its door would front the street, but in fact, the library is on the second floor of a building. By chance, I see the small bronze plaque marking its location and step into a shadowy recess, then go up a set of stairs until I find the main door. I walk into the sight of shelves and a long reading table flanked by comfortable chairs, into the smell of old books and newspapers and magazines. Patrons sit lost in their reading at the table. I rake my gaze over them, a little electric current of expectation running through me. Everyone I see looks like an American, maybe long-staying tourists, or expatriates, or just walk-ins, like me. But not one person looks like Pa. I take a look around the place. There are three rooms chock-full of books, most in English, it appears. My mind fills with the image of Hub and his books. Hub reading in bed, in the barn, on the tractor. Hub trying to read at the table and Ma yapping and batting his book away. Put that thing down! Food's on the table!

When I walked in, I had spotted what I'm sure was a librarian at a desk in a corner of the main room. I go up to her now. She peers at me over the top of her half-moon glasses. "Yes?"

"I have a problem and I need your help," I say, a direct line from one of the workshops I teach, the reason behind the line being that people are usually eager to help others solve their problems. It makes them feel needed.

She raises her eyebrows. She lowers her glasses, which are looped around her neck by a beaded chain so that they rest against the flowered fabric stretched across her bosom.

I extend a hand to her. "I'm Annie Hart Rush," I say. "I'm here from Minnesota."

She takes my hand. "Mildred Pierce," she says. "Like in the movie."

I smile. "That's something," I say, referring to her name. I've never seen the movie, but I recognize the title. "I bet you could write a book about having a name like that."

She nods, her only concession to my attempt at a bit of humor. I decide to take a more serious tack. "Here's what I need, Mrs. Pierce. I'm looking for my brother. He's also from Minnesota, but he's been living in Oaxaca. I wonder if you might know him?"

"Your brother's name?"

"Hubert Henry Hart, but we call him Hub. Hub Hart."

"Don't you have your brother's address?"

There's a chair beside the desk. One of those ancient schoolhouse ones with dull, stainless steel legs and dark green leather for a seat. "Do you mind?" I point to the chair.

"Be my guest."

I take the chair. Conspiratorially, I lean in toward her. "Here's the story. My brother has been estranged from the family for some time. Now my mother, our mother, has died, and I need to let my brother know."

Mildred Pierce is silent, obviously taking all this in, then she says, "I'm sorry about your mother."

"Thank you. It's been hard. Hub's my only sibling. He needs to know that Ma has died."

"How do you know your brother is in Oaxaca? You say you've been estranged."

"He mailed a postcard from here. I got it two weeks ago. That's why I made the trip. I'm here to find him."

"And he didn't write his address on the card?"

I shake my head.

"And so you want to learn if he's someone I might know?"

"Well, I was thinking that maybe Hub came in and signed up for a library card. Reading books was one of his passions. He used to read all the time."

"So, you want me to check to see if your brother signed up for a card. Is that what you want?"

"If you could, it would be a great help. I'd be most grateful. You see, just before she died, I promised my mother I'd find my brother." Lamely, I raise a hand as if making a pledge.

Mildred Pierce goes silent again, then she lifts her glasses, unfolds the arms and adjusts them before her eyes. The colorful beads of the chain hang down from her face like suspension cables on a bridge. "Might I see some identification?"

I open my purse and extract my wallet. I pluck out my Minnesota driver's license. Luckily, I've kept Hart as my middle name. I hand the card to her.

Mildred Pierce studies the card. "Hopkins?" she asks. "Where is that?"

"It's a suburb of Minneapolis."

"I have a cousin who lives in Edina. That's also a suburb, right? My cousin lives in a high-rise. Assisted living, it's called."

"Edina is very near Hopkins. I'm practically your cousin's neighbor."

"Small world," Mildred Pierce observes. She reaches for a square metal file that sits on the desk. She pulls it toward her. Flips open the lid. Index cards crowd the space inside. There are alphabetized card dividers. "Your brother's name again?"

"Hart." I spell it out. "Hubert Henry Hart." It might be this easy. Walk into a Oaxacan library. Find my brother's name in a card file. Get his address. Go to him. The enormity of what I soon might learn quickens my pulse.

Mildred Pierce's hands are spidery, the backs knotted with veins. Her nails are lacquered a soft shade of pink. Like the interior of a seashell. She pokes a nail behind the card divider that separates the "H"s from the "G"s. From the looks of it, there are not many cards assigned to the "H"s. I hold my breath as she goes through them.

"I don't see a 'Hart' here," she says after a moment. She looks up at me, over the edge of her glasses once more. This time there is kindness in her gaze. "I'm sorry."

I exhale and sit back against the chair. What a fool I was to think it would be easy. I shake my head in disappointment. "I promised Ma," I say, really to myself.

"I have an idea," Mildred Pierce says. "If your brother likes to read, you might inquire at the bilingual bookstore. It's just down the street. It's called 'La Casa del Libro.' Enrique Wilson owns it. He knows everyone in town. Enrique might know your brother."

"That's a good idea. I'll try that." I rise and then an idea of my own strikes me. "Do you think I could leave my name and where I'm staying, here, at the library? I know it's a long shot, but if Hub does come in for a card, you could give him the information."

Mildred Pierce slides a leaf of paper across the table toward me. "Write it down. I'll place your note in the 'H's, in the place his name would go."

I sit down again. Take the pen she hands me. I write: "Hub, it's me, Annie. I'm here in Oaxaca, at Casa Amapolas. I leave on December 21st." I include the phone number. "Please call me." I sign my name. I'm about to fold the paper over when I add, "Hub, it's been such a long time."

It's green sauce night (mole verde con hierbas) at El Naranjo. The restaurant on Trujano features the seven moles of Oaxaca, one for each night of the week. A group of us from the casa crowd around a table set in a charming patio with a fountain, its edge brimming with flowerpots. I sit next to Joe. We all sip margaritas in glasses rimmed with a crust of salt. My drink is both tart and sweet and very cold. The margarita is taking the sting out of my disappointing day: no luck at the library, no luck with Enrique Wilson at the bookstore. My only hope at either place is the notes for Hub I left at each.

"Chris and I found the greatest carving today," Karen, the newly-wed from New York, is saying. "It's a big rooster with polka dots."

"Actually, the rooster is being carved for us," Chris says. He's an engaging-looking fellow with thinning hair, despite his youngish age. "We saw one at the carver's studio. The man said he'd make one special for us."

"You went to the carver's studio?" I ask.

"Oh, sure," Karen says. "Most of the artisans have open-door studios. Usually, they're out in the villages."

Chris adds, "This one is on the way to Monte Albán."

"If you're looking for good carvings," Karen says, "you should check this place out. It belongs to the Huerta family. An old man and his wife. Also their two sons. It's one of the sons who makes the roosters."

"We're picking ours up in a couple of days," Chris says. "If any of you want to go with us, you're welcome."

"I might do that," I say. I've decided to return home with the pottery mermaid I spotted yesterday. Maybe if I added a wooden mermaid carving, I'd be on my way to starting a collection.

Our dinners are served. We all have ordered the pork loin with green mole. The dish is bright green and a delight to the eye. When I lift a fork to my mouth, I'm in heaven. Tender slices of pork are smothered in the tang of cilantro and parsley, in the sweetness of tomatillos and onion, in the fire of serrano chiles. And these are just a few of the ingredients.

"God, this is good!" Miriam, the guest from Houston, exclaims.

Joe says, "You know, this restaurant offers cooking classes. If you want, you can sign up and learn how to make the moles."

"Let's get some information," Paul says to his partner, David. David says to the rest of us, "Paul's my gourmet cook."

After dinner, we stroll out into the balmy night and head for the zócalo, the plaza, three blocks away. Joe and I take up the rear. As we walk along, I readjust the shawl I've wrapped around my shoulders.

"By the way," Joe says. "That shawl looks good on you. The colors and design are striking with your hair."

I look down at the swath of fabric draped along my arms. Against a black background, silk embroidered flowers stand out. Anemones maybe, with rusty-colored petals, their centers showy spokes in honey and sage. "Thanks, Joe. I got it at the museum store next to the Santo Domingo church. It was a forty-dollar bargain, my consolation prize after talking to that bookstore owner."

"Yeah, you had a tough day."

"I don't know, it seems I'm running out of options. My only hope is the ad. It'll start running tomorrow." It feels good to be walking next to Joe, talking about my troubles. He's an objective, patient listener, and it's just now dawning on me that I've been needing someone like this. Someone who doesn't share a history with me. Someone who, after I return home, I'll probably never see again. There's a certain safety in that. I feel as if here, in this place so far away from all that's real to me, I can be anyone or anything I want, and who would know the difference?

"Remember, you've got to give the ad time," he says. "Even if your brother sees it, that doesn't mean he'll drop everything and rush over. He's been gone a long time. Chances are he'll need to adjust to the fact that you're so near."

"I hadn't thought about that." In my mind, Hub would read the ad and then immediately appear. It hadn't occurred to me that he might have to think twice about seeing me again. Worse, that he might decide not to see me at all.

"Well, it's just a point of view."

We walk along in silence for a few moments, stepping around the occasional missing square in the sidewalk, at times nudging against each other when we do. After a bit, Joe says, "I've been thinking. There's a place on the outskirts of town we might try. The Centro Cultural de Oaxaca. It's a meeting place for non-Spanish-speaking visitors. It also provides a number of free programs for the community at large. I've presented two lectures on anthropology there already. In any case, we could drive out there and check things out."

"I hate bothering you with this, Joe. Why don't you give me the address, and I'll just hop a cab."

"Are you kidding? You think you can cheat me out of seeing the look on your face when you finally find your brother's name on some roster? No way."

I smile. "Well, okay."

The others stroll in a bunch up ahead. Someone must have cracked a joke, for David is now laughing hysterically.

"You know what, Annie?" Joe says. "More than anything else, you should just do what you can about your brother and then try to have some fun. If you want, we could go out to Monte Albán or to Mitla. Those are two fine pyramid sites. Or we could make a trip to the villages and meet the carvers, or the potters, or the weavers."

"You're right. I should do what you say, surrender to the cosmic will of Mexico."

"There you go," Joe says.

At the zócalo, we sit at one of the iron tables under the arches that front the garden. I order a hot chocolate. The zócalo is filled with people. It's past eleven and there are people enjoying drinks and even meals at every table. People stroll around the garden plaza. They relax on park benches. It's a wonderful thing to see, this communal camaraderie so late at night, under the stars.

A small girl, maybe seven or eight, approaches our table. She carries a basket filled with gardenias. "¿Florecitas?" she says, lifting her basket so we can take a closer look.

Joe picks up a small bunch. He asks how much and pays, adding a few extra centavos, which makes the girl smile, though she lowers her head to do it.

"Para tí," Joe says, handing me the bouquet.

"Oh," I exclaim, touched by his thoughtfulness. "This is so nice." I poke the stem of the flowers behind an ear. "Gracias, Joe."

"Por nada," he replies, leaning back in his chair. His tanned face shows a sweet expression.

I have to keep myself from grinning foolishly. How fortunate can I be? It's the dead of winter and I'm sitting beneath the sky of my dreams, indigo and star-studded, in the company of a new friend, gardenias perfuming my hair.

 Back at the casa, before going to bed, I sit on the veranda with my laptop. I open up the e-mail I'd filed earlier from Sam.

"Dear Annie," he writes.

Just want you to know I mailed out the cards today. Ten days before Christmas, just like you instructed. I can't believe there were so many. But then, you always send to everyone. You little miss perfect you. Everything's okay here. But we're all missing you, even if it's only been a few days. Milly's doing a great job. Today, when I came home from work, I could smell the cookies baking as I got out of the car. There was a pot roast in the warmer. Smashed potatoes and green beans. Green beans with little hunks of ham, just the way you fix them. Yum yum. The boys and I ate until we burst. Even Elvis got some. I know, I know I shouldn't have, but hey, the commander's gone, so we snuck in a treat. Well this is all the news. All my love is for you. Sam. P.S. The kids send their mommy big fat kisses. I do too.

"Dear Sam," I write back.

Thanks for sending the cards. I wish you and the kids were here. This is such an amazing place. Unlike the Mexico I discovered back when I lived in Cuernavaca. You know that old saying, the place that time forgot? That's Oaxaca. Modern, but still traditional. Well, this is all for now. Time for bed, I'm getting sleepy. I wish I was going to be snuggling in beside you. Hey, I have an idea. Why don't you fly down? I'm not kidding. I love you. Annie. P.S. Give my kids big fat kisses from me. And a big long juicy one for you.

 Popeye yaps when the gate squeaks open. He trots from the kitchen as Luli comes through the door, home from work. She is a slight woman, skin the color of mahogany, ebony hair cascading to her shoulders. Luli's belly is bulging now. "Pareces pita con nudo," Hub likes to say to her. You look like a rope with a knot.

Luli steps into the kitchen, into an aura of domestic tranquility. Hub's vibrant paintings hang on the walls, mounted in rows and columns right up to the ceiling. Still lifes, portraits, landscapes. On the counter, the radio softly plays a ballad. The aroma of sautéing onions and tomatoes wafts from a skillet. Uberto sits on a stool at the table, drawing with crayons on a sheet of pink construction paper. "Mira, Mamá," he says when Luli lays her tote bag down. He lifts the drawing for her to see.

"Que bonito," Luli says. "¿Qué es?"

Hub answers for him. "It's one of Jesus's animals, verdad, hijo?"

Hub is at the counter, dicing serrano chiles for the salsa for supper. To-night he's making enchiladas verdes.

Uberto nods. "It's a dragon with fire in his mouth."

Luli kisses her son on the head. He has so many curls, some mis-take him for a girl. "Jesus had a dragon?" She goes over and kisses her husband. To do it, she has to crane her neck and lift her face to his. Her eyes are dark and luminous. She closes them and Hub kisses each eye-lid. Luli steps over to the table again and pulls a stack of hot tortillas, wrapped in a cloth napkin, from her bag. Every day, after work, she stops to buy fresh tortillas for their supper.

"I found a book at the library," Hub says. "It's called *The Bestiary of Christ*. It describes animals mentioned in the Bible. It might be an idea for our radish tableau. Uberto is helping me draw them. We're going to show them to your father."

"Why don't you just show him the book?" Luli says.

"It's still at the library. I haven't signed up, so I didn't take it out." He liked to go into the library, sit in a chair with a book in his lap. Or he pored over the American newspapers. Not the latest editions, but current enough. Sometimes, he struck up a conversation with a tourist. Sometimes, they left the library together and went over to El Mariachi and had a Dos Equis. He doesn't make a habit of this, but sometimes it's good to talk with another gringo, to have a long con-versation about gringo things, like perhaps gringo football. Los Vikin-gos, to be exact.

"You should get a card at that library. It has books in English. You can't get books in English at the Biblioteca Nacional."

"I know." What he doesn't know is why it's taking him so long to do it.

"Here's your newspaper." Luli lays a copy of *El Tiempo* on the table.

"Good news," she adds. "Some gringos came in and bought two of your paintings."

Hub stops dicing. "You're kidding."

"No. They bought the still life with the mangoes and the one of the church."

"Which one?"

"The one of San Antonino church."

"Oh, that one. Well, good." He goes back to dicing. He is pleased with this news. It has been almost two months since he's sold a piece of art. A month since he's done any house painting. The dearth of work was beginning to worry him. Especially with the baby's arrival only a few weeks away.

"I'm going to change." Luli leaves the room and soon you can hear water running in the bathroom. She returns in comfortable clothes: Reeboks, loose pants, a sweatshirt that a client in California had given her. Luli stands beside Hub and helps ready supper.

"Good thing that sweatshirt's big," Hub says. Luli's stomach stretches out the fabric, as if she'd stashed a basketball under it. "How was our baby today?"

"Kicking all day."

"She wants to come out," Hub says.

"I want it, too."

After dinner, Luli puts Uberto to sleep on the big bed in their bedroom. When she and Hub are ready to retire, Hub will transfer his son to the sofa in the living room. Because the house is small (three rooms, a bath), every square inch counts. In addition to the sofa, the living room holds the television (bought new and carried all the way from

San Diego despite its bulkiness), as well as Hub's easel and canvases and his art supplies. His art is of vibrant colors in imaginative combinations. Magenta and ochre. Turquoise and jet. Emerald and orange. In addition to paintings, he creates retablos. Some consist of tin squares painted with miniatures and including blocks of text extolling some received blessing. Others are small, painted cabinets decoupaged with found art. The walls of the house, all of them, serve as a gallery. Even the bathroom. His most personal work is a large painting of rolling farmland with a fringe of trees at the top and the blurred image of a green tractor plowing up a black field. This painting is not for sale. It is signed "Hubert Henry Hart," and not "Enrique" like all the others.

Tonight, Hub and Luli relax on the sofa under this painting. She's stretched out, her head in Hub's lap. Popeye lies next to the TV, head resting on his paws. A movie with Clint Eastwood is playing. It seems funny to watch him open his mouth and speak Spanish. He's doing it now. He aims a big-barreled gun at the head of a bad guy. "Déle pues, hágame mí día." Clint's top lip curls as he challenges the miscreant to "make my day." When the movie is over, Luli yawns and runs a hand over her belly. "Go to sleep, little girl," she says.

"Is she moving?" Hub spreads a hand over his baby. He can feel the rippling movement of her.

"Do you really think we'll have a girl?" Luli asks.

"Seguramente," Hub says.

"I want to have a girl for you."

Hub nods. He strokes his wife's forehead. "But the truth is, no matter what we have, it'll be okay with me."

"¿Seguro?"

"Seguro," Hub says.

Luli closes her eyes, as if taking this in. After a moment, she opens them. "When we have the baby, will you let your mother know? Your sister, too?"

Luli had asked him this before, four years ago, when Uberto was born. That time, when she asked, he had not answered and she had not pressed him.

This time, however, he says, "If it's a girl, I will tell them."

I've decided to take Joe's advice and loosen up and try to have some fun. I'm propped against the bed's headboard, paging through the *Oaxacan Handbook,* looking for places to shop or visit. I'm going to make a list. There's a knock on the screened door. "¿Señora?" It's Prudencia on the veranda, the woman who sweeps and swabs the floors, who serves the meals.

"¿Sí?"

"Teléfono, Señora."

The ad! I spring to my feet, the handbook clattering to the floor. I don't bother with it. "I'm coming."

The only guest phone at the casa rests on a little table placed on the veranda across the patio from my room. I hurry over the trellised walkway to get to it.

"Hello?" I say into the mouthpiece. My hands are shaking.

"¿Annie Hart Rush?"

The voice is deep, a man's. His English is heavily accented. He speaks the name "Hart" without pronouncing the "h." "Rush" sounds like "Roosh." This voice is obviously not Hub's. My heart sinks. "This is Annie. Who is this?"

"The notice. In the paper today. I have information."

"What sort of information?"

"Come to Portal de las Flores, the café on the zócalo, in front of the entrance to el Hotel Señorial."

I repeat the name of the café.

"Yes. Across from the bandstand."

I think this is the place where we had drinks last night. "When?" I ask.

"Come now. I wait an hour."

"How will I know you? What is your name?"

"I am Jorge. I will be at a table. I will have a red umbrella."

"An umbrella?"

"Bring money."

"You want money?"

"Bring five hundred pesos."

The line goes dead and I stare at the receiver in disbelief. I lay the phone in its cradle. Five hundred pesos? That's about fifty dollars. Is this a joke? I look at my watch. It's twelve-thirty. Joe is away, but he's scheduled to be back at two, for lunch at the casa. If he were here, I know he'd go with me. Joe present or not, I have to check this out. I start back to the room, but Prudencia is mopping the walkway and I can't readily cross over. She makes long, wide strokes that turn the tiles blood red. I take the route around the veranda. I pass Paul and David's room; they'll be leaving early tomorrow. As I go by, I catch movement behind their screen door. On impulse, I turn and retrace my steps. "Knock, knock," I say through the screen.

"Come on in."

It's David. He's obviously packing. Sheets of bubble wrap and newspapers are lying about. On the floor, suitcases yawn open. David, fists poked into waist, shakes his head. "What were we thinking? We've got way too much." Merchandise is piled on the beds, the chairs, the dresser. "Packing'll be a challenge."

"I always pack too much," I say. "Listen, you know that café we were at last night? Do you remember its name?"

"You mean Portal of the Flowers? I think that's what it's called."

"Oh, good. That's what I thought. I have to meet somebody there, and wanted to make sure." I look at my watch again. Twelve thirty-five. I tap the case. "Listen, I've got to run. Good luck with all that."

In my room, I open the armoire. I unlock and pull out the security drawer that contains my valuables: passport, airline tickets, a few pieces of jewelry, traveler's checks and cash. I lift out the envelope containing the Mexican pesos I've exchanged. I thumb the edge of the bills and extract five one-hundred-peso notes. I lay the envelope back in the drawer, slide it closed and lock it with the key. I shut the armoire, stash the money and key in my purse, then hurry off to the café.

Down Avenida Independencia, past la Soledad Church, then four blocks to the post office, right at the corner, across the tree-lined promenade, to el zócalo. The day is hot, the sun glaring. Perspiration slips between my breasts. I pluck at the fabric plastered to my skin, giving it a few tugs to circulate some air. I hitch my purse up on a shoulder, clasping it tightly under an arm. The square throngs with people. Tourists meander along the sidewalks, locals park themselves on the garden benches. On the colonnades, under the arches, people enjoy refreshments or an early lunch.

I step out of the sun. The sudden shadows are momentarily blinding. I lift my sunglasses and perch them on my head. Squinting, I look down the length of this colonnade. The entrance to the hotel is at the other end, the Portal de las Flores just in front of it. I go toward it, weaving around the bunched tables of one café and then another. The closer I am to my destination, the drier my mouth becomes. When I reach it, I duck into the hotel's doorway, allowing my gaze to sweep the many people sitting at the little tables. Thanks to a long-standing ordinance, the street around the square is devoid of traffic. Sunlight bounces off the cobblestones. The pale blue domes of the bandstand kiosk rise beyond them. I wipe moist palms against my skirt.

On the corner, at the edge of the colonnade, sitting half in the sun, half out, there is a man with a cigarette. My eyes fall on the unopened red umbrella spanning the tabletop. I take a deep breath. In with the good air, out with the bad.

"Are you Jorge?" I ask when I reach the table.

The man looks up, eyes darting. He rises. Mashes his cigarette out with a heel. He is in his forties, perhaps. Long, lean face. Clean-shaven, but with a hint of five o'clock shadow. He wears pressed trousers, a white shirt, a tie with a geometric design. He looks very different from what I'd imagined. This man looks like a bank clerk, or maybe a government employee. Does he look like someone to be trusted?

"Señorita," he says. He makes a sweeping gesture for me to sit. I take the chair across from him. The umbrella lies like a barrier between us.

"You have information?"

He settles back into his chair. Sunlight falls in a diagonal line across this chest. "This man you want, this Ubert Enri Art, I give you where he works. I give you, how do you say, la dirección."

"The address."

"Yes, the address."

"And you want money for this address?"

A nod of the head. "Five hundred pesos."

I hesitate, so as not to appear eager. Of course, I would have paid double that amount. "Describe the man I'm looking for."

"Un norteamericano. Alto." He lifts his hand high to show how very tall.

"What color eyes?" I ask. "What color hair?"

When he speaks, there is no hesitation. "Like yours."

"Let me have the address."

The man slips a hand into the pocket of his shirt. He extracts a card. Holds it up momentarily for me to see. Then he sets it, facedown, on the edge of the table. He rubs fingers with a thumb, the universal sign that means "money."

"Is that a business card?" I ask.

"A place of work."

"The place where Hubert works?"

"Sí."

"Okay." I have wedged my purse between myself and the side of the chair. I reach in and find my wallet. Set the wallet on my lap. Pull out the bills I've set aside. "Give me the card, I give you the money."

Over the red umbrella, an exchange is made. Five folded bills for a cream-colored card. I read the information on the card. "Where is this place?" I ask. In the blink of an eye, the bills have disappeared.

"On the road to Monte Albán." The man stands. He picks up the umbrella. "Con permiso, Señorita."

Like a gentleman, he dips his head to me.

 "I think this is the place." I point out the side window of Joe's Cherokee. We are on the southern outskirts of town, at a cross section of roads crowded with businesses: a machine shop, a tortilla shop, a tool and die shop, a dentist's clinic, identified by the huge molar sketched on the wall. To signify the pain, bolts of lightning shoot out from the tooth. To illustrate impending relief, a menacing drill bears down upon it. The cantina advertising is painted, it appears, by the same quirky mind and creative hand that had worked for the dentist. On the cantina wall, a drunkard weaves his way down a street. You can tell he is weaving by the squiggly lines demonstrating his progress. You can tell he has enjoyed a cerveza or four by the lightning bolts forming a crown around his head. It is midafternoon and the molten sun bears down upon the road tar, upon the gravel littered across the wide shoulder that ends at the establishment doors. Then there is the dust. The afternoon palls with it.

"There, on the corner," I say. Joe pulls off the road and we bounce over the gravel. He drives up to a long, low building overspread by a thatched roof. "Well, here we are." Joe slides the gearshift into Park. "You okay?"

"My heart's flying out of my chest." On my lap is the latest photo I could find of Hub, a high school yearbook picture of him at seventeen. Long, unkempt hair. A scowl. The blank-looking eyes.

Joe pats my shoulder. "I can imagine."

I lower my head and swallow hard. "God, I feel sick. Like I'm going to throw up."

"Breathe in slow. Take your time, there's no hurry."

We sit for a while; outside the car, radios blare, machinery screeches, dogs bark, buses grind through gear shifts. "You know what?" Joe says at length. "Why don't you wait here and I'll go in and pave the way. How does that sound?"

"Oh, God, would you? I'd be so grateful. Here." I hand over Hub's photo.

Joe stashes it in his shirt pocket. He pulls the keys from the ignition. "I'll be back." He climbs down from the car, poking his head back in before he closes the door. "Don't worry, okay?"

"Okay." I watch him go around to the entrance. He is an angel in roomy walking shorts and a red-striped shirt. A bilingual angel. I close my mind to what might be happening inside. I focus on the thought of a happier Hub. Hub pitching bales down from the hayloft. Hub golden with sun, his eyes shining. Maggie and I liked to hide up in the loft, trying to entice the feral barn kittens. "That's a joke," Hub would call out to us. "Don't you know those things are wild?"

"Maybe it's futile," Maggie would say, "but it doesn't hurt to try."

"Futile," another of Maggie's big words.

My thoughts are interrupted by a metallic rapping sound. I look out the side window of the car, and standing by the door is a child. A small girl, maybe three or four. She looks up at me with soulful eyes, her tiny palm turned up in hopefulness. I dig into my purse, then slowly open the door. The girl backs away as the door swings wide; her eyes are now downcast. Still her little hand is turned up.

I hunch down beside her. "¿Cómo te llamas?"

There is no response. Not even an upward glance.

"Yo me llamo Ana," I say. "¿Y tú?"

Still no response. Only the round earnest face, the smudged cheeks, the tangled mop of ebony hair.

I fold the ten-peso bill and lay it in the girl's hand. "Para tí."

Brown fingers curl closed. Black eyes glance quickly at me. A fleeting smile and she is off. I watch her go across the gravel, her turquoise flip-flops *scrunch-scrunching* as she does.

"Oh, there you are. I came back and I didn't see you in the car."

Joe comes around to the open car door. I lay a hand over my mouth, to stifle what . . . a whoop of joy, a groan of despair? "What happened?"

Joe shakes his head. "I'm sorry, Annie."

"What did they say?"

"They said no one by that name has ever worked there. They looked at the picture and no one came to mind."

"They were sure?"

"They were sure."

I lean against the car, the metal hot against me. I look up the dusty road, at the ever-moving humanity, people on foot, in cars, in buses, all weighed down by their own true stories. Still, the world keeps spinning. Despite tragedy and sorrow, the world does not stop for anyone. "That son of a bitch."

"Your brother?"

"No, the asshole at the café."

"Yes, well, the world's full of them. Anyway, it could have been a genuine lead."

"Yeah. But it wasn't. I don't know, maybe all of this is futile."

"Know what? I think you need a hug."

He steps so close, I can see into his eyes, deep-set and flecked with amber. At their tanned corners, tiny white lines radiate. I smile at him. Suddenly shy, as the little girl had been.

The hug feels very good.

Im feeling punk today. I cant get much wind. I sound like a locomotive. Uhuhuhuh. Something like that. I keep checking my nails to see if there pink. If they get purple thats bad news the doc says. Im suppose to call if it happens. But maybe I wont. Im getting tired of breathing hard. Its my own fault. Cant blame any-one but me. Doc says to quit. Annie too. But its too late now. Whats done is done. Im not quitting now. Id die without my ciga-retes. Ha. Thats pretty funny. Annie went on a trip today. To new york city to teach one of her classes. She asked me to go. Maybe I should of went. I never been on a plane. Ma she said you come and we can stay in a fancy hotel with a big deep tub. You can take a long bath in bubbly water. We can pick up the phone and order from the restarant and they bring food up on a cart. You can have your food in bed. That would be something. Me eating in bed. Its not natural. I cant imagine handing somebody a plate while there

sitting up in the bed. Cant imagine myself being served like that at
all. My whole life Ive been putting food on tables. On the farm I did
it. In the cities too at the school. I used to stand behind those steam
vats, heat rising up from them, that silly looking net mashing up
my hair. I dished out food for the kids. Beef stew noodles green
beans mashed potatoes. Not that many of them pointed to that.
Most of them wanted the pizza slice or the hamburger and the
french fries. Myself I had no apetite for any of that. These days all
I want is frosted flakes. Maybe with a half banana. Annies kids
like it too. Those sweet boys so big and bright. I don't know why Im
rambling like I dont have any sense. I think Ill stop for a while. I
hear the mail coming through the slot.

Im back. I cant believe it. Hub sent another postcard. This one
came from San Diego. A fancy hotel is on the front. Im looking at it
now. Its called the Coronado. I yam what I yam is written on the
back. Those words always make me think. How are you Hub I
want to ask not what. Are you still my son? Do you still remember
us? Do you think someday you can forgive me?

 Once again, this familiar scene: me, lying on a bed, curled into a ball of pessimism and despondency. Updates of my trip crawl across the screen of my mind, like script on the bottom of the news channel: "Man with red umbrella hoodwinks naive Minnesotan." "Long-lost brother remains lost." "Surviving sister losing hope." The sun set some time ago, and as the room grows dark, I close my eyes and carry myself back home, to my own house, to my own bed. I lie very still, conjuring up Will and Jack, straining to hear them do what they do after they've had dinner: Finish up homework. Play with the Nintendo. Bicker and fuss. I picture Sam, down in the den, watching the History Channel, or maybe Larry King. In my head, I call out to Sam. Please come. I need you. And then Sam slips through space and settles on the bed beside me. He takes me in his arms. Holds me close. Says, Hi there. Remember, this is one boy who'll never ever leave you.

The supper bell clangs, so it must be eight o'clock. I'm not hungry.

I don't want food. I don't want company. My screen door frames a landscape, like a painting: a patio in melancholic lamplight, a green blur of trees, a covered birdcage, like a hanging spook at Halloween. Soon, screen doors creak and then clatter shut. Soon, on the veranda, there's the patter of footsteps, the snippets of conversation: ". . . she said she'd have it ready by tomorrow afternoon . . ." and ". . . it means the city of the dead . . ." and ". . . are you kidding? I'd never tell him that . . ." Soon, quiet returns, and I continue musing.

I want to see my brother, though my feelings for him continue to seesaw. At times, I want to run into his arms and lay my head on his chest. At those times, I don't care what Hub has done. Why he left. Why he hasn't returned. But at other times, I want to pummel his chest with my fists, demanding explanations. One thing is certain now, I want to find Hub for my own sake and not merely because I promised Ma. But the prospects for finding him grow dimmer day by day. This afternoon, on the way back from the place where Hub wasn't, Joe and I stopped at the Centro Cultural. I think Joe was as crushed as I to learn that no one there had ever heard of a Hubert Henry Hart.

I'm scheduled to leave in less than a week. If I don't find him by then, I'm not sure what I'll do. Stay and give it more time? Throw in the towel for now, then maybe return? I don't know. I just don't know.

Sometime later, how long? who knows, the screen door frames a shadow.

"Annie? Are you in there?"

It's Joe. And he's whispering, as if he thinks I'm asleep and he's afraid to wake me.

"I'm here."

"You didn't come to dinner."

"Why are you whispering?"

A little laugh. "Yeah, you're right. Anyway, are you okay? Don't you want to eat?"

"No, I'm not hungry, but I'm okay. It's just that I'm a little sad."

"Hey, listen. Let's walk down to the ice cream stands. I bet you could go for an ice cream."

"I don't think so, Joe."

"Aw, come on. A walk will make you feel better. An ice cream will make you feel even better than that."

And so I go. Out the door with Joe, down the hill, up the wide flight of steps to the nieverias, the ice cream stands, that sit in the shadow of Soledad Church. We stand in line, because there are a lot of people out enjoying the night and stopping for a cone. I ask for a pineapple one and Joe has the mango. We take our treats to one of the benches and for a time we sit in silence, twirling our cones and making them disappear. "That was good," I say, dabbing my mouth with the little paper napkin from the nieveria.

"See. I told you," Joe says, as he finishes his. He gives his fingers a lick.

I look up at the night, past the tops of trees that, in December, wear no snowy icing. Over what looks like a battlement wall, the church towers rise. I point to them. "Do you think it's open? Can we go in?" I'm chagrined to admit I'm not much for churches and prayers and candles, but tonight I need the fortification all of these may bring. I hope that God puts up with people like me, people who only turn to Him when the going gets rough. I have to admit, when it comes to religion, I'm a fair-weather friend.

"It's always open," Joe says. "Good idea, let's go in."

We go around the wall and I pause for a moment to admire the grandeur of the edifice. It's a Baroque church—a basilica since the sixties, Joe has said—with two four-storied towers that rise about an equally lofty but recessed entrance. Bottom to top, the towers' rose-colored stone is exquisitely scrolled and sculpted. Deep, vaulted niches hold carvings of saints. On the second level, spanning the breadth of the church, is a parade of scenes depicting the Virgin Mary, all carved in high relief. There are many churches in Oaxaca City, sometimes two on a single block. La Basilica de Nuestra Señora de la Soledad is almost four hundred years old and houses the image of the patron of the city: Our Lady of Solitude.

We step into a vaulted and arched interior, the air redolent with candle wax and murky with its smoke. There are few people in the church: Some sit in the main pews, some kneel at side altars. Somewhere, someone quietly prays aloud. Maybe reciting the rosary. The echo of the prayers is very soothing. Joe and I go down the principal aisle, toward a resplendent central altar. Over it stands a gilded glass chamber holding the statue of Our Lady. She wears a cloak, ornately embroidered with black and golden threads. Her porcelain hands and face are delicately rendered. Joe has said that her five-pound crown is made of solid gold, that it's encrusted with six hundred diamonds.

We slip into a pew, Joe genuflecting and crossing himself before he sits beside me. For a while, we remain there, in easy silence. I feel comfortable with Joe, a miracle because I've only just met him. Yet he has been nothing but generous with his time and kind with his concern. It's obvious that God, in his goodness, has overlooked my fickle attitude and blessed me with a man like Joe to help me find Hub.

Joe leans over. "I'm going to light a candle."

"Okay."

Joe walks up to the front where two broad candle stands flank the railing before the altar. He nears the left one and soon I see the little spark of a long match going off, then a tall red glass gleaming with new light. Joe crosses himself once more and kneels on a wooden prie-dieu. I watch him as he prays, bent head over clasped hands. There is something touching about this scene. To see a man in prayer is to see a vulnerable one. Sometimes I think it's good for men to surrender to their own vulnerability. Had Pa done it, maybe he'd still be alive. I picture Pa here, kneeling before the figure of Our Lady of Solitude. Were this really so, I know what he'd be thinking. He'd be thinking he was guilty. He'd be asking for forgiveness. It's all my fault, and I'm sorry, so sorry, the words tumbling over and over in his head.

I leave the pew and go up and light a candle, too. There's room on the bench and I kneel beside Joe. "Are you feeling better?" he asks in a low voice.

"I'm feeling better," I reply, for what's the use of saying otherwise. I lower my head, the same words that must have tumbled in Pa's, now tumble in mine. The prie-dieu is narrow and I'm grateful that it is. Joe's side touches mine. He has a wide shoulder I can lean on. I say a little prayer to give thanks for this.

 I'm on top of the world. Or so it seems, given I'm sitting on the South Platform at the Monte Albán archaeological site. Five of us from the casa have come out to see the ruins; Joe is both our driver and our guide. We've been exploring for hours. We've learned that this city on the hill reigned for twelve hundred years starting from 500 B.C. That it was populated by the Zapotecs, who harvested corn and beans, squash and chiles on the hillsides and in the adjacent valleys. From where I sit, I have a perfect view of their spectacular achievement: plazas, staircases, tombs, a ball court, all stone. Stone lugged, chiseled, carved and piled, one huge slab atop another. It gives me pause to gaze upon this wonder. All those people, that civilization, gone. When I think of them, of what is before my eyes and of what's not visible, the subterranean passages and labyrinths they laid out under the city and that extend who knows how far, well, then, all my troubles seem rather small. At this moment and at this place, anyway.

It's late afternoon, and the sun has lost the brunt of its ferocity. Light lies in golden shafts over hieroglyphed stone and over the close-cropped grass of the central concourse and the plazas. Up here, the sky is big, big and the surrounding valley is ringed with hills, furred and velvety with trees. The air is hushed, perhaps in reverence.

"It gives you pause, doesn't it?" says Mickey, who's been sitting by my side. Mickey is a newspaper reporter from New Jersey who arrived at the casa just yesterday. She appears to be in her fifties. But who can tell these days? "You took the words right out of my head," I say.

"Probably out of lots of people's heads."

I nod. "It's all amazing. Oaxaca's amazing. Is this your first time here?" I've brought a bottle of water and I pull up the plug and squirt myself in the mouth.

"Yes. I usually go to San Miguel, but this time I thought, what the heck, Mickey Lou, be a little adventuresome, try something different. And so I did, and I'm not sorry. How about you? You must've come many times."

"No. I'm like you, first time."

"But your husband, he knows everything about the place. *He* must've come many times."

I frown, not understanding, and then it dawns on me what she means. "Are you talking about Joe? Joe Cruz?"

"Isn't he your husband?"

I frown. "He's not my husband."

"Boyfriend then. Significant other."

"He's not either. He's just a friend. I met him when I got here."

Mickey raises her eyebrows. "Oh."

"Why do you ask?" I don't know how to feel about all this.

"I'm sorry. I don't mean to imply anything. It's just that the two of you seem close."

Across the grassy esplanade, I think I see Joe with the other two we've traveled with. They're sitting on the North Platform and they're looking this way. On impulse, I lift a hand and give a wide wave. Soon one of them waves back. I'm pretty certain it's Joe.

"There's good karma around the two of you," Mickey adds.

"Well, that's good to know." I squirt myself with water again.

The five of us who went out to Monte Albán are sitting around the table at the casa enjoying an after-dinner coffee. After our trek, we've decided not to go down to the zócalo tonight. Me, I'm turning in early. I could use ten hours' sleep. We've had a very pleasant supper. Mickey, prompted by me, regaled us with some of the odd stories she's written for her newspaper. One of them involved a man who robbed a convenience store. He might have gotten away, except that he returned to the scene a few hours later to buy a bottle of Sominex. He was nervous, he said, and couldn't sleep. We went on to talk about Mexico in general, and Oaxaca in particular.

Now, Harry, from South Carolina, asks, "Has anyone been down to the coast, to Zipolite Beach?"

His wife, Ingrid, says, "We're thinking about going. Maybe after the New Year. I hear all you have to do is get on a bus."

"Or you can fly, you'd get there much quicker," Joe says. "There's a plane that goes to Huatulco every day. That's not far from where you want to go. Door to door, Oaxaca to Zipo, it'd take about two hours. Tops."

"Is that right?" Harry says. He has a face that puts you in mind of a hound dog. Loose flesh, bags under the eyes. That kindly, yet a tad bereft, look.

"I'm actually driving down day after tomorrow," Joe says.

At the news, you could push me over with a feather. "You are?" I hope my disappointment doesn't show in my voice.

"No big deal. I'll just be gone overnight."

Before I can ask more, before Joe can add anything, Ingrid tilts her head. "What's that?" she says.

Something's happening outside. People singing.

Teresa, the evening server, comes in from the kitchen to refresh our coffee cups. Joe asks her about the singing.

"Una posada," she says. "Allí, en la casa del frente."

"Boy, are we in luck," Joe says. "It's a posada, at the house across the street."

"What's a posada?" Ingrid asks.

I've read about them in my research. "Isn't it a reenactment of Saint Joseph and the Virgin Mary looking for lodging in Bethlehem?"

"That's right," Joe says, "and the posada is the place where they're invited in. That means there'll be a party. Let's go have a look."

There must be fifty or so people, all silent now, on the street outside. They have formed a procession. Most of them are children, all of them carrying lighted candles that spread shadows upward on their faces. Mickey, Ingrid and Harry start across the street, weaving their way around the people, while Joe and I go down the sidewalk to get a better view. Four older children seem to be the focus of the festivities. They stand by the wooden gate of the house chosen for the posada. One of them lofts a pleated-paper lampshade glowing with candlelight. Another holds a statue of Saint Joseph. A third, a statue of the Virgin Mary.

"Those four represent the peregrinos, the pilgrims," Joe explains. "They'll sing a song and ask for lodging. I can translate, if you want."

"Please." It is a tender sight. Children's sweet voices asking the innkeeper for lodging: My name is Joseph, my wife is Mary. She will soon be the mother of the Divine Son. In the name of heaven, we ask for a room.

There are a few more back-and-forth refrains. Then, from over the gate, comes the final response: Sainted pilgrims, come in, come in. We might be poor, but with much love, we offer you a corner of our humble home.

The gate opens and all the people start in. I can't see beyond them to the inside. "It must be huge in there. Looks like there's room for all of them."

"Like the song implies," Joe says, "humble places are made spacious by love."

"Ah." What he said and the way he said it touches me. "What will happen once they're in?"

"They'll kneel around the family's Nativity scene. You know, like the one Ginny has out in our garden. They'll all say a rosary, then the fiesta begins. There'll be a piñata, cold drinks, good things to eat, fireworks, music. You know? A fiesta."

"That's wonderful."

"My grandmother, she was from Puebla. That's north of here. Abuela used to have a posada every year."

"What a tradition."

"Yeah." Joe is leaning against the casa wall. He's lifted a leg and placed a foot against it, too. Now that all the candlelight has disappeared from the street, I can't clearly make out Joe's face, but I sense a shift in his attitude.

"All of this makes me homesick," I say. "It's all so much about family."

"You're right."

There it is again. All the energy drained from Joe's voice. I hesitate a moment, thinking that perhaps Joe will say something more, but he does not. I decide to forge ahead. "I miss my husband. I really miss my kids." In the past, Joe and I have not spoken much about our families. He knows, of course, about Ma's death and my promise to her and about Hub. But I have not gone on to tell him about Maggie or Pa. Sam and the kids, I've mentioned them only casually. About him, I know very little, and because he's not been forthcoming, I have not pried. For the most part, I'm gregarious, but I like to keep private things private. It's obvious that Joe is like me in this regard. I think that's why we've gravitated toward each other. Why there's good karma around us, as Mickey said.

"How old are they again? Your kids?"

"Jack is nine and Will eight."

"Good ages," Joe says.

In the dark, I see him push off from the wall. Throw his shoulders back. "Well, I think I'll turn in." He starts off, not waiting for me.

Joe's abruptness, his quick retreat, catches me by surprise, but I make no comment, I just follow after him as he goes into the house. Under the trellised walkway, we bid each other good night.

I know what this silence is about. I carry a secret too weighty to share. Maybe the same is true for Joe.

I'm soaking in the tub when I hear Joe on the veranda again. "Annie, are you there?" I've shut my room's door, but here, in the bathroom, next to the ceiling, there's a high, open window, like a porthole. Joe's voice floats in through that.

"I'm in the tub," I call out. "Is everything all right?" It's maybe ten o'clock. Don't most bad things happen in the dark of the night?

"Could you come over after you're through? I need to talk to you. It won't take long."

Strange, I think. "Sure," I say. "Just give me a couple of minutes."

"Okay. I'll be out on my little patio. I'll make some coffee, if you want."

"Not for me, thanks. I'll bring over a hot chocolate." I lie in the water, listening to his receding footsteps, wondering what this is all about. I finish bathing and pull on fleece warm-ups, a T-shirt. I apply a quick swipe of lipstick.

As he was on the night when I arrived at the casa, Joe is sitting in the shadows when I walk up to his room. The small candles lined up on his windowsill are lit, providing a flickering illumination. Music plays low on his CD player. Something by Enya, I think. I recognize the haunting, mesmerizing melody. When Joe sees me, he does a gentlemanly thing and starts to rise. "Don't get up," I say, and I take an equipale chair. I set my mug of chocolate on the table. "Are you okay, Joe?"

Joe clears his throat, as if to pave the way toward uttering something important. "Listen, I owe you an explanation."

"Why do you say that?"

"Out there on the street. I was rude. I'm sorry."

"Oh, Joe. You weren't rude. I didn't take it like that."

"It's just that . . ." Joe's voice drops off.

"Look, you have nothing to explain. Really, I mean it."

"Well, maybe I don't. But still . . ." There is a pause, a long pause, before he starts again. "This is hard for me, but I'm just going to blurt it out because I need to." Once more, he clears his throat before continuing. "The thing is, almost three years ago, I lost my wife. My son, too. He was five. His name was Pete. Petey, we called him."

I give a gasp. "Oh no."

"There was a fire. Some kind of problem with the furnace. Anyway, I came home to a blaze. I tried rushing in, but the heat kept driving me back."

"Oh, God." Recognition and grief strike, almost like a blow, in the pit of my stomach. Maggie on the tractor. Me reaching out to her. My arm not long enough to grasp her hand before she slips down.

Joe says, "My only consolation is that they died of smoke and not of fire. That's what the autopsy reports said: smoke inhalation."

In the murkiness of his patio, Joe is but a wide shadow. His cowhide chair complains when he shifts his weight in it. I go to his side. Bend awkwardly over. Stretch an arm along his back. "Oh, Joe, I'm so sorry."

"I guess I just wanted you to know." He lifts a hand and pats mine, resting there on his shoulder.

A great motherly love rolls over me and I pull his head against myself and cushion him against my breast. As if he were Will or Jack who'd come sobbing to me, I hold him. After a time, I gently pull away, dig a tissue from my pocket and quietly blow my nose. Despite the dark, I make out Joe's hand as he passes it over his face. I go back to my chair. Drop myself down in it. In the surrounding garden, night creatures make their small soft sounds. The night intensifies the jasmine's perfume. From the music player, Enya chants something about angels.

"You know," I say, finally breaking the silence we've been keeping. "I was born a twin. An identical twin. My sister, Maggie, died when we were nine. We lived on a farm. It was a tractor accident. I was with her on the tractor when it happened. Pa was driving."

Joe makes no reply to my confession, but I can see him lower his head. I can see his shoulders start to heave.

"I stretched out my hand to grab her when she started slipping, but I wasn't quick enough. My arm wasn't long enough." I can't remember the last time I gave voice to these words. Even in the therapist's office, even with the therapist poking and prying and cajoling, I never once said them.

"Jesus," Joe whispers.

"Yeah, I know," I whisper back.

When I return to my room, I write an e-mail to Sam. It goes on and on. It's all about longing. It's all about desire. It's all about how much I love him. How much I love the kids. How my life would be nothing if anything happened to them. In the e-mail, I tell Sam to check the furnace. I write, "I know I'm being goofy, but check it for funny noises. You got to promise me, okay?"

Joe's confession has made me sad. All night long, I tossed and turned, my head filled with fire and the churned-up earth a farm harrow leaves behind. This morning, Joe's not at breakfast and after I finish mine, I go over to his place to see if he's okay. He is. He's dressed and hauling boxes out of his room and onto the patio. "Morning," he says, no shadow of our late-night conversation in his demeanor. That's a relief. I'm not a person who likes to rehash past conversations. What's said is said, and I like to leave it at that. All that "processing of issues" people are so fond of, I have a few words to say about that: Forget that crap.

"You weren't at breakfast," I say, steeling myself against his saying he's packing up and moving on.

"I made some coffee, want some?" He points to the Krups, its little red light glowing, the carafe half full.

I pour myself a cup, noting the plate of sweet rolls, the bowl filled with fresh fruit sitting beside the coffeemaker. "You had room service."

"I did. I went into the kitchen early and Prudencia fixed me up. Help yourself, there's plenty."

"Thanks, but this is just fine," I reply, lifting my cup. I go over to the table and sit down. "So. What's up?"

"I'm getting ready for Zipolite."

"Ahhh," I say. He's not moving out; he's just going to the beach. I don't fully understand what's happening with me. A week ago, I'd never heard of a man named Joe Cruz. Now the thought of his leaving is unsettling. "What's with the boxes?" There are three sitting on the patio. Big ones. Like the ones computers come in.

Joe kicks one softly. "Christmas treats for the kids at Piña Palmera. That's a rehabilitation center for children that's built under the palm groves at Zipolite Beach. It's quite a place. Every time I come, I make a trip down there and bring what I can. This time it's goodies I bought at Target."

"Can I see?"

Joe opens one of the boxes and pulls out a T-shirt printed with Superman. "All the shirts in here show sports and action figures. Kids love that." He lifts the lid of another box. "This one's filled with jelly flip-flops and lots of those big watches with the jelly bands." He picks out a watch and shows it to me. It has a lilac wristband and a thick face, like something Dick Tracy would wear. "And this box has those portable cassette players with the earphones. I put music tapes in them." He plucks a cassette out of the box and ejects the tape inside. "This one has 'N Sync." Joe closes the boxes up, interlocking the flaps. "All this stuff will be added to the gifts the kids'll get on el Día de los Reyes. That's the Day of the Magi, on January sixth. In Mexico, kids get their presents then." Joe shrugs. "Anyway, I had lots of fun picking all this out."

"That's so generous of you, Joe."

"Yeah, well . . ." He goes to the side table and pours himself some coffee. "I still need to run over to the market across the highway and get supplies for the cooler." He comes over and joins me at the little table.

"How long does it take to get there?"

"To Zipolite? Oh, maybe eight hours. I like to take my time. The way down to the coast is beautiful country. Have you been?"

"Never. I've never been to any Mexican beach, if you can imagine that. I've only been to Mexico City and to Cuernavaca. No beaches there."

"Listen, I have an idea. Why don't you come?"

"Me? Come to the beach?"

"Yes. We'd leave tomorrow and come back the next day. I'm staying at Gloria's."

I feel a thrill of excitement. I can't believe it. Sun. Sand. A Mexican beach. "Oh, but Gloria's not expecting me. I couldn't impose . . ."

Joe chuckles. "No, no, Gloria's is a place to stay. It's really called Posada Shambhala. Gloria owns it and runs it. It's a little slice of heaven. I'll call and get you a room."

"Oh, I don't know, Joe."

"Tell me something, Annie, did you bring a bathing suit?"

"Yes I did, but for what, I don't know."

"Well, now you know. You brought it for Zipolite."

 We leave town, Joe and I, in his Grand Cherokee. CD in the player, we head toward the Southern Sea, the ancient Mexican name for the Pacific. We left about six hours ago, switching on the music the second we pulled past the casa gate. We listen to Bonnie Raitt, the Gypsy Kings, k.d. lang, the Buena Vista Social Club. Rhythms throb in the car as we travel a route nothing less than spectacular. Joe was right. We pass through dusty grassland, which gives way to an expanse of desert, populated intermittently with ejidos, small communities of huts and sheds ringed by cacti fences. At most every one, scrawny, old dogs lolling in the sun lift their heads to note our passing. We climb the Sierra Madre del Sur, up into the coolness of pine forests, the Cherokee parting cloud banks that in some spots hover only yards from the road. Deep gorges with jaw-dropping views plunge down on both sides of us, no guardrails in evidence. Here and there a sobering sight: a small white cross to mark the scene where some unfortunate plunged over.

Now, as we descend the far side of the sierra, the air turns sultry, and we are greeted by thickets of banana and acacia trees. In the distance, the ragged tops of palm groves thriving on the coast hula in the breeze, enticing us. I pull my sweatshirt over my head, thrilled because at Christmastime I can be in just a Speedo swimsuit and a pair of roomy shorts. No clumsy moon boots today, only my thick-soled flip-flops.

"Get ready for a vista," Joe says. We round a bend and there, filling up the far horizon, lies the Pacific, deeply blue, glimmering and silvery with sunlight.

"Holy cow," I say, not because I've never seen the sea before, but because the sight of this sea, on this day, seems such a blessing. Since our heart-to-heart two nights ago, Joe and I have found a warm connection. This is an unspoken thing, but I feel a bond, and I know he does as well. We both have been through fire—he a literal one—and who except someone who has experienced it can know the pain of such a trial? "It's awesome," I exclaim. "No other way to put it."

"Yep," Joe says. "We'll be in Puerto Angel in a few minutes. We'll have lunch at Gloria's."

"Good, I'm hungry." It's now past two, definitely time for something more than a snack from the cooler in the back. It's packed with Bimbo bread, a jar of peanut butter, jalea de fresa, strawberry jam. There are also bottles of spring water and sodas and cans of Jumex juice, including my favorite, nectar de melocotón, the peach nectar. Joe's treats for the children are in the back as well. That he's invited me along for this delivery is opportune. I welcome a break from searching for Hub. I want my shoulders to lose their tightness; I want the anxiety gnawing at my gut to disappear. I look forward to sinking bare toes into sand, to watching the sun set over water, to turning myself over to the curative powers of the sea.

As the travel handbook indicated, Puerto Angel is a small fishing port set around a halcyon blue bay. The town is still recovering from Hurricane Pauline, which struck two years ago. But according to Joe, business establishments were soon up and running, trees and vegetation soon flourishing again. Despite the upheaval, Joe says Puerto Angel has returned to the laid-back place it's always been. He says, "In PA, the sixties are still alive and well." No fancy resort hotels here. Instead, the guidebooks tout rustic cabañas, single rooms or, most popular of all, hammocks under palapas, palm-topped huts, set beneath the coconut trees growing along the beach. As we drive down the main boulevard (a fancy name for a simple, paved street), one of the area's two beaches lies at our left. A substantial pier juts out into the horseshoe bay; small fishing boats bob gently on the water. We pass tourists' rooms on our right, a post office, a grocery store, a bus stop. Though it's the holidays and the high season, few people mill about. I imagine most are having lunch or, possibly, a siesta. For a few minutes we lose our sea view as we drive around a naval station. Joe has said it's common to see groups of sailors, equipped with M-16s, parading up and down the beaches. Though simply part of military maneuvers, these displays help keep crime away, Joe adds.

We drive on, crossing a bridge over an arroyo, go around a promontory and down a stretch of road to Zipolite Beach, a long, gently curving strand of honey-hued sand. Dozens of palapas are set right on the beach, each a giant palm-frond umbrella. Now, at mid-afternoon, the surf is thunderous; the glare so bright, I squint behind my sunglasses. Craggy cliffs reach toward the beach, the shoreline softened by the palm groves backing it.

Joe drives down to the end of the beach and then up a densely treed hillside to Gloria's, formally called Posada Shambhala. "My goodness," I say, for even out the window, the wonder of the place is immediately apparent. "I can't believe this," I say, as we step down from the car. Perched atop the hill, Shambhala is an enclave of cabins and huts and terraces spread at various levels under papaya, coconut and palm trees. The beach, the crashing surf, the sea crags rimmed with sprays of foam offer a spectacular vista below us.

"This is quite the place," Joe says.

We stand at the edge of the parking lot, looking over our surroundings. I'm in shorts and a swimsuit; Joe's in walking shorts and a tank top, his arms and chest tanned and well muscled. I wish Sam and the kids were here to enjoy this; all three dressed in light summer clothing, just like Joe. "You're right," I say. "This is a little slice of heaven."

Joe nods. "As you might imagine from the name 'Shambhala,' this is a Zenny kind of place. There's yoga classes, and coves and crannies for meditation. The food's vegetarian. Macrobiotic, if you want that. There's no alcohol, not a whiff of marijuana. All the rooms are thatched and plainly furnished. There are no private bathrooms; instead, the facilities are shared. Hope you don't find this inconvenient. I've stayed here a number of times and find the simplicity refreshing. That's why I wanted you to come."

"Simplicity's good," I say, thinking of my own too-complicated life. Oh, but that my days might merely consist of a stretch of sand, a book, a breeze, the lulling sound of rocking water. "So what exactly does it mean, the word 'Shambhala'? Doesn't it mean 'peace' or have something to do with enlightenment?"

"You're right, it means that, but it also means something like 'surrendering to the buddha nature.' "

"Ah, is that the same as surrendering to the cosmic will of Mexico?"

Joe pulls his sunglasses up and places them on his head. He smiles broadly. "You could maybe put it like that."

"Well, there you go." Surrender. It's all about surrendering. But surrendering to what? The crashing sea is wild music. The air is hot and moist and smells of brine. My winter-parched body drinks in the moisture. To all this, I could surrender. Better yet, I will *try* surrendering to all this.

"Let's eat," Joe says, and I eagerly follow him down a narrow, blossom-lined path to the restaurant, a huge palapa with an open terrace looking out over the water. The quintessential Mexican decor delights me: rustic, thick-legged tables and chairs lacquered a bright purply blue, lilac place mats and tangerine-colored napkins. The place is crowded and buzzing with conversation, the patrons as colorful as the decor. Young and old are dressed comfortably in beachwear: bikinis, one-piece suits, tank tops, shorts, muscle shirts. A well-traveled backpack leans against almost every chair. All degrees of tanned skin are evident, from the deeply brown to the golden. At the edge of the terrace a couple sits at a table enjoying drinks in tall, frosted glasses. She is as pink as steamed shrimp, the sight of her a precaution.

Joe and I must wait for a table, but soon one opens up and we are sitting on the terrace, under the palms. We both order the fresh tuna salad (atún is the area's main catch) with avocado. Plantain chips come with it. We also ask for fruit plates and naranjadas, orangeades, made with mineral water. When our food arrives, hardly a word passes between us as we greedily dig in. We both make soft grunts of satisfaction.

After we've cleaned our plates and are enjoying a coffee, I ask, "So, tell me. What's the plan?" Joe has not really said what our agenda is, other than delivering his treats to the children's center.

"Well, here's the scoop. I should drive on out to Piña Palmera and drop off those boxes. The director is expecting me. While I do, you can settle in here if you want."

"Heavens, no. I want to come along. I'm very curious about the center."

"Okay, great. After we do that, we'll check in here. But there's a catch to the arrangements. You'll be staying here. I'll be staying in the car."

"The car? What are you talking about?"

"Well, I made my reservation months ago, from San Francisco. I made it for a single, of course. When you said you'd come, I called to see if there was another room available, but it's high season, the holidays, and all the rooms were taken. So, I went ahead and reserved a space at Gloria's campground. You can stay in the room assigned to me, and I'll just park in the camp and sleep on the futon in the back of the Cherokee. It's no big deal. I've done it a million times. In fact, I always travel with the futon, my pillows and blankets. You saw the stuff there, when we were loading up."

"But it's not right, Joe. You have a room, it's not fair for me to take it."

"Yes it is. Besides, the camp is just down a path and minutes from here. It's right on the beach. I can park with the back toward the water. Put on a CD, lift the back hatch up and lie looking at the surf. I've done it before. It's wonderful, actually."

"Wait a minute, wait a minute. If it's that wonderful, maybe I should take the Cherokee."

"No way, my friend. Tonight, it's me getting the room with the best view."

Hub is in a hurry; he has parked the VW in a no-parking zone. Hub holds his son's hand as they both take the stairs, two risers at a time, to the library. Uberto steps wide in order to keep up. "Where are we going, Papi?"

"Up to the library, to get the book about Jesus's animals."

"But Papi, why are we running?"

"Because the library's about to close."

As they rush through the door, Hub glances at his watch. Seven minutes to five. The weary afternoon light spills in through window blinds. It paints diagonal stripes on the reading table. The place is nearly empty, only a woman rising behind a desk. She's short and round, her hair blue-black, like the peel of eggplants. She's tidying things up. An opened purse sits before her. It waits to be snapped shut, slipped over the wrist, carried down the steps and into the weekend. The woman glances up, knits her forehead. "We're closing."

"I know," Hub says. "At five. But there's still a little time and I'll only take a minute."

Uberto bounds over to her. His curly-topped head barely clears the desk. He grasps the edge of it with pudgy hands, vaults words over the edge. "Queremos el libro de los animales de Jesus."

"It's called *The Bestiary of Christ*," Hub tells her. "It's right over here." He steps quickly around the corner into the adjacent room. He goes directly to the book, which, luckily, is still in the spot where he placed it four days ago. He pulls the book from the shelf, takes it to the desk, lays it in front of the woman. "This is it. This is all we want." He smiles broadly to attempt to win her over. "Oh, and we also want to sign up and get a membership card."

"You don't have a card?"

"No, but I want one."

"Are you a tourist?" The woman's face is freckled. What shows of her chest—a very wide V—is freckled as well.

"No. We live in Oaxaca. In San Antonino del Valle."

"And you don't have a card?"

"No, but we want one. Don't we, son?"

Uberto nods vigorously. His long curls bounce on his head. He looks as angelic as a brown Shirley Temple. "We want Jesus's animals."

The woman has been standing. Now she sits herself down. "It's ten dollars to join."

"Okay, but can I pay in pesos? I don't happen to have dollars."

"Do you have identification? I'll need to see that."

Hub fishes a finger into the back pocket of his jeans. He extracts his wallet. Hands over his U.S. driver's license. Adds his Mexican Carnet de Identificación. He counts out ninety pesos. Lays the bills on the desk.

"You're Hubert Hart?" She looks up from the ID and stares at him.

"Hubert Hart," Uberto says, pronouncing it "Uber Art."

"That's me. It's my son's name, too."

"I see." The woman nudges her purse aside. She slides a metal file box toward her. Opens up the lid. Flips through the index cards. Stops at the "H"s.

Hub relaxes. He's made it. He's going to get the book, a good thing, because the library is closed until Monday and don Efrain and the men need the book for their carvings. The Night of the Radishes is less than a week away.

"There is something here for you," the woman says, a lilt of surprise in her voice. "A note. It's been placed here in the 'H's."

"A note? For me?"

"It says 'Hubert Henry Hart.' That appears to be you."

Hub frowns. What in the world? He takes the note, sees his own name, unfolds the slip of paper. When he reads what is there, it shocks him so, he wheels around, thinking he'll catch whoever has made such a terrible joke.

Stunned, the blood still roaring in his ears, Hub is behind the wheel again, Uberto in the back. The VW idles in front of Los Tules Gifts and Art Gallery. In a moment, Luli will walk out of Los Tules's door and Hub will lift *The Bestiary of Christ* from off the front seat. Tucked between its pages is his note. He read it twice, once at the library, the second time when he got into the car. Now the note lies trapped between book pages, and he can't wait for Luli to pluck it out and read it to him. If the note is even there. If it actually exists. He thinks, perhaps, that it does not. He thinks he's caught in some kind of time warp, like on *The Twilight Zone,* where things are not ever what they seem.

The car door creaks open (he has meant to oil that door) and Luli squeezes half of herself in. "¡Ay," she exclaims, "gracias a Dios!" It is her last day of work; she won't be going back until a month after the baby is born. Hub lifts the book off the seat and Luli folds the rest of herself in. Her musky-flowery scent drifts into the car with her. Her belly is so huge she can't sit straight. Instead, she scooches up and leans back, her legs spread a bit to accommodate her baby. Without looking back, she greets her son and he wedges himself between the seats and kisses her cheek. "You sit tight back there," she says. Hub hands the book to her and she lays it on the wide shelf the middle of her body has become. "You got the book," she says. "Papa will be glad."

Hub nods. He shifts into first and steps on the gas. "Before we go home, we need to make a stop." He drives down Independencia, turns left at Diaz Cordaz, left again at Morelos. They near the church of la Soledad. Luli makes the sign of the cross as they go by. "¿Donde vamos?" she asks.

Hub makes no reply. He continues up Division Oriente, makes a left at Negrete. He pulls up to a wide service gate. Switches off the car.

"Did you get another job?" Luli asks. "Isn't this Casa Amapolas? Didn't you do some faux painting here?"

"Where are we, Papi?" Uberto asks.

Hub reaches for the book, opens it to the note (incredibly, the note is there), hands the note to his wife. "Read it," he says. "Read it aloud."

Luli keeps her eyes on Hub as she unfolds the paper. He holds her gaze for a moment, then lifts his chin to prod her along. Luli turns to the note and reads, "Hub, it's me, Annie. I'm here in Oaxaca, at Casa Amapolas. I leave on December 21st. Please call me. Annie Hart Rush. Hub, it's been such a long time."

"Why are we stopped, Papi?" Uberto asks, and now neither one of his parents responds to him. His parents are now staring at each other. His mother's hand is stretched across her mouth. His father's face is very still.

"Where did the note come from?" Luli asks at length.

"Somebody left it in the library."

"Your sister Annie?" Luli almost whispers the name.

"Well, I guess we'll find out," Hub says. He opens the car door. "Want to come along?"

Hub and his family stand before the purple door of Casa Amapolas. Hub rings the bell. The electric sound it makes might just as well be coming from his heart. After a moment, Prudencia swings open the door. He recognizes her from a few years back, when he worked painting a few rooms. "¡Ay, Señor Enrique, Señora! Pásele, pásele." Prudencia swings the door wide so that they all can enter. She exclaims over Uberto. She points to Luli's belly, nods her head in approval. "Uno nuevo. Que bueno."

They all stand in the entry, all nodding and smiling. Everything is as he remembers it: The desk against the wall. The big table against an opposing wall. The pamphlets, maps, brochures fanned out on it. And through the archway, the trellised walkway. The patio. The gleam of oxblood tiles surrounding it. Hub feels jelly-kneed. In a matter of minutes, his whole past might come rushing back to him. "I'm looking for someone," Hub says.

"A ver," Prudencia says. "Tell me."

"Annie Hart Rush. I'm looking for her. I think she's staying here."

Prudencia widens her eyes. "Ah, la señora Roosh." She smiles, as if pleased to have been of service.

"La señora Roosh, está 'quí?"

"No. No 'sta."

"She's not here?"

Prudencia replies, "No, no, she's here, but today she's in Puerto Angel. She and el señor left this morning, bien temprano, very early."

"She's in Puerto Angel?"

"Yes, but they return tomorrow."

"Okay," Hub says, "okay." He lays a hand on the desk, casually, so as not to give away how much he is shaking. "Okay, then we'll be back tomorrow."

"By nightfall," Prudencia says. "They should be here by then."

 It's a half hour before sunset, and we are on the beach, setting Joe up in the back of the Cherokee, which is now free of the boxes we dropped off a few hours ago at Piña Palmera. Spread under palm groves, with grand views of the ocean, the nongovernmental center provides free medical care, meals, special education, physical and occupational therapy to needy disabled children and their families. When we drove up, the director came out to greet us. She was delighted with the gifts Joe brought, grateful once more, she said, for his steadfast generosity. The director led me on a tour of the place, and I left touched and impressed. I didn't say it, but I plan to make a nice donation. I'll make it in Maggie's name and in her memory. I know Ma would be happy about that. After all, it's her money that will make the gift possible.

We are parked on the spot of sand closest to the shrub-lined path leading up to the restaurant. The way its rear hatch is lifted, its front doors flung wide, the Cherokee looks like a black metal monster gulping for air. And who wouldn't? A dull heat beats down on the beach; the sand traps some of it, reflects the rest of it back. I'm in my bright yellow Speedo; twice I've had to run into the surf to cool myself off. On the last time, I neglected to wear my flip-flops and much to Joe's amusement, I did a little Dudley Moore-hopping-across-the-hot-sand dance all the way into the water. My suit is one of those that dries in minutes, but I'm sweating so much that I can feel the moisture slickening and salting the inside of my thighs, the plunge between my breasts, the nape of my neck, my upper lip. Joe appears to be of a drier sort. I see no sweat shine on him as he carries the cooler around the car and sets it on the front passenger seat. He's tucked his open suitcase under the steering wheel, its lid resting against the back of the driver's seat. It's all very convenient. All Joe has to do is reach over the seat for his supplies and to restock the CD player. The Bee Gees are on now and they are warbling away. Their high harmonics float out over the sand, across the waves, toward the sun starting its slow descent at the top and back of the world. Gulls drift like blown leaves; like the Gibbs, they perform their own melodious screeching.

We share the beach with many others. Cars, RVs, SUVs, all surrounded by sea lovers. Big tents and small, like net mushrooms, rise in the shade of the coconut trees. And stretched under palapas are the string hammocks. I note a bright turquoise one spread open by the tourist lying in it. From here, the person looks like a huge pork loin encased in stretchy webbing. Down a ways, and set back from the shore, a team of six leap and spike a ball over a volleyball net. The men are golden, graceful and sleek as Baryshnikovs. Their gleeful shouts ride easily on the air currents. Beyond them, and set back under the trees, is the large palapa housing the privies and the cold-water showers.

Joe has folded the backseat down and my homemaking and nesting skills have kicked in, big time. I'm inside the car, on my hands and knees, my back only inches from the ceiling. I'm happily tugging his futon around to find the best position for sunset and ocean viewing. I spread a deep blue sheet over the mat. I find the pillows, plump these up and prop them against the back of the seat. To make a night table, I wedge the square box containing emergency supplies between the side of the futon and the car door. Joe has one of those round, battery-operated, push-on lights. It has adhesive strips on the back and I affix it against the side window. I press on the plastic dome and, voilà, light! I press again, and the light goes off. I spy a few books in a corner and I stack them on the box, the better for Joe to reach for them.

I have brought my own reading matter to Gloria's. My mother's notebook. At the last minute, I slipped it inside my tote. I've made no promises to myself about starting it, but it's here, waiting, in case I feel the urge. I quickly note what Joe's brought along: *Travels with Charley* by Steinbeck, and two dog-eared books of poetry: one by Robert Bly, the other by Mary Oliver. I think that what we choose to read tells a lot about us. Learning what books a person loves is like glimpsing into his or her psyche. Like maybe opening a dresser to spy on its contents, the condition of the items, the way they're stored. In neat piles? Kind with kind? Scattered about? Or all balled up so badly it's as if someone took a beater to it all?

It occurs to me I'm playing house, and I chuckle at the realization. I know I'm playing house because I have the urge to rush out and look for pretty flowers to pick and poke into a can and set beside the books. If there were artwork, I'd display it. And shirred curtains would be nice. I look up and find Joe standing beside the car, leaning in and staring at me. He's caught me being my own super-fussy self. I put on an innocent face and smooth the sheet on the futon. "There," I say, and, "I think the push-on light is in just the right spot for you to read by." Joe says nothing, he just keeps staring, and now I'm suddenly abashed at the way I've simply taken over and set things up as I wish. Did I even ask Joe what he would have done? My assertiveness is so apparent to me that I'm immediately contrite. I drop back on my heels, blow a wayward strand of hair away from my face. "We can change things around if you like." I point out my efforts with a raised hand. "This is only, like, a suggestion."

"No, no, it all looks good."

"Are you sure?" I like Joe. I want Joe to like me.

"I'm sure." He comes around the car, and I follow him with my eyes, twisting around to look over my shoulder when he reaches the back. "You want something to drink?" he asks. "The show's about to start." Our plan is to sit in the back with the hatch up and watch the sun go down.

"How about a ginger ale?" I say. We had stopped at the little store in PA on the way back from the children's center and stocked up on fresh ice.

"Ginger ale it is." Before plucking the cans from the chest, Joe switches off the CD player. "Sunsets have their own sweet music," he says.

We sit in the back, our bare legs dangling as if we're on a dock about to fish. I've propped my soda can between my thighs and, after the first icy shock, the can begins to cool me off. Up and down the beach, all eyes are turned to the horizon. The pork-loin man has extricated himself from his casing, the volleyball guys have interrupted their game. Unbelievably, two black cows have ambled down from the hillside and have folded themselves up on the sand, their heads pointing toward the sea. I smile at the sight of them, so serenely observant.

"Look at those cows, Joe."

"They're the Zen cows. They've been coming down to the beach for years. We'll have a good sunset tonight. The cows know."

"Amazing."

The day goes hushed; it turns the hue of hammered gold. The sea is blue velvet, its surface impenetrable. Like a child, Joe lifts his legs up and down. He says, "Look at the sky. Look at those pinks and corals." We are silent for a moment, then Joe adds, "There it goes," and we watch the orange platter of the sun balance itself for a moment on blue water.

"Wait for the flash," Joe says.

I know about the flash. That phosphorescent dazzle the sun sometimes throws off as it slides behind the world and disappears from view. We see the flash now. A green resplendence that lasts but an instant.

"I love that," Joe says after a moment. "If I were asked to make a drawing of hope, it's that green flash that I would draw."

His comment gives me pause. "But Joe, the flash is something momentary. Sometimes it happens, sometimes it doesn't. Is that what hope is like for you?"

Joe stops swinging his legs. He looks at me. "Hope, when it comes, happens in a flash. The trick is to grab on to it when it presents itself. The trick is to make it linger."

Maybe it was the daylong drive, maybe the change of scenery, maybe even the slant of the sun; how, on the coast, the sun shoots straight down with hardly a structure to deflect its glare. Maybe it was the enervating sea air, maybe all of it in combination, that deflated my buoyant spirits. Tonight, Joe and I sit on the restaurant terrace, under the palms again. I've dressed up a bit, maybe to cheer myself up: loose linen slacks, a halter top, a cinnamon-colored scarf draped over my shoulders. We've both ordered the zesty pescado a la Veracruzana: red snapper, Veracruz style, with onions, tomatoes, cilantro and chile. We're halfway through dinner when the shade drops further down on the windowpane of my mood, leaving me in a shadowy place and suddenly bereft. Triste, it's called in Spanish. That's what I am, triste, triste. If I could, I would bury my face in my hands and weep.

Joe notices the change in me right off. He lays a quick hand over my own. "What's wrong, Annie?" I shake my head, not knowing the what, but suspecting the why. Perhaps I miss Sam, Will and Jack. Of course I miss them. I've been away for seven days, seven fruitless days. There have been a few e-mails. No phone calls. My scheduled return is three days away. That will make it four days before Christmas. It's not difficult to imagine what I'll be returning to: my precious family, yes, but also to the frenetic chaos of the holidays. Worse, I'll be stepping into, once again claiming, my own obsessive nature, the need I feel to make everything I do the best it can be. No, that's understating it. Perfection, that's what I strive for. Perfection in everything. And now I've traveled to Mexico in search of my brother and that quest has not been perfect. In fact, it appears that I have failed.

"I was thinking about Christmas," I say to Joe. "Only days away, and so much to do." The cookies I'll bake, ice, sprinkle, rise in endless towers before me. The holiday menu is an interminable list of specialty items to track down. This at Byerly's, that at Lunds, this other at Whole Foods. And there's the ham to buy, to score, to stud, to glaze. The rush out to the tree farm, to find the just-right specimen. Chop chop chop in the freezing cold. Noses dripping. Hands numb. Feet, ice blocks practically. My God, I'm exhausted just contemplating the ritual. And yet, like a low-grade fever I try to ignore, something else niggles at me, too. Anger. Anger at the load I bear alone.

"So, you're going back as scheduled." Joe makes it a statement of fact and not a question.

"Yes." I pause, because the assertion exhausts me further. "I guess I am. Brother or no brother, I guess I'll head home. I can always come back."

"Well, when you get home, you should do as the Mexicans do and keep your Christmas simple this year. Gather your family around you. Have a nice dinner. Wait until the Day of the Magi for gift-giving."

"Ha! That would be the day, my kids waiting until after Christmas for their presents." As for keeping things simple, how can I do that when my life is one mad dash from one clanging bell to another?

"I suppose," Joe says, "kids want their presents." He looks down at his plate. Spears a broccoli floweret.

I stifle the need to apologize for mentioning my kids and thus reminding Joe of his own lost child, for sometimes the best way to compound a problem is to keep mentioning it.

"I already did the Christmas shopping. All the presents are wrapped and labeled and at my friend Milly's, next door. I even bought the cards, wrote little notes in them, addressed and stamped them. Sam sent them out for me."

"Boy, you're a veritable human tornado. Even from afar, you're pulling the strings."

"I guess I am, but I wish I weren't. A human tornado, that is." I have the last bite of fish. Follow it up with some rice. Then a long drink of lemonade.

"It's all about guilt, you know," Joe says.

"What's all about guilt?" I set my lemonade glass upon the lilac-colored place mat.

"Trying to be perfect."

"Is that what I'm doing?" Though I know that this is so, I ask the question just the same, because it's good to get another person's take on things. "Explain." We have both laid down our forks. Our plates are clean. A candle in its glass holder glimmers in the center of the table. Joe and I look across it into each other's faces. His expression is earnest and maybe even a little sad. I don't have to see my face to know I'm reflecting the same look back to him.

"Well, trying to be perfect is all about wanting to be loved," he says. "If we're perfect, people will love us. If they love us, they won't abandon us. And God knows, *we know*, we deserve to be abandoned. We deserve it because we feel guilty."

The intimate turn of the conversation has caused the rest of the diners to drop away. It's as if our own small table has levitated off the patio, and Joe and I are alone, up above the softly swaying palms, up closer to the sky. "And what are we guilty of, Joe?"

"Well, I'm guilty because I didn't prevent my family from dying."

"And I'm guilty because if it wasn't for me, my sister would be alive. My father, too." Tears slip down my cheeks and I quickly brush them away with a finger.

"Your father? Your father also died on the tractor?"

"No. He died three years later. The guilt really got to him. He put the end of a rifle in his mouth and pulled the trigger. He was down in the basement when he did it."

"Holy God."

"I know." I dab my cheeks with the napkin.

"Let's take a walk," Joe says. "You're finished, right?"

After signing for the meal, we go down the path that leads to the beach. It gets cooler as we near the water, and so I swirl my silk scarf around my neck. The Cherokee is parked not too far up the beach, and we walk over to it and leave our shoes beside it. We amble off, away from the campsite lined with vehicles and palapas. Away from the music coming from the different camps and rising over the beach to collide, one melody with another. The moon is three-quarters full and makes the night milky with its light, painting a shimmering trail on the water.

As we stroll along, white foam rolls gently across our feet. The water that follows is cool. Because I'm comfortable with him, I've slipped an arm through Joe's as we proceed, leisurely and silently, toward the flank of the mountainside jutting down like a giant creature's paw right into the water. Joe and I, two guilty souls buttressing each other. It's clear to me that until now I've never met another person who, because he's weighted down with the same burdens I've endured, truly understands what I bear. Not even Ma could do that for me. Ma's burdens were different from mine. Ma's grief was pure and unobstructed. It was not encumbered by guilt and the self-reproach that guilt brings. That is, not that I could ever tell. Perhaps, when I finally have the nerve to really read her notebook, I might learn otherwise.

The beach ends in a warren of rocks and boulders. Sea spray laps around them. I can make out the chalky barnacles clinging to their edges. A cluster of stones, each of different heights, form a natural staircase up to a large, wide boulder, flat as a tabletop. "Let's sit up there," I say on impulse, and soon we are perched on the rock, shoulder to shoulder and cross-legged. From this vantage point, the beach is a frothy band of phosphorescent light. Far off, at the end, the campsite twinkles. Above us, the vault of the sky is salted with a thousand stars. The rock under us is cool and substantial. My hair is pulled back with a scrunchy and I remove it and pull it over my wrist. I give my hair a quick shake and it falls around my shoulders. "There," I say. "I'm now the Little Mermaid sitting on the rock in the Copenhagen harbor."

Joe looks at me. For an instant, he lays a hand against my hair, then withdraws it. "You're much prettier, Annie," he says. "Also, you're not made of stone."

"Thanks. That's sweet." I'm touched by his words. "But you know, sometimes I feel like I *am* made of stone. Like I'm all tight and knotted up inside. Stony."

"You know what makes for all that stoniness, don't you?"

"No, what?"

Joe gazes out across the water, staring at some far-off point on the horizon. He's wearing a cabled fisherman's sweater. Charcoal gray. Slacks the same color. Were he not sitting next to me, his figure would be lost in the duskiness. "Anger. Unexpressed anger, it boils up like lava and turns to stone. What we need is a jackhammer to bust it up."

"I don't get it."

Joe turns to me again. "Don't you see, what's tight and knotted up inside us is really all the anger we've stored up. Let it out, and we bust it up. Like with a jackhammer."

"But using a jackhammer is heavy work, Joe. Besides, jackhammers make a god-awful racket."

"Well, I'll tell you what, keeping all that anger in is even harder work. And there's no louder sound than the silent roar of unexpressed emotion."

I take all this in, trying to digest the gravity in it. After a moment, I say, "Joe, are you sure you're not really a psychiatrist, instead of the anthropology professor you purport to be?"

Joe chuckles. "Well . . . ," he says, and leaves it at that.

I hug my legs to my chest. "I hate anger. I hate it when I feel it, I hate it when I hear it. When I see it, like on TV, say, like if I'm channel surfing, and happen to light on a talk show and catch people screaming at each other and being ugly and confrontational, I turn it off. I just can't stand it. It actually makes me sick to my stomach." Just talking about it now is like the lightest sweep across a raw and humming nerve. "But I know I'm angry," I continue. "Deep inside, I'm very angry."

"I think you have a lot to be angry about."

"You think?"

"Yes, I think."

We are silent for a while, and then Joe asks, "You want to try something?"

"Try what?"

"Try naming the things you're angry about."

"Oh, I can't do that." I feel the old familiar tick of anxiety at just the thought of doing such a thing.

"Why not?"

"Because I just can't."

"Sure you can. Come on, name one thing you're angry about. Just one, that's all."

Something moves inside me, like when I stand next to a window that's dozens of stories up. When I look down, I feel the draw of something reaching up to me, something urging me to let go and leap into the void. "Well, okay," I say, "but just one thing." Still, it takes me a few moments. "I guess I'll start with the obvious. I'm angry at my brother."

"Why?"

"Because he up and left. One day he was home, the next he was gone. And he left without a reason, when Ma and I needed him the most. He didn't even say good-bye. I know he was sullen and snarly. He was seventeen, for God's sake. And talk about angry. He had a punching bag down in the basement and he was always down there giving it a million whacks. Sometimes the house shook as he whacked that thing, again and again and again. Still, he could've said something before taking off. He could've warned me he was leaving." I hear myself. My voice is taut and strident.

"He should've, but maybe he couldn't."

"No, Joe!" I'm not interested in excuses for my brother. The fact that Joe has offered one pumps up the pitch of my emotions. If I were standing, I would poke my fists into my waist for emphasis. Maybe even stamp my foot. "And what were those postcards all about? You know what Hub did? Over the years, he sent postcards to my mother, so she knew he was all right. But what about me? No postcards for me!" My voice rises in volume, pinched and edging toward hysteria. The sound of my own voice sends tiny sirens wailing away inside me. "And you know what my mother did? Ma never once told me about them. All those years, and she never said a thing. It was only hours before she died that she let me in on her secret. Talk about angry! I'm angry about that." I roll back upon my heels. From this position, I gather more steam. "And while I'm at it, I might as well add Pa to all of this. Sure, I know how he felt, all that guilt and remorse after Maggie died. But what did he do? He took the coward's way. Put a rifle in his mouth, and bang! no more guilt, no more responsibility. Well, you know what? I hope he's frying in hell. No, I mean it! I hope he's frying in hell for all the shit he put us through."

I'm out of breath. Out of strength. I allow myself to fall against Joe, and he takes the whole of my weight. Holds on to me as I continue ranting. "You asked what I'm angry about. Well, I'm angry about that. No, wait! That's not true! I'm more than angry. I'm enraged, I'm outraged, I'm furious. At Hub, yes, but also at Ma and Pa. I tell you, I'd kill those two! I'd kill them if they weren't already dead."

The world goes hushed at this terrible pronouncement. The stars stop wheeling. The sea quits rocking. The breeze goes still. The rock upon which I sit shifts, and I plummet into regret. I clutch the nubby yarn of Joe's sweater. Hold on to him with all my might, before remorse carries me off. "Oh, my God. I didn't mean it. I didn't mean it, Joe."

"Sushsushush," Joe murmurs. He strokes my hair. Over and over, Joe strokes my hair.

 My room has a narrow bed, a small dresser, a chair. The planked floor is bare and worn to gloss by the sweep of brooms and mops and feet. In this simple landscape, I lie in bed, awaiting sleep. When Joe walked me here, me leaning against him all the way down the beach, I said I'd be fine when he asked if I wanted company. He'd be happy to sit in the chair and watch over me, he said. But I thanked him for the kindness he'd already shown and sent him off, to the Cherokee and to rest. Now I'm not so sure I don't want him here. My eyes are swollen, my throat aches, my heart's cracked open once again. I feel all akilter. As if my life has careened around a bend, and it's tipping up on its side, and one small nudge will send me plunging over the edge. In my mind, I prepare a white roadside cross for myself.

Despite the temperature, I'm wearing Sam's flannel shirt over warm-ups. "Goddamn it, Sam, where are you!" And this is not a question, but an accusation. One thought of Sam, all cozy and oblivious in our bed, and the sniffles start again. I lift a corner of his shirt to my nose and inhale his lingering aftershave. I need Sam. If there were a phone around, I'd call him right now. I want to lie in your arms, I'd say. In our bed, my face snuggled to your neck. I want to smell your smell. I want you to rock me, stroke me. Comfort me. I fix on this, hoping it's enough to soothe and lull me into sleep. Then Ma's face rises before me, Ma's skin white as milk, her nostrils pinched with the effort to breathe, and I hear the terrible things I screamed about her, down there on the beach. My throat is raw, as if I've swallowed razor blades. I curl into a ball. I sob, quietly at first, then wildly, my mouth agape, my body convulsing. "Oh, Ma. I'm sorryI'm sorryI'msorry." The words come in hiccups and gasps, and to keep myself from choking, I stand and swallow hard. I pluck a tissue from the pocket of Sam's shirt. I blow my nose. I start to pace. Round and round my tiny cell. I pace right into a flash of inspiration, into the way toward some atonement. I light the lamp on the dresser, find my tote bag and slip out Ma's notebook. I pull the chair under the light, sit and flip through the pages. A date catches my eye. April 24, my birthday. I read on:

Today is April 24 1998 my girls birthday. Annie is 33 today. Maggie is 33 in heaven. Its been 24 years since my Maggie was gone. Not one day has passed when I havent thought of her. All I have to do is look at Annie and theres my Maggie staring back at me. It helps that Annie looks so hearty and so hail. When I look at her it helps take away the godawful pictures that come into my mind of my darling, all chewed up from the tractors harrow disks. Elmer carried her home from off the field, but she was already gone. It was a mercy really. I was in the kitchen snaping the ends off the green beans when I heard the horriblest wail like the mama cat in the barn

pitched that time her kittens got run over by the truck. Hub was in
his room with a sore throat, and we both rushed outside to find
Annie doing the wailing. Blood all over her and her running with her
arms outstreched like she was trying to grab on to something. Like
her sanity most probably. God knows we all went a little crazy after
that. But Lord why am I thinking of these awful things when its my
Annies birthday and theres plenty to celebrate with that.

Dear God in heaven. The words have leapt from the page. I can no
longer hold on. It is this, this blow, that sends me careening over the
side. I place Ma's book on the bed and turn away from it. Away from all
the hurt that it contains. I rush from the room, quickly closing the
door behind me. I run down the veranda, my bare feet slapping against
the wooden floor. I run past the long row of rooms, out onto a small
patio, then back under shelter, around the restaurant, and down the
concrete path to the beach and toward Joe's Cherokee, glowing from
the push-light I attached in the back. I can make out the car's rear window, raised like the jutting bill of a sports cap. My bare feet sting from
the run over concrete but are soothed the moment I hit the beach. I
stumble on, my legs going soft, my lungs burning as if I were a sprinter
going across the finish line.

I half collapse against the car. "Joe!" I manage to call, "Joe!" and
then I slowly slide, down the car's black shine, until I'm but a heap on
the sand.

I feel the car jostle and then Joe is beside me. "Annie, what's happened?" His voice is filled with alarm.

I shake my head. I nod. I open my mouth to speak, but nothing
comes.

Joe kneels before me. He takes my shoulders in his hands, gives me a gentle shake. "Annie, listen to me. Are you hurt? Did something happen up there, in your room?"

I shake my head. I take great gulps of air.

"Okay, now, calm down, Annie. Calm down and tell me."

"I read something." My voice could be coming from a mouse, it sounds so small and squeaky.

"You what?"

I clear my throat and try again. "I read something. In my room."

"You read something in your room?" The light coming from inside the car is enough to illuminate a tender arc around us. In this light, I see Joe's face, his brow knit in concern. He's in his shorts. No shirt. I can make out his chest, his thick shoulders. "What did you read? Tell me what you read."

"Okay."

Joe pulls himself up. "Look. I'm going to sit right here beside you. I'll put my arm around you and then you can tell me. Are you okay with that?"

"Okay." I wait until he's repositioned himself, his back against the car, his legs splayed out, like mine. I wait some more, until he's circled my shoulder and I tilt my head against him. I don't know how late it is, maybe one, maybe two. The surf is down and the shoreline has moved yards and yards away from us. Under me, the sand is cool and faintly damp. The sea makes its gentle lapping.

"Tell me, Annie."

What I will tell, I've never told before. Not even Sam has heard it. I know that once I tell it, I'll never utter it again. I brace myself against the coming shock of my confession. I begin with Ma's notebook. I say to Joe:

"Ma left a notebook after she died. I've tried reading it, but every time I try, I lose courage and have to stop. I brought the notebook to Mexico, thinking that Hub and I could read it together. But now I can't find Hub, so I brought the notebook here. Tonight, when I couldn't sleep, I opened it, and there, on a page, was Ma writing about Maggie. About the day my sister died." Once again, I feel I'm free-falling. I find Joe's hand and hang on.

"Annie, listen, you don't have to go on. You can stop if you want."

"No, Joe, no. I have to do it, really." I pause for a moment, gather my wits, before setting off again. "When I was nine, we lived on a farm. Ma and Pa, Hub, Maggie and me. That winter, we had lots of snow, then, with the thaw, there was lots of mud and plenty of floods. The roads were a mess that year. So were the fields. But luckily, years before, Pa had buried clay pipes in the fields to carry any pooling water into drainage ditches.

"By the middle of May, it was finally dry enough for tilling. Pa had bought a new John Deere. We really needed one, because the old one had conked out on us. The new one was shiny green. The back tires had a curved wheel cover, green with a yellow stripe. The fender was wide, like a bench, the perfect place to sit when we rode along."

I stop for a moment. I let go of Joe's hand and pull a tissue from my pocket and blow my nose again. I lean my head against the side of the car. Look up into the vast and immutable sky. Maggie, are you up there, Maggie? Can you hear what I'm saying? You know what I'll tell. I close my eyes, clutch Joe's hand again.

"That day, right after breakfast, Pa was out in the barn hooking up the disk harrow to the tractor. Maggie and I were in our room, arguing. I remember that well. We were arguing about going on the tractor. I wanted to ride on it, but Maggie wouldn't budge. She was on her bed stringing beads for her Indian bracelet. The bracelet was yellow and green and it had black blobs on it that Maggie insisted were like arrowheads. I tell you, Joe, I'll never forget that thing."

Telling it like this, it's as though I'm living it again. I stop speaking for a bit, allowing myself to fall back into the past, to walk right into the farmhouse, into my bedroom and into my own sad story.

You're a big baboon, Maggie. I don't know what you see in that old thing of yours. It doesn't even look like a bracelet.

It does so. Take it back right now.

I will not, you big baboon.

From down in the kitchen, Ma hollers, Kids! Kids! You stop that racket up there!

Outside, the tractor roars to life, and I rush to the window and catch Pa driving it slowly out of the barn. The tractor's newness stands out in the sun. The harrow, hoisted up and disengaged, is attached. Those rows of disk blades, those sharp edges.

You put that bracelet down, Maggie. I want to ride the tractor and you're going with me.

No, I'm not. I told you I'm not.

Yes, you are. If you don't go, I'll tell Ma what you did to her vase.

You better not.

I most certainly will.

You both get on out of here, Hub shouts from his room. How can a sore throat get any rest with the likes of you two bickering?

At the vivid memories, I'm shot through with remorse. I tell Joe how it was. How mean and contrary I had been. How I had forced Maggie to do my bidding.

"And so you both got on the tractor," Joe says. "And your father let you do it."

"Yes." I can still see Pa, sitting high in that scooped, metal seat. He gave us a toothy smile as he put the thing in gear. You girls hang on tight back there, he said. I shake my head. I feel the blood rushing into my ears, like bees buzzing, and I continue:

"We had been riding for maybe half an hour. The morning was warm. The sky was blue with not a cloud to spoil it. Even Maggie was enjoying herself. She sat on the fender, holding on to its edge, her face lifted to the breeze and to the sun. We bobbed along, past rows of budding trees, past the barnyard, crowded with Guernseys waiting for Hub to lead them out into the pasture. Behind us, the soil was black and rich and fragrant. Pa's harrow blades slashed into the plowed soil, churning it up and smoothing it out.

"Then, in a blink, the tractor hit a section of pipe that had wormed its way up to the surface of the field. When the tractor bucked, Maggie lost her grip. She slid back, her legs flying up. I yelled out. Pa looked quickly over his shoulder and his eyes went wide and wild and then he froze. He didn't stop the tractor. He didn't throw the clutch. He didn't disengage the harrow. An instant later, when we rolled over a second piece of pipe, Maggie jerked back, her eyes as wide and wild as Pa's."

I raise a hand to my head. Poke my chin into my chest. My chest feels so full, I think I will burst. I struggle to finish. "I reached for my sister, Joe. I held on to the lip of the fender. I stretched out as long as I'd go, my arm, too, long and pointed like a gaff. For just a second, Maggie's arm flailed up toward mine, but it was no use. When Pa finally threw the clutch and the tractor stopped, the harrow blades had already chewed her up."

 Confessing depletes me. I climb into the Cherokee and lie on the futon, which just this afternoon I had made comfortable for Joe. He clambers in and presses the push-on light, and the car goes dark. He lies beside me, his body against the back of mine, one arm arcing around my head, the other resting over me, as if to keep me from flying off.

For a time, only our breathing fills the space. Mine, ragged and harsh; his, one smooth exhalation after another. Joe's breath is warm against my neck. It soothes and comforts me. After a time, my breathing eases. The moon turns darkness into shadow and I make out the side of the box I'd earlier placed between the futon and door. I reach to touch the box, to make sure that I'm here, that I've not been struck dead for the sins I've committed. I draw my hand back and find Joe's lying innocently against Sam's shirt. I clasp his hand. "Joe?" I say, my voice as thin as onion skin.

"I'm here." His voice is as quiet as mine.

"I never in my life told anyone that. Not even Sam, and now I can't imagine why. For twenty-five years, that's been my secret."

Joe squeezes my hand in response.

"You know what?" I say. "Somehow I feel better for having told."

"It's the jackhammer effect. It works on guilt, as well as anger."

"Boy," I say.

Joe squeezes my hand again. After a moment, he says, "You know what? I have a secret of my own."

I know too well the fragile wall we can erect between the desire to confess and the fear of doing it. Sometimes all we need to remain quiet is the sound of another's voice, and our resolve toward revelation crumbles. So I say nothing. I simply wait.

Soon, Joe says, "For days before the fire, Grace—that was my wife's name—Grace kept telling me about the furnace. She said the furnace was making noises. 'That thing's making funny noises, Joe,' that's the way she put it. 'What do you mean?' I'd ask. And she'd say, 'Weird knocks. On and off, I hear weird knocks.' "

Over my shoulder, Joe's voice grows weary. "Grace told me this at least half a dozen times. I listened for the knocks but never heard them, so each time she'd complain, I'd say, 'Oh, it's probably the heat calibrator. Don't worry about it.' "

Joe's voice catches, and he pauses and then he gives a cough. " 'Heat calibrator.' I don't even know what that is. I guess I made it up. I made it up because Grace was always worrying about something. After Pete was born, she worried about additives in the food, or pesticides in the water. She worried the brakes might not hold in the car, that someone might steal into the house and carry Pete off. And then she worried about the knocks the furnace was making. She said she worried something would catch fire."

Joe slides his arms away from me. I feel him turning onto his back. "I can't tell you how many times I've played Grace's words over in my mind. 'That thing's making funny noises, Joe.' Over and over, like a scratched record."

It is so still in the car, I'm sure I hear the beating of my heart. I hear Joe gulp. He coughs again. He then asks a question that totally surprises me. He says, "Do you like poetry, Annie?"

I roll over and lie on my other side so that I'm now facing him. He's drawn his knees up into tents. He's thrown an arm over his face.

"Poetry?"

"Yeah, poetry. It's saved my life, one poem in particular. It's called 'Wild Geese,' and it's by Mary Oliver. It goes like this:

> *You do not have to be good.*
> *You do not have to walk on your knees*
> *for a hundred miles through the desert, repenting.*
> *You only have to let the soft animal of your body*
>   *love what it loves.*
> *Tell me about despair, yours, and I will tell you mine . . ."*

Joe's voice cracks and he begins to weep.

The wrenching sound he makes breaks me again. "Oh, dear God," I say, and I'm pulling him toward me. I'm pressing my face into his neck.

Joe holds me, tight, tight, then, as naturally as breathing, we lift our faces to each other. "Sweet woman," Joe murmurs, and we kiss. A long, mournful kiss filled with longing.

I lay his hand against my breasts. Even through the fabric of my shirt, I feel the heat of his palm. We are sailing away, floating out to the horizon on a wave, when Joe suddenly draws back. "God!" he exclaims. "What am I doing?"

His voice jolts me. We roll onto our backs. "Oh, God, Annie, I'm sorry."

"Don't be, Joe. Please don't." I fumble for his hand and won't let go. We lie side by side, our breathing slowing. The car fills with the sound of us returning safely back to port.

Don Efrain's shed is a typhoon of activity. He and his sons are busy carving wooden figurines to use as models for their radish carvings. Hub and Uberto, and the little cousins, are sanding the models as they are made. Hub has joined the men at the worktable. The boys are in the yard, working in the shade of one of the guayamuche trees. This year, the family's tableau will feature the Holy Crèche. However, to lift it out of the ordinary, theirs will include, in addition to the usual animals watching over the Christ child, a number of fabulous beasts from the book Hub borrowed yesterday from the library: a unicorn, a griffin, a dragon, a centaur, and a winged horse.

Don Efrain holds up the winged horse he's completing. "El caballo angélico," he says. "The angel horse." The animal is a hand-span high, a hand-span wide. It's caught in mid-trot, forelegs bent. He will soon add the wings, elegantly spread, like swans' wings.

Mauricio is fashioning a griffin. It has the head and wings of an eagle and the body of a lion. Across from him, Rogelio is bent over the centaur he's carving. Like the one in the book, his is a deer-centaur. It has the head, arms and torso of a man, but the hindquarters of a deer.

Don Efrain bobs his head enthusiastically at the work they're producing. He grins at his son-in-law, bestirring the gray thatch that shades his upper lip. "You brought us a good book, Enrique."

"I'm glad," Hub says. He's gladder, still, that his mother-in-law has finally cracked a smile at something he has done. Besides dreaming up figurines on their own, don Efrain and his sons are always on the lookout for imaginative illustrations in books and magazines. So Hub is pleased that he has been of help, and none too soon. The Night of the Radishes is only four days away. Hub sands the spiraled horn of the unicorn, but his heart isn't in it. Since his visit yesterday to Casa Amapolas, his mind has been filled with nothing but the thought of his sister so near. Last night, he tossed and turned and got little rest. To keep from disturbing Luli, he left the bed and went to drop into the big chair that was in the living room. Across from him, on the sofa, Uberto slept peacefully under the painting of the farm, the field, the tractor. Hub laid his head back. Closed his eyes. The painting pulled Hub into a troubled dream.

He was in the house on Holmes Avenue. He was riding a little green tractor, like the ones made as riding toys for children. Around the living room he was riding, into the dining room, around the table, past the hutch and into the kitchen. Round and round on the little tractor as shiny new as the big one had been on that terrible day.

His mother strode in wearing her school cafeteria uniform. The plastic card was attached to her left pocket with a pin. "FLO," the pin read.

"Out out out!" his mother yelled. She'd taken the broom from the closet. She rushed after him, making sweeping motions with the broom. "Out of here! Out of my life! Now! Out of here, now!"

In the dream, as in real life, Hub had done her bidding. He had left, not on a Trailways bus, but on a little tractor. Out the front door, across the porch, over the steps, up the sidewalk, down the road into oblivion.

Now, his sister has shown up and his past is on the verge of colliding with his life. For almost twenty years he has locked his past up, kept himself from opening the door on any part of it. His only concession has been to send, now and then, a message to his mother. To let her know he is okay. To let her know he is what he is. And what he is is a thirty-seven-year-old Mexican man. That's what he's become. And he's never been happier.

Hub glances out the shed door to see his boy sitting in the dappled shade of the tree. His precious son is an elegant blend of Luli's Mixtec beauty and his own cranelike lankiness. His face is a study in concentration as his hand slides back and forth over the figurine he's sanding. Hub loves his son. He loves his wife. In but a week, there'll be another child to love. He hopes it'll be a daughter. If it is, he'll sometime soon make the trip to Minneapolis, to reunite with his family, to face up to the past he's left behind.

Until then, he'll stay in Mexico. When evening comes today, and Luli asks if they'll be driving to Casa Amapolas, he'll say no. No, they will not. If she goes on to ask why (and knowing her, she will not), he will tell her it's a matter of fate. Yesterday, when he found Annie's note, he'd rushed over to meet her. But Annie wasn't there and he won a reprieve. Now he's been given more time to prepare himself for such an eventful reunion. It's a blessing, really. So, yes, for now, he thinks it's best to stay put.

 My world is rearranged. This is not a bad thing. More like deciding to move an ungainly sofa that for years has been parked in the middle of a room, blocking the traffic flow. Moving it to a corner, or better yet, to another room, or maybe even out the front door and into Goodwill. Oh, how right the room seems then. You stand back, admiring the transformation. Telling has unblocked me, made me lighter, and therein lies the path toward an eventual transformation. I can see now my mother's inclination toward the same kind of change. Ma filled a notebook with her own telling, and when I'm home, no matter what the cost, I'm determined to give it the same respectful attention that Joe granted me last night. As far as what happened between Joe and me after our telling, that long kiss, then that quick holding back, well, that's almost beside the point. Or that's what I tell myself, anyway.

Awakening at first light, still in the back of the Cherokee, the day pristine with promise, I'm drained, lethargic, spent. I feel empty, but again, this is not a bad thing, because it offers me hope that I can be refilled. We're returning to Oaxaca City today, so I rouse myself into action. A more welcome scenario would be to spend the day lolling on the beach, catching the waves heading in and heading out. As we ready ourselves for the trip, Joe and I don't mention last night, though for a moment, when he first said good morning, his face crumpled as if he wanted to say "I'm so sorry" again. I shook my head, set a finger against my lips, to keep him from it. I will not put a name to what transpired between us, except to say that kindness comes packaged in a variety of ways. When I fly home the day after tomorrow, Sam and my boys will meet a woman on the way to becoming a different sort. A woman capable, at long last, of being more tender with herself.

And so we're back in the Cherokee, Joe behind the wheel, me beside him, an Enya CD in the player. This sweet, celestial music suits our shyer, more sensitive selves. It serves as a perfect background as we continue to pass stories back and forth.

"You know," I tell him, "despite what you say, there's no question I've kept you from your work. I've been in Mexico eight days, and I don't think I've ever seen you working. I bet you'll be glad to see me gone so you won't have all these interruptions."

"Actually, I finished before you came. You arrived at a good time." Joe takes his eyes off the road and sets them on me. "And no. I won't be glad to see you gone. I'm going to miss you, Annie. You've been a much-needed compañera."

"Same here," I manage to mumble. His frankness touches me, and I slide my eyes away from his, so he won't see in my face that my thoughts have turned to last night, to our long, deep kiss. For a time, I study the road ahead, how the car swallows up the road's middle line. After a moment, I ask, "You're doing a paper on Mixtec anthropology, right? That's a very broad subject. Enough for a book."

Joe says, "Well, not really. Truth is, when you first asked, I just gave you my easiest answer." He looks my way again. "Now that I've gotten to know you, I'll tell you what I'm really doing. That is, if you want."

"Well, of course I do."

"I'm writing a long paper on 'el susto.' "

"El susto? What's that?"

"Literally, it means 'fright.' But it's actually the name of a folk illness that has to do with soul sickness, with the separation of the soul from the body. Susto can happen following a sudden frightening experience. Or it can come about from a magical intervention, like someone putting a curse on you. But like I say, it can happen following an accident, or a death, or the witnessing of something tragic and dramatic."

"Like someone seeing their twin sister being cut up by a harrow?"

Joe nods. "Or like someone coming home and finding their house on fire and their family trapped inside."

"Oh, Joe." I lift a hand and lay it briefly on his shoulder. In my mind, I add two other possibilities: like maybe someone doing homework up in her room when a rifle blast goes off down in the basement? And, like maybe if someone has to watch her mother suffocating to death? "And what are the symptoms of this susto?"

"Well, you can imagine," Joe replies. "It runs the gamut. Depression, anxiety, insomnia, anorexia."

"I can't believe it."

"Yeah, well . . ."

My mind swirls with the list of my complaints since Ma died. Check, check, check and check, all the ones that Joe mentioned. "And what's with the separation of the body and the soul? What's that all about?"

"Well, in Mexican folklore, there's the belief that trauma can cause the soul to disconnect from the body. El susto is the condition of living out this separation. In severe cases, susto moves up a notch, and then it's called 'espanto.' That elevates the condition from fright into terror. Pretty heady stuff, all of this." Joe shakes his head before continuing. "You know, my grandmother Cruz, the one I told you about, she believed in all kinds of folklore. She had potions for all conditions and sayings for everything. I guess my interest in all of this came naturally from her. And since Grace and Petey died, I've been a bit obsessed with el susto."

"That's not surprising. But are you saying you've been suffering from this susto? Is this what you're saying? That your soul is not connected to your body?" I can't believe that he would think such a thing.

Joe grips the wheel with arms locked straight, as if to steady himself. "Listen, what is guilt, if not fear? Fear—no, not fear, but dread—dread that we have done something wrong. In my case, that I've committed a wrong so terrible that it caused the death of my family."

"But Joe, you didn't kill Grace. You didn't kill Petey. It was an accident. Sure, you could've called the furnace people, and they could've fixed whatever was wrong and then it *still* could've exploded. Another thing, Grace herself could've called the furnace people. She didn't, so does that mean she was responsible for the accident as well?" The words rush from my mouth like water spurting from a runaway garden hose.

Joe slides his eyes off the road and pins me with his gaze. "Well, then if that's true, then it wasn't you who caused the death of your twin sister. Your sister's death was an accident, too. You didn't pull her kicking and screaming from your house and hog-tie her to the tractor. Your sister went meekly on her own."

Our mutual statements stun us into an abrupt silence. We are climbing up the sierra again. Leaving behind the sultry glint of the sea, we come into cool forests. Pine trees tick by in a blur as we proceed. Somewhere in the shadow of those trees, birds gurgle innocently. In any case, this is what I imagine, what I want to believe. After a while, I say, "You know what? I think we're both crazy nuts."

"You're right-on about that."

"Okay, so tell me. Let's say we're both suffering from el susto. So what's the remedy? I hope there's a remedy."

"Oh, there is, and that's the good news."

"Tell me."

"It's a simple remedy. It lies with a healer named doña Clarita. She's one of the reasons I come to Mexico."

"What's she do?"

"She does a ritual called a 'barrida.' It means a sweeping. What she does is listen to your story, then she lays you out and sweeps the susto from your body."

"How in the world does she do that?"

"With a broom. Usually it's made of rosemary leaves. She uses it to sweep all the bad stuff out. After a few times, the susto's gone and the soul can join the body again. I know it sounds crazy, but it's worked for me."

"You've really done this?"

"I have."

I don't know about my soul, but thanks to the bit of therapy I've recently had, I'm aware that since Maggie died, I've pushed most of my emotions up into my head. So for me, it's body and mind that've been disconnected. To think there might be someone who can sweep the two back together seemed like a good thing. In any case, I figure it can't hurt. "Joe, I know I only have a day, but do you think I could see your doña Clarita?"

Joe smiles triumphantly. "We could try," he says. "I'll drive you out there tomorrow, and we can see what develops."

"Do you think she'll mind that I'm a gringa?"

"Are you kidding? Why would she mind that?"

"Well, okay, good." I grin back at him. "The cosmic will of Mexico, eh, Joe?"

"The cosmic will of Mexico."

We arrive at the casa just as the sun slips under the horizon. I'm looking forward to supper. A long hot bath. Then sleep. I don't think I got even an hour's rest last night. When I flip on the room light, I see a note has been slipped under my door. Just seeing it makes me imagine the worst: Something bad has happened at home. I open the note. The message is from Prudencia.

The note is dated yesterday. It's in Spanish, but I can easily make out its contents: "El Señor Enrique vino a verla." Mr. Enrique stopped by to see you.

I turn the paper over to see if there's more, but no, just the short, cryptic note. Enrique? Who's Enrique? My mind fills with possibilities. It could be another opportunist, like the man with the red umbrella. But, from nowhere, comes a connection. Enrique. Spanish for Henry. Henry, my brother's middle name. The realization is earthshaking. I stare down at the paper. "El Señor Enrique." My excitement builds and my next thought is to find Prudencia and ask what the man looked like. But it's almost seven o'clock, so she's gone for the day. Then another idea occurs and it sends me scrambling through my tote bag to find the small notebook, where I've been keeping a record of expenses and information.

I riffle through the pages until my eye falls on what I'm searching for. "Enrique Wilson, La Casa del Libro." Mildred Pierce, at the library, had given me his name and suggested I visit the bookstore and leave a message for Hub. So that's who came by, the Enrique from the bookstore. I plop myself down on the edge of the bed. Enrique Wilson might have information about Hub, another exciting possibility. I want to make time leap into tomorrow, to ten o'clock when Enrique Wilson opens his bookstore. But I know there's nothing I can do now. I know another night will pass when I'll get little sleep.

 I startle awake. Just like my Jack, whose eyes open each morning with a snap, mine do the same. I look at my travel clock. It's almost nine o'clock. I can't believe I slept through the clanging breakfast bell, through other guests strolling by on the veranda. I scramble to get up, get showered, get dressed. I have a million things to do today, but before all else, it's the bookstore and a talk with Enrique Wilson. Until then, I won't allow myself to hope that Prudencia's note was about Hub. It boggles the mind to think I could lay eyes on my brother on this, my last day here. But then, maybe not. Aren't I in cosmic Mexico?

Joe and Ginny Powers are the only ones left in the dining room when I stride in. "There you are," Joe says and waves me over. "I can't believe I overslept," I say, taking the chair across from them. "I had trouble getting to sleep, but when I finally drifted off, I slept like the dead." On their plates are the remains of an egg dish, a few crusts of toast. "Am I too late?"

"Heavens, no," Ginny says. She lifts her cup. "I'm having more." Ginny is her usual sunny self. Her periwinkle blouse is starched and carefully ironed.

"I am, too," Joe says. He looks scrubbed and fresh. I can still see the comb's path through his full, wavy hair.

Prudencia waltzes out of the kitchen with a pot. "Buenos días, Señora," she says, and pours coffee all around. I greet her and pull her note from my pocket. I thank her for slipping it under my door. "Is the señor Enrique who dropped by the señor Enrique who owns the book-store?"

Prudencia knits her brow, then shakes her head. She smiles. "No, es el pintor." She asks what I want for breakfast, and I order tostadas and jugo, toast and juice. "Muy bien," she says and disappears through the kitchen door. I am totally perplexed. Enrique is a painter? I don't know any painters.

Ginny obviously notes my confusion. "Is there a problem?" she asks.

"Well, I don't know. It's just that Prudencia left me a note that said . . . Wait. Here, you read it." I hand Ginny the slip of paper. "I don't know an Enrique, so I assumed it was Enrique Wilson, from La Casa del Libro. But she says, no, that el señor Enrique who came by is a painter."

Ginny looks up from the note. She lays it on the table. "Oh, that might be the Enrique who did our faux painting about two years ago. He also does real paintings, the kind that hang on the wall."

When Prudencia brings my orange juice and buttered toast, Ginny asks her for more information. It turns out the person who showed up is indeed the person who had done the faux painting. This time, he brought his very pregnant wife (Prudencia sets her hand way out from her belly to show it) and their young son. I can somewhat follow Prudencia's explanation, but I'm glad when Ginny retells it and makes it clear. Her eyes light up when she says, "Despite his name, Enrique's an American, you know. Come to think of it, he's from Minnesota!"

"What?"

"I'm sure that's right. When he was working here, we used to talk. I think he said he was originally from Minneapolis."

I brace myself for the answer to what I'll ask next. "What did this Enrique look like?"

Ginny sips her coffee. She sets the cup down. "Well, let's see. Slender. Tall. Long blond hair, the same honey-colored hair as yours, as a matter of fact. He also wore it pulled back in a ponytail, sort of hippie-like."

"Do you remember his last name?" In my mind swims the image of Hub in his senior-year photograph. I try to reconcile how he looked then with the image of him now: a grown man with a wife, a child, another one on the way. Can this be possible?

Ginny shakes her head. "I'd have to look it up. I'm sure I have it. Probably in my accounts payable records. I keep all that on my desk."

I look down at my hands. I think I see them shaking. "Ginny, I hate to bother you with this, but it's very important. Do you think you could get that information for me?" I could tell her all about my brother, but I haven't up to now, so I think I'll wait until I know for sure that "el pintor" is Hub.

"Sure can, hon." Ginny does not rise from the table. She continues sipping her coffee. As if she had all the time in the world.

"No, Ginny. I mean now. Can you get it right now?"

"Oh. You mean like right this minute?" She's tilted her head to look at me, as if she suspects I might be kidding.

"If you wouldn't mind. I'll wait here while you get it. It's very important."

"Well, okay." Ginny frowns, but still she finishes her coffee. She pushes back her chair. "I'll be right back."

"That was your brother who came by, wasn't it?" Joe asks, leaning toward me across the table. "All the color's drained from your face."

I nod. My mouth has gone dry. I raise my hands for Joe to see. "Look. My hands are shaking."

"I know," Joe says. He nudges over the jam jar. "Eat your toast. Drink your juice. It'll settle you down."

Like an automaton, I follow Joe's suggestion. I spread jam on the toast. I bring it to my mouth. It crumbles when I take a bite. I brush crumbs from my blouse. I wash the toast down with juice. I feel suspended between then and now, between what used to be and what is. The thought of what might be is nerve-racking. In addition, eating is not helping a bit.

Ginny returns with a thick file folder. She sits back down. "Let's see," she says, opening it. "I think Enrique was here sometime at the end of ninety-seven. In October, maybe." She sorts through the pages. "I know he painted the bedrooms on the west side of the patio. Your bedroom was one of those, actually."

I concentrate on my breath. Breathe in softly. Blow out gently.

"Here it is," Ginny says. Her red-lacquered fingernail rests on something written on a page. "Hart," she says. "His name is Enrique Hart." She claps for more coffee, and Prudencia comes out of the kitchen again and refreshes the cups. When she gets to me, I smile and lay a palm over my cup. "No, gracias, Prudencia."

"El pintor se llama Enrique Hart," Ginny says to her.

"Ey." Prudencia nods. "Y se acuerda, tiene un perro, Popay."

Ginny gives a chuckle. "That's right. Prudencia's reminding me that Enrique has a dog called Popeye. The mutt was here every day that

Enrique was. Cute name for a dog, don't you think? So, how do you know this Enrique Hart?"

I feel strangely calm. Like I'm caught in the eye of a storm. I sit very still to keep from flying off. "Enrique Hart is my brother," I reply. The name "Enrique" feels odd in my mouth.

I write Sam a quick e-mail.

> Sam, something incredible has happened. I'm close to finding Hub. I found out he has a family. A wife named Luli who's pregnant. A son. I don't know his name. Joe Cruz (remember I told you about him, he's been so helpful) is going to drive me out to Hub's place. It's in a village called San Antonino, about half an hour from here. If it turns out I do find Hub, then I'm not coming home tomorrow. I'll make reservations for later. Stay tuned. Keep your fingers crossed. How I wish you were here. All my love, Annie.

 Once again, Joe and I bounce along a Mexican road, looking for something and somebody. This time it's Hub's house in San Antonino. Ginny could not provide the exact address, for in this part of the world there is no need for anything so precise. Instead, she suggested that once we reach the village, we stop and ask for directions. To "la casa del gringo or la casa de Luli" is what she said we should say.

Like thousands of other such villages in Mexico, San Antonino is a quaint, dusty place of old adobe buildings, in various states of disrepair, rising along a half dozen transecting streets. We drive past a white-washed colonial church—tall, narrow, two bell towers, a few cantinas, a barbershop, a farmacia, which is more like a sundries store than a pharmacy. The village is known for its embroidery-making, and a number of shops display colorfully decorated dresses hanging from poles hooked to the tops of opened doors. A small breeze sets dress hems flapping like brightly stitched flags.

"I'll stop and ask here," Joe says, as we pull up to a taqueria at a corner. "Tacos La Preferida" is written in uneven script at the top of the door. Joe leaves the motor idling and jumps down from the Cherokee. I roll the window down and catch the satisfying odor of tortillas frying in bubbling oil. I watch Joe round the front of the car and disappear into the taco shop. Once again, he's in his uniform: khaki walking shorts, a pastel knit shirt, Birkenstocks. What would I do without Joe's help? From the first moment, he's been a godsend. Now he's fast becoming a soul's companion, and the soft spot I've developed for him is growing at an alarming rate. I think of the men I've met over the years in the workshops I've led. Some have possessed a certain endearing quality that had a lot to do with how open and honest they were. A few of these men had intrigued, even beguiled, me. I recall coming home with the thought of one in particular swirling in my head. But that was years ago, and that man's name, what he looked like, is lost in the recesses of my mind. Not so with Joe. I will go to my old age remembering Joe Cruz.

He now emerges from the shop. He is grinning. When he climbs back into the car and shuts the door, he continues to grin.

"What?" I will not allow myself but the smallest hope. "Seeing is believing" is the peg I'll set my hat upon.

"Your brother's house is 'la casa del cacto pintado,' the house of the painted cactus. It's down this road, the taco man said. Just a little way past the outskirts of town."

It's amazing. A concrete-block wall with cacti painted on so realistically that it looks like a hedge. On the other side, a house. Small, compact, also built of concrete block. The house is the color of pumpkin pie; its door and window sashes, peacock blue. Joe has driven up slowly and cut the motor. We sit beside a curlicued iron gate, and I feel dumbstruck by the anticipation of who might materialize from all this living color. I turn to Joe and catch him studying me.

"How you doing?" he asks, reading my mind.

"I'm scared to death."

"I can imagine."

"Maybe there's no one home. There's no orange Beetle." At the breakfast table, Prudencia had reminded Ginny that el señor Enrique drove "un Bolsbagen color naranja."

"It could be parked in back," Joe says.

"That's true."

"You know what? I think it's finally show time. Time to get out of the car and swing open the gate. Time to walk up to the house and knock on the door."

"God, Joe."

"You can do it."

"I'm glad you think so. Listen, when I go in, would you wait for me out here?"

"Of course. You think I'd leave you stranded?" Joe shakes his head.

"Or maybe you could leave and then come back."

"You know what? I could go over to la doña Clarita's, the healer I told you about. Her place is in Ocotlán. That's not far from here. I could drive over to check if she has time to see you. You still want to go, right?"

"Absolutely. And since I'm not leaving tomorrow, I'll have plenty of time."

A dog startles us. A big black one barks at the gate. "Where did he come from?" I poke my head out the window. "Popeye? Are you Popeye?"

The dog yaps even more furiously. I can see through the gate. Down the walk past the dog, the house door opens. A woman appears. She steps out into the sun, a hand over her eyes as a shield against the glare. The woman wears jeans and a voluminous blousy top, an embroidered one.

I would leave the car, but I fear the dog, so I lean out the window. "¿Es usted Luli?" I call this out over the racket the dog is making.

The woman cranes her neck toward me.

"¡El perro!" I point to the dog.

"¡Popay!" The dog trots back to its mistress. It wags its tail, quiets.

Carefully, so as not to re-arouse the dog, I slip out of the car. I stand respectfully next to the door. "Soy Annie, de los Estados Unidos. Soy hermana de Hub . . . de Enrique." I pause. "Are you Luli?"

The woman nods and walks up to the gate. She hooks a finger through the ironwork. "Annie Art," she says. "Sister of Enrique."

I go to her, tower over her, wish crazily that I were shorter. I extend my hand through the gate and she gives my hand a squeeze. "Mucho gusto," I say. "I'm your sister-in-law. Soy su cuñada." The words bloom like an offering from my mouth.

"Ey," Luli replies. She smiles a dazzling smile, and for a moment we simply gaze at each other, taking measure of what it means to be standing face-to-face.

Finally, I ask, "Is Enrique here?"

Luli shakes her head. "But soon he will return."

"You speak English," I say, and then immediately wish I hadn't put it so condescendingly. I try again. "You speak good English."

Luli smiles at my inane remark. "You wait for your brother?"

"How long before he returns, do you think?"

"Half an hour maybe. You wait in the house." Luli lifts her chin in the direction of the car. "The man in the car, he can come in, too."

"This is my friend, Joe Cruz. He's also staying at Casa Amapolas. He's been good enough to drive me." Joe gives Luli a little wave and calls out, "Mucho gusto." Luli nods in response. She invites him in, but Joe explains that he has an appointment and will be back to fetch me later. I watch Joe pull away. I catch the silly grin stretched across his face.

Luli opens the gate and we awkwardly embrace. That's a very pregnant belly under that embroidered blouse. Popeye sniffs me but is docile, given his mistress's welcome. "Pásele," Luli says, and walks me toward her peacock blue door. On the way, I ask about the cacti hedge.

"Enrique painted it," Luli says. "In the house, we have many of his paintings."

I sit at the kitchen table, Hub's creations a swirl of color everywhere I look. Luli goes right to the stove and heats up the coffee. She serves me some in a china cup she has to fish from the back of a tall cabinet. To do it, she stands on a step stool, not allowing me to help her. I'm a total wreck. All my workshop philosophies are of no benefit to me at all. I wish I could stand alone before Hub's paintings, gleaning meaning out of each and every one. Somewhere, in some image, I might find the answer to the mystery of his escape. Instead, I sit across from my newfound sister-in-law as if it's the most natural thing. As if I'd been on my way to the store and just dropped in for a quick cup and a casual chat. But no, here I am, having crossed three thousand miles and closed the breach of twenty long years. Here I am, in suspended animation, every nerve poised to the sound of an orange Beetle rumbling down the road.

Since Hub left us, whenever I imagined a reunion, it was either Hub bursting through Ma's door, calling, Maaaaaaa, I'm home. I think I've had about enough of being gone! Or it was Hub ringing the doorbell of my Hopkins house, maybe one of the kids answering his ring.

Most probably Jack, one eyebrow raised, asking sassily, And who might you be? And Hub shooting back in his own sassy way, Hiya there, kid. It just so happens I'm your long-lost uncle. Over the years, it's these scenarios I've envisioned. Never could I have guessed, never even dreamed, what is happening now. Me, perched on the edge of this chair, my heart beating very fast, or maybe not at all.

"You're going to have a baby," I say to Luli, the import of this striking me at last: My brother is having a baby.

"On December twenty-six," Luli says.

It takes me a moment to compute this in my head. When I do, I give a little yelp. "Oh, that's in less than a week!" All these years, and my brother has had a real life. He owns a house. He has a wife. A small son. Another on the way. "Where is your son?" Ginny Powers had told me about the son.

"He's with his father. The two are inseparable." To show me how much, Luli lifts a hand and presses two fingers together. "Así. Like this."

"Oh." Again, the only sound I can manage.

Luli twists her head, suddenly listening. "Enrique's coming."

I feel the blood drain away from my face. I stand, wanting inexplicably to run and hide. In the yard, Popeye starts to bark. Soon there's the crunch of tires rolling over gravel.

"You wait here," Luli says. "For your privacy, Uberto and me will go to neighbor house. Okay?"

I seem nailed to the floor when Luli goes out of the room, but when I hear the slam of the car door, I bolt. Out the kitchen, into another room. This one long and crowded with painting supplies, an easel, canvases stacked against the wall. A large TV under a window. A sofa. A big chair. Outside, the creak of the gate. A child's giggles. "Mámi, Mámi." I turn and face the sofa. Above it a huge painting. A field of roiled brown earth. A green John Deere tractor painted hazily to show movement. The sight of the painting almost brings me down. I make it over to the sofa. Drop upon it.

Soon, there are footsteps, then a pause. I keep my eyes glued on the TV, on its curved black screen. I do not rise. When my brother comes near, when he lowers himself beside me, I do not turn to face him. He sits so close, I feel his shoulder set against mine. His hip alongside mine. When he lays an arm around me, my heart expands like a fireworks burst and the TV swims before my eyes. I drop my head, the tears coming fast, slipping, hot, down my cheeks and onto my lap.

"I'm sorry, Annie." Hub's first words to me in almost twenty years.

I nod. I reach a hand to pat his, draped over my shoulder. "I'm sorry, too, Hub."

We sit like that, my hand over his, our lives lining up once more beside each other. It strikes me that, soon, Hub will ask after Ma, and I will tell him what I've come all this way to say. And so, inevitably, Hub squeezes my hand. "How's Ma?"

It's now I turn to face him. Now I see how much he looks like Pa. Same long face, nut brown and creased by the sun. Same dark, brooding eyes. Hub's pale hair is pulled back into a ponytail. A broad part down the middle of his head shows his freckled scalp. I lay a hand along his cheek. "Ma's gone, Hub. That's what I've come to tell you."

My brother's face crumples. His lower lip quivers, like Will's lip does when he's just about to cry. Hub lowers his head and his shoulders begin to shake. I dig some tissues from my shorts pocket. Hand him one. Use another to dab my own tears.

"When?" Hub asks after a moment.

"In March."

"What happened?"

"Emphysema."

"Goddamn cigarettes."

"Goddamn cigarettes," I say, but thinking, "God damn you." The sight of him, tall, lean, tanned, him here, on his couch, in his room, in his house, all of him, all of these possessions are an affront to my familial dedication and loyalty. All the time I was slaving and coping and worrying and grieving, Hub was painting pictures and living his life, free from all I was enduring. This internal rant starts a slow leak in my ballooning emotions. It's time to let it all out, I think. Go ahead, girl. Out with the bad air. "Ma choked to death, Hub, if you want to know the truth. She choked to death, that's the long and short of it." I hear the harshness of my words, how I've repeated them for emphasis, and I feel only a momentary guilt at not softening the way I give him the news. I think, Good for you, Annie Rush. Good for you for telling it like it was, and of course I go on. I go on to tell about the months and months of Ma's illness, how her lungs slowly filled, the difficulty of her breathing, the nightmare of her life. I spare no detail. Not one gory bit of information. "So, that's the way it was. It was awful."

Hub's long face has grown longer still. "How long was she sick?"

"Five years."

"Oh, God. I should've been there."

"Goddamn right you should've been!" At last, my past on its way to claiming the revenge I know I rightfully deserve.

"I'm so sorry."

"I'm sorry, too, Hub. I'm sorry . . . no, you know what? Here's the truth, I'm furious. Positively furious. At you!" I've knotted my fists and can feel the sharpness of my nails digging into my palms. "I'm furious because you left me all alone to deal with Ma. It wasn't easy, you know. It was hell actually. Ma was no picnic after Maggie and Pa died, after you took off. All she'd do was sit, mope and smoke. When she got home from working at the school cafeteria, she wouldn't eat, she hardly wanted to cook, and most times, being the good daughter, I didn't press her. I'd just go get something out of the fridge and fix it for myself. At night, she'd sit there in the dark. Rocking back and forth in that old rocker in the bay window. The smoke of her cigarettes fouling up the house. I tried everything I could to get her out of her shell, to make her happy, to help her see that, even though Maggie and Pa and you were gone, I was there." I pause, take a breath. "Jesus! Hub, I was there! I was the only one there!"

Hub reaches for me, but I draw back. "No! Don't come trying to make up for things now. Where were you all those years I needed someone? You were living the high life in Montana and Florida and California, all those places you sent postcards from."

"You got them."

"Ma got them. You sent them to her. All those years, and never once a postcard for me."

"What do you mean? I sent them to both of you."

"No you didn't. You sent them to Ma."

"Well, yeah, they were addressed to Ma, but they were meant for the two of you. That was understood."

"Well, guess what? I never saw them. I never saw them until the day Ma died."

Hub's jaw drops. "Are you telling me she never showed them to you? All those years and Ma never showed you one?"

"That's right. All those years and I didn't know if you were dead or alive. Sometimes I'd think of you so hard. I'd close my eyes until I'd see bursts of color and I'd wish and wish and pray and pray. Come home, Hub, I'd say. Please, please come home. I'd even ask Maggie to help me find you. I'd say, Maggie, find Hub. Tell him to come home. And then I'd open my eyes, expecting you to be there. And you never were, Hub. You never, ever were." Now my face crumples, my mouth twists and I'm making those pitiful sounds I make when my heart, once more and for the hundredth time, neatly breaks in two.

Hub drops down from the sofa and kneels before me. He wraps me in his arms. "Oh God, Annie," he says.

I lay my head on my brother's shoulder. "You never once came home, Hub." I mumble this against his neck. "Some days I thought you were dead. I thought I'd never see you again."

Hub holds me; he rubs little circles against my back. When I've quieted down, Hub brings a chair from across the room and sets it before me so that we're sitting knee-to-knee, face-to-face. "Listen to me," he says. "I want you to know something. Something very important."

"What?"

"It wasn't only postcards, Annie. It wasn't only postcards I sent Ma."

"What do you mean?"

"I wrote Ma letters. When I was in the Army. I wrote her once from there. And when I was in Montana and then from Florida. And I also called her. I called her once."

"You've got to be kidding." In all of Ma's papers, there was no evidence of this.

"No, I'm not. Granted, I addressed the envelopes to Ma, but I always included you. 'Dear Ma and Annie' I wrote in every one. And the time I called and she picked up, I said, 'Hi, Ma, it's me,' and then I hung up. I got so scared that I hung up."

This news stuns me. It absolutely stuns me. "She never told me. Not once, about anything."

Hub shakes his head. With a finger, he wipes the wetness from his eyes. "God. Ma really must've hated me."

"Hated you? Why?"

"Because of what I did. Do you think I wanted to leave? I didn't want to leave. Ma threw me out, Annie, that's what really happened."

My world is turning upside down. "I don't get it."

"Look, I did a very bad thing. But I was just a kid. A stupid kid full of rage at what had happened to us."

"What did you do?" I can't even begin to imagine.

"I said something really brutal to Ma. One day, when I got home, and she was sitting there, like you describe, a cigarette hanging from her mouth, all that smoke, like a screen around her, I asked her something. I can't remember what, all I know is that she pissed me off. It pissed me off to see her and how she was letting herself go, how she was letting us both go, *swoop*, down the drain with her."

"What did you say?"

"I said I knew why Pa had killed himself. I said, 'Pa killed himself because of you, Ma.' I said, 'If I had the guts, I'd kill myself, too.' I said, 'You make me want to stick a rifle in my mouth just like Pa did.' I said, 'I don't blame Pa at all. At least he doesn't have to live with you anymore.' " Hub shakes his head. "Those words are etched in my memory. There's no force on earth that can erase them from my head."

I feel my eyes widen. "Where was I when this was going on?"

"I have no idea. All I know is that she threw me out after that. 'Guess what, mister!' she yelled. 'You don't have to live with me, so get out of my life! I never want to lay eyes on you again!' Of course, I did what she asked. That was all the excuse I needed, being the crazy, mixed-up kid I was then."

I am in shock. I don't know how to respond. Finally, I say, "I can't believe it."

"Believe it, Annie. That's what happened. I figured Ma would have told you."

"You know what? When Ma was dying, and she asked me to fetch the postcards, I asked her why she had never shown them to me. All she did was shrug. I asked her if that was all she'd got, if you had sent anything else, and Ma just shook her head. She shook her head no."

Hub says nothing, only looks at me, and I can see in his face that he's telling me the truth. "I can't believe it," I say. "Why would Ma lie like that?"

"I don't know."

I feel the rage boil up in me again. Now it turns to my mother's omissions. Jesus! What had I done to be so cruelly treated? What had I done? The answer strikes like a thunderclap. I had lived, that's what I'd done. I feel the sourness rise up in my throat, and I stand and wiggle around Hub and start to pace across the room. "She hated us both, Hub. After Maggie died, Ma hated everything."

"Ma had no reason to hate you, Annie. You were a perfect daughter."

"I might have been perfect, but there was one thing Ma couldn't stand and I just realized what that was."

"What?"

"She couldn't stand that every day I lived I was the identical reminder of what she had lost."

At the admission, I drop back onto the couch, the reel of my life with Ma unrolling before me: Me fixing supper. Me doing the wash, the ironing. Me doing my homework with my hearing pitched toward Ma. Then, when I'd moved out to go to college, me phoning up to check on her. Me bringing her takeout. Me coming in and straightening up the house. And when Sam and I were married, me walking down the aisle alone. Ma standing in the pew. The whole church had its eyes on me as I came toward the altar. But Ma, Ma had her eyes on the floor.

Hub says, "You don't know that that's the truth, Annie. That's only something you surmise."

"Well, it must be some kind of truth, or why else would she have kept news of you from me? Isn't that something you would do to somebody you hate?"

Hub is silent for a moment. "You got me there," he finally says. Then he moves off the chair and sits on the couch beside me. "Well, I know she hated me. I have proof positive. She threw me out."

"But Hub, I didn't throw you out. Why didn't you try to find me? Why didn't you call me?"

"I should've. God knows, I should've. But when Ma never answered my letters, I just figured you knew everything. That she'd told you everything, and that you felt the same as her."

"Well, you were wrong."

"Yes, I was wrong, and I'm truly, truly sorry." His voice drops to a raspy whisper and he says, "Can you forgive me?"

I look into my brother's eyes and see the need in them. "We all need forgiveness, Hub, so I forgive you, if you can do the same for me."

Hub frowns. "What in the world would you need forgiveness for?"

"You'd be surprised," I say, and I would go on but there's a commotion in the kitchen and Hub's son bounds into the room, Luli after him. "I'm sorry," she says. "He wanted to see his papi."

Uberto wedges himself between Hub's long legs. He is a beautiful boy: curly black hair, deep-set eyes, round brown face, Botticelli cheeks. "Uberto, this is your auntie," Luli says.

"Shake your auntie's hand," Hub says. "Your auntie is my sister."

"Hola," I say.

Uberto looks sidelong at me. He thrusts out his hand shyly.

"I'm happy to meet you, Uberto." His little hand is soft. I can feel no bones in it at all. "You know what? You have two cousins. Jack and Will. They are nine and eight. They'll be so happy to meet you someday."

"Your note," Hub says, "the one you left at the library, you signed your name 'Rush.' "

"Sam Rush is my husband."

"Just think," Hub says to Luli and his son, "we have a whole new family."

"And so do I," I add.

Later, when I'm back at the casa, I sit on the veranda in front of my room and compose an e-mail to send to Sam. "I found Hub," I write.

> I'm just back from his house. He has one, can you believe it? Also a wife, a four-year-old son, and another on the way. Due date in less than a week! He wants me to stay for the birth of the baby and maybe I will. Hub is coming over day after tomorrow, when he's back from a trip he and his father-in-law have to make to get wood for their carvings. When Hub comes over, we're going to sit and do more talking. We did a lot of that today. I'm going to show him that album I made and also give him his cigar box, the one Ma had kept. He'll be so surprised. So, I'm going to change my reservations. How long I'll stay, I don't yet know. I wish you were here. Do you think you all could come? A silly wish, I know, but still. I miss you all. Your Annie. P.S. I'm going to do something incredible tomorrow tonight. I'm going to go see a healer. Her name is Clarita, which means clarity.

 *Ive been wishing my Annie could have another baby. Shes young enough for it. I love Jack and Will its not that. Those are two precious babies. Will brought over his teddy bear the other day. He calls him Cooper and sleeps with him every night, but that precious boy put Cooper in my lap and said grama you can have Cooper hell help you breathe right. Of course I wouldnt have it tho I thanked Will for the thought. I said you keep Cooper just bring him over for visits and Will said that would be okay. God love that precious child. But I want a little girl grandbaby. One to call Maggie again. Maybe thats not a good idea I dont know. All I know is I want my little Maggie again even though I dont have much time. If Annie got pregant tomorrow Im so bad I wouldnt be around when the baby was born. Breaks my heart to think of it. I think about Hub somewhere in the world and wonder if he has a family. I wonder if he has a good wife and*

some sweet babies. Maybe he has a little girl. Maybe hes called her Maggie. A new Maggie with green eyes and hair the color of corn silk. Now that would be something. How I wish I could find out.

 Here I am, lying flat on the ground on a plastic sheet doña Clarita spread out for me. "Pa que no te ensucies," she said. So you won't get dirty. Between me and the plastic is a cross the healer created from two lengths of aluminum foil she snapped off a roll. We're in her altar room, one of several tin-roofed rooms built behind a tall wooden gate and around a grassless patio made pretty by geraniums and common daisies growing in pots and manteca cans. A lone tree, a lime from the looks of its fruit, shades the area. Joe sits on a bench under the tree, the moon filtering light through the branches, waiting for the healer to sweep me clean of el susto, which in my case at least, has caused me to live divorced from my body.

In preparation for the ritual, I sat under the tree myself, and doña Clarita (a birdlike woman in her fifties perhaps, with, of all things, one wandering eye) held my hands (her hands were hot, her grasp firm) as I recounted my story. I told it in English, which was not a problem, she said. A true story is a story, no matter what language is used to convey it. And it's not so much the story's content that's important, she went on. What's important is that it be told. That it be brought up from the heart, pushed out by the breath, released into the air. Freed. Freed to mingle and collide with all the other freed stories permeating the air around us. It's where stories belong, doña Clarita said. Outside us, or simply etched in our memories, not trapped and calcified within, weighing us down like sea anchors.

Doña Clarita's altar room smells of burning candlewax, the pungency of incense and the fragrance of rosemary branches tied together into bundles. The room is smoky and dim. Flickering votives set along the altar's shelves provide the only light. Objects crowd the shelves: photographs, holy cards, figurines, rosaries. When I first stepped in, I didn't pause to study what surrounded me, I simply laid myself down upon the shiny foil cross as doña Clarita directed me to do, trying with all my might to trust what I was doing, to trust what was being done to me.

I don't know exactly what is happening tonight, I only know that for me it's time to let go of the paralyzing grip the past has had on me. What does it matter the method I use? How unorthodox or strange the method seems?

Doña Clarita circles me. She intones what I think is the Apostle's Creed. "Creo en Dios Padre, Todo Poderoso." I believe in God, the Father Almighty . . . The words are a comfort, though I don't know them by heart, but it soothes me to make out what she's chanting in Spanish: "el cielo y la tierra," heaven and earth, "el Espiritu Santo," the Holy Spirit, "la Virgen María." Three times she says this prayer.

"Do you know el Padre Nuestro?" the Our Father? she then asks in Spanish. And I nod and close my eyes and we both say the well-known words, our two languages blending into one heartfelt prayer. Again, as with the other, it takes three recitations.

Now we leave the familiarity of common prayers and step off into new territory as doña Clarita sweeps me clean. She uses a rosemary bundle to do it. She brushes it vigorously back and forth over my body. The branches are prickly and sharp, the feel of them keeping me alert. As she works, I allow the images of my troubled past to float up into my consciousness. I don't hold them back. Maggie on the tractor, her outstretched hand, her innocent eyes, wide with fright. Pa sitting on the leather sofa in the funeral home, his hands bunched upon his lap, the rubbing rubbing, as if he were Lady Macbeth. Pa poking a rifle barrel into his mouth, his hand, also outstretched, his finger reaching for the trigger. Ma huddled on the back stoop of the farmhouse, the plume of smoke leaking from her lips, like her very soul escaping.

And Hub. I think of Hub, and I ask God, I ask the Universe, I ask the cosmic will of Mexico to help me surrender any anger I might still feel toward him. Help, help, I ask all the powers that be, help me truly love my brother again.

Swish, swish goes the prickly, fragrant broom, and I imagine all the grief and rage and pain lifting up from me, imagine it all whisked away and dissipating in the air. And how soon? I ask myself. How soon will I fall back into my body? How soon before my body can truly love itself again?

"You must return twice more," doña Clarita says, almost as if she's divined my questions. "Three times you must tell your story. For there to be wholeness, things must be done in threes."

To end this first time, doña Clarita does something that surprises me. She jumps over me. Three times. Once across my head, then across my middle, then finally, across my feet. She is spry and agile. I watch her leaping over me, her long, skinny braids flying up as she does.

When we're back under the lime tree, and I've given doña Clarita three times her customary charge, she presses an offering of her own into my hand. A whole nutmeg. "Carry it with you," she commands. "It will help keep el susto away."

Back in the car, I lay my head against the seat. I'm limp. There's nothing left for me to feel. Joe turns the key and the engine roars to life. We drive off toward the casa. In my hand, the nutmeg seed, a brown, furrowed talisman.

 Joe has been kind enough to make himself scarce while Hub and I share the privacy of his patio. Moments ago, my brother walked across the garden and through the opening in the hedge. Now, he sits, just inches away, all knobby-kneed and freckled, his face ignited with a look I can only call happiness.

"I have something for you." I hoist my tote bag off the floor and set it on my lap. I pull out Hub's old cigar box. "Remember this?" I ask, handing it over. Also in the tote are Hub's postcards, Ma's notebook, plus an album filled with photographs of her and Sam and the kids.

"Is this what I think it is?" Hub says, taking the box. He opens it and studies the inside of the lid. "I can't believe it!" He looks up at me. "Where did you find this?"

"Ma had it."

"Wow, look at that. 'I yam what I yam.' Remember that?"

"You're a can of Spam," I retort, and we laugh.

Hub lifts out the Hank Aaron baseball card and lays it on the table. Then the one aggie marble. Then his Boy Scout neckerchief ring. "I'd forgotten all about this. This brings back so many memories."

"I bet. Ma kept the box, all these years, on the top shelf of her closet. She asked me to fetch it just hours before she died. That's when she asked me to find you. She said, 'Promise me you'll find your brother.'"

"She did? She actually said that?" On Hub's face a cloudy look, as if he really can't believe Ma would say such a thing.

"Yes, she did. And you know what? I think Ma died with lots of regrets. At the end, I think she was wishing she'd done things differently."

"We can only hope."

"We can only hope," I repeat. I dig into the tote again and pull out Hub's postcards, held together with a rubber band. "And here are these."

Hub slips off the band and fans the cards out on the table. "Will you look at that. That's a big part of my life lying there."

"Tell me about it, Hub. Tell me where you went and what you did. I used to lie in bed, thinking about you, wondering where you were sleeping. If you had a bed, a blanket. If you were cold. That's what I used to think about."

"Sometimes I didn't. Sometimes it was just me on some floor. I took my old sleeping bag. That old brown one with the bucking broncos. So I had that."

"I remember that thing. Remember that summer when I pitched your tent out in the yard? I used your sleeping bag, too."

Hub nods. "I remember I used to come out in the middle of the night and try to scare you."

"And I remember I hated you for that."

"Yeah, well, who could blame you? I was a real ass."

I chuckle. "I think I might have to second that. So, when did you join the Army?"

"Not too long after I left. It was the best thing I did. For three years, I had a roof over my head, three squares a day, and lots and lots of discipline. I thought about re-upping, but then I decided not to. The Army gave me some skills, and I figured it was enough to get me going. After the Army, I could cook and I was pretty good at repairing cars, so I just went from place to place, taking any job I could in machine shops, car repair shops, in diners and cafés."

"But you never stayed too long in one place. That's easy to see from the postcards."

"Nope. After a while I got the wanderlust and I decided to follow the sun. I was sick of all the hard weather, so I ended up in Florida. That's when I started to paint. I was staying at a rooming house owned by a painter. The old man used to let me come in and watch him. He let me study his painting books. He had loads of them. Then he got so that he'd let me dabble with his paints. He used to encourage me, tell me what I was doing right and how I could improve. One day he told me I had the soul of a painter. I'll never forget that." Hub shakes his head. "I loved that old man."

"What happened to him?"

"I don't know. After I left Florida and moved to California, I lost track of him. He's probably dead by now."

"What made you move to California?"

"I don't know. The wanderlust again maybe. Besides, Florida isn't the easiest place. California's much better. When I got to San Diego, I knew I'd found my place. That's before I'd come to Oaxaca, of course.

Now, I've found my home. At heart, I'm an old gringo-Mexican, that's what I am."

We go on like that, me asking questions and Hub filling me in on what's transpired in his life. We take a break and I make coffee on Joe's Krups and then he asks me about Sam, about the kids. He wants to know if I work and then wants me to tell him all the things a corporate trainer does.

After we run out of steam from all the telling, Hub says, "I think we'll need a lot of days to tell all our stories." He gathers up his postcards and childhood treasures and puts them back into the cigar box. "Thanks for bringing this all the way from home. It means a lot to me."

"Well, I knew it was the right thing to do. After all, remember, I once stole it from you." That hot summer day. Maggie and me in the tree house, it all comes alive again in my head.

"You didn't steal it," Hub says.

"Sure I did. Don't you remember? You were so mad when you found out."

"No, no. I don't mean that it wasn't stolen. I mean it wasn't you that stole it. It was Maggie who did."

"It was not."

"Of course it was."

A ringing sound starts and I look around for the source, suddenly distracted.

"Oops, that's my cell phone," Hub says, and pulls the phone out of his pocket. He lifts a finger to me. "Let me get this real quick." He lifts the phone to his ear. "Bueno," he says.

While Hub tends to business, I'm thinking that I have not told Hub about his inheritance, about the fact that Ma has left his room untouched. I don't know why I haven't, maybe it's because these are two huge things and I'm perversely enjoying having the power to keep them to myself for a little while yet. Across the table from me, my brother's expression goes from pleasant inquisitiveness to sudden concern. "¿Cuándo?" he says. He listens, then says, "Sí. Okay. Ya vengo."

I understand enough Spanish to know my brother's now on his way to somewhere. Hub turns off the phone. "That was my brother-in-law. Luli's gone into labor."

"Oh my, where is she?"

"She's at her parents'. The midwife's on her way. I have to go." Hub stands up.

"Of course. Can I come too?"

"Would you?"

"Wild horses couldn't keep me away."

 *Its hard to admit the terrible things Ive done but time is getting short and I dont want to die without confessing. Maybe the catholics were right about that. Maybe Martin Luther shoulda thought twice about confession. Id give anything to kneel down in a little booth and get forgiveness and a blessing. If I wasnt hooked up to this horrible machine Id march into a church and tell a priest what I've done. It doesnt matter Im not catholic but a Lutheran. A sinner is a sinner and all Gods creatures merit some kind of forgiveness.*

My most horrible sin was sending my son away. Ive thought back time and time again on what he said to me. He said it was because of me that Elmer took his life. I know Hub was a kid when he said it. I know he had no sense and that what he said he said in anger and a kid shouldnt be totally responsible for the things he does then. But I think Hub was sort of right. I know Elmer put a

shotgun in his mouth because he felt responsible, but after Maggie died I didn't help him any after that. After Maggie a black cloud settled over me and try as I might it followed me around. Still does if you want to know the truth. All you have to do is look at me sitting here in this easy chair this infernal machine going the noise it makes my constant companion. Its all my fault Im dying like this. Maybe Elmer and me were alike in that respect. He took the fast root in killing himself while I prefered the slow root. Bullets and cigarettes in the end are both the same.

I hate to admit what I did after Hub left. He sent a letter and I tore it up. It came from Fort Riley Kansas I remember that. When I came home and found it laying on the floor under the mail slot I saw red and tore it up. Into a million little pieces. Then I tried like crazy to put them back together but it was no use. I kept all those little pieces for a very long time but then one day I threw them out because just seeing them made me so much sadder than I already was. I've kept one little piece, the biggest one. Its between the pages of the bible. I kept it for the words. I wish that I. Thats what it says.

Hub called me once. I know it was him but then he hung up. Then there was a few more letters which I didnt tear up. I think one was from somewhere out west and the other was from Fla. By that time I had cooled down so I woulda answered them but there was no return address. I dont think I have those letters anymore. Ive looked and looked but cant place them anywheres. All this I kept from Annie. Maybe it was wrong. I did it first to spare her. Now when I think back on it I think I shoulda said something. But now its too late. Whats done is done. Maybe one day if she reads this shell see what I did and that I meant her no harm. Still I know Ive *not been a good mother. I hope Annie can forgive the lousy way I was. I hope Hub can too. I keep thinking when I pass that Elmer and Maggie will be up there with there arms open. Its what keeps me going if you want to know the truth.*

 If you'd told me months ago that three days before Christmas and nine from the millennium, I'd be away from home in Mexico, standing in a bedroom doorway holding my nephew's little hand while his mother, propped up in bed, squeezes her eyes shut as she endures a contraction, I would've said that you were crazy. No way, José. As Joe has suggested, I think I'm finally surrendering to the cosmic will, not of Mexico, but to the cosmic will of life itself. From this moment on, I vow to step off my usual path. I'll welcome and accept all that comes to me.

Hub has pulled a chair up to Luli's side. He's spread a hand over her big belly, rising, like a gigantic loaf of yeasty bread, up under the sheet. "Breathe, breathe, breathe," my brother murmurs, and Luli nods and takes in air and softly blows it out. Her face is shiny with perspiration; her hair, gathered into a ponytail, is damp as well. An arc of framed photographs crowns the wall behind her—ancestors keeping a sober watch over the family. My brother has explained that the photograph haloed with black paper flowers shows the likeness of Luis Eugenio, Luli's youngest brother, who died three years ago. On the dresser, the ubiquitous votive candles. Luli's mother, doña Fausta, and Licha, the midwife, are also in the room. The women seem perplexed, maybe even a bit vexed, that Hub is solicitous and underfoot. All afternoon, he's been in and out with a cool cloth, a calming word, a soothing hand. The men of the family are in the shed out back, clearly the place where Oaxacan men belong during a birthing. The men seem respectful of Hub's need to do otherwise, but I'm sure they miss his help in preparing for tomorrow night's Radish Festival.

When Hub and I arrived, there were introductions all around. Don Efrain and his sons were all sweetness and hospitality. The grandsons, looking older than Uberto, stood under a tree, watching me. The dogs, Popeye included, were not as shy. They came right up and sniffed my thongs, my toes, my legs. The men pushed them away, then pumped my hand and smiled broadly. They led me to the radish patch to point out this year's bounty: a splendid bouquet of radish tops crowding the growing bed. Don Efrain remarked how fortunate I was to be here today, of all days. By evening, he said, there was sure to be a new baby. And the start of a prizewinning radish tableau as well.

Doña Fausta, obviously distracted by her daughter's labor, received me with reserve and politeness. She offered me a Coke, insisted when I demurred, then tipped a tepid can over the rim of a plastic glass printed with Bugs Bunny munching on a carrot. I thanked her and raised the glass to her. She gave me a quick tour of the living room. In the corner stood a white plastic Christmas tree decorated with tiny blue bulbs blinking on and off. On a long side table, the room's focal point, was a large Nativity scene, this one with a rough-hewn crèche holding a baby Jesus as pink and hefty as a newborn, a ceramic figure that is clearly her pride and joy. She lifted it from its crèche for me to hold and admire.

Now, I'm trying to stay out of everyone's way. My personal contri-
bution is keeping Uberto entertained and out of the bedroom, where
he insists on climbing up on the bed and sprawling next to his mother.
"Let's go see the baby Jesus," I say to him. Luli, her contraction over,
smiles at me appreciatively and urges her son on, "Go with your auntie.
Mámi'll be right here." I gently pull Uberto away from the door and we
step over to the crèche, a trip we've made maybe half a dozen times.
"Soon your mámi will have a baby just like that," I say to him. Uberto
and I speak in a mixture of Spanish and English, with lots of gestures.
Despite the obstacles, we're communicating quite well. "Let's go look at
the pictures," I say, and we go out to the front porch and sit on the
steps. I've brought the album I made for Hub. Uberto has looked
through the photographs a number of times, but now it's he who turns
the pages. He says, "Minneapolis Minnesota, Minnesota Minneapolis,"
shooting me a glorious smile. Tapping a photo with a finger, he tells me
who's pictured there. "Mis primos," Uberto says. "My cousins, Will y
Jack." Uberto takes this job seriously. His brow furrows in concentration. His curls are as damp and springy as his mother's. We page
through the album once more, start to finish. Uberto names the kids,
Sam, Ma, Pa, Maggie, even Elvis. He giggles at the sight of old Elvis. I've
included a number of photos of Hub when he was a baby and, later,
when we lived on the farm. In one he stands in front of the red barn,
his arm crooked to make a muscle. Under the photo, I've printed "I
yam what I yam." When we get to it, Uberto crooks an arm like his
father. "Iyamayamayama," he says, and we both giggle.

"What's so funny?" Hub comes out to join us. He drops down
beside me, and I lay the album in his lap and show him the picture.
"Wow," he says. "Where did you get this?"

"Ma had lots of pictures. I filled up an album for you. There's everyone in here."

"This is great," Hub says, and before he can begin to look through it, doña Fausta calls out "¡Enrique!" and he jumps up and hurries in. I listen for anything that might mean Luli's condition has changed, but nothing more comes from inside the house. As for Hub and me doing any talking, it's been like this since we were interrupted back at the casa. There are so many things Hub and I need to discuss. We have so much unfinished business, my mind brims over with thoughts and questions. And there's the big news I'll be giving him: He has an inheritance coming his way. A house and its contents, with which he can do as he pleases. But all this will have to wait until the baby comes. Until we can sit down and talk quietly and at length.

I slip the album into my tote bag, and Uberto and I go around to the back to watch the men again. When we walk in, all three look up with questions about Luli in their eyes. "Todavía nada," I say. Nothing yet. Luli's been laboring all day. Last time I saw the midwife (it was during our quick lunch), I noticed what looked like concern in her face, but I said nothing. I have no idea how midwives work, what the procedure is, but Licha seems to be a capable and confident woman. I'm sure that if problems arise, she'll take no chances and step aside so that Hub can take Luli to the hospital. In any case, this is what Hub has said.

I look around the shed, at the drawings of Christ's animals pinned to the shelves. The place is amazing. It's a swirl of color and texture and design. I spot a few mermaids I'd like to have. One of them rests against a rock and is strumming a guitar. I note that the men's work has progressed from harvesting the radishes to carving them. An ancient Coca-Cola cooler sits in a corner, its cord plugged into two extensions that have been snaked over the shed's crossbeams to draw power from the ceiling light fixture. The cooler hums. I peer inside. In its cold water float radish roots and what look like sealed plastic bags. These radishes don't look like any radishes I've ever seen. These are long and thick, some are gnarled. Their skins range from bright red to pink to white. Don Efrain says their flesh is firm and woody, qualities that make for easy and precise carving. "Claro," he says. "Of course, these radishes are not for eating."

He's at the table, working on a winged white horse. I pull up a stool and watch him. His grandson nudges against him. "Look," don Efrain says, to both of us. He's used the thick middle of a radish for the horse's barreled body. The legs are carved out of more slender radishes. In fact, thanks to fortunate turns in the tubers, this horse will be rearing up on its hind legs. I ask how he'll attach all the parts and don Efrain points to the boxes of wooden toothpicks, which he'll use as dowels. I nod my head in appreciation. "Muy bueno," I say, wishing I had the vocabulary to tell them all how clever and creative they are. Luli's brothers are carving the more common Nativity figures. Mauricio, a dove and a cow. Rogelio, a little drummer boy with three tiny stars down his chest and fringed pantaloons. Our conversation consists of simple comments, enthusiastic nods and smiles, which, amazingly, are all we really need to understand each other.

Don Efrain slips the completed segments of his horse into plastic bags and drops them in the cooler. "Para que no se me sequen," he says. So they won't dry out. He goes on to explain that each creature will be assembled in the booth before the contest starts. The booths are traditionally constructed clear around the zócalo square. The Huerta family's booth is number twenty-five. "Veinticinco, un número dichoso." Lucky number! Don Efrain raises his thick eyebrows like Groucho Marx. He starts on the horse's wings. I can see the drawing he's made for a guide. They'll be carved from the thick skins of pink radishes. In the drawing, the cutout wings look like lace.

Hub walks in and takes a stool. Uberto comes around the table and insinuates himself between his father's legs. "How's Luli?" I ask.

"I don't know," he says, worry written all over his face.

"What do you mean you don't know?"

"Licha says that the baby might be coming feet-first."

"My God, Hub, that's a breech birth. That could be a problem."

"I know. She's been trying to turn the baby around, but it's a big, big baby and she's not having any luck. Luli's pretty exhausted."

"So, what'll happen now?"

"Licha's going to give it a bit more time. If things don't change soon, we're off to the hospital."

"Okay, that sounds right. What hospital are you going to? I suppose the one where her doctor is. Luli's been seeing a doctor during her pregnancy, right?"

"Well, yes and no," Hub says. "We belong to the IMSS. That's the national health plan. Luli's been over there for checkups a few times, but the place is a madhouse. And you don't always get the same doctor. You just see whoever is available when you get there. And usually you have to wait for hours and hours. And you always get the runaround if you need any tests. We thought we might need an ultrasound, but forget that. No way could we ever get a doctor's approval for that. So, that's why we have Licha. Licha's available whenever you need her."

"The place sounds awful. But the IMSS isn't the hospital, right? The hospital would be different."

"It's the same place," Hub says. "If we have to go, we'll be stepping into chaos. That's the way national health is."

"Aren't there any private hospitals?"

"Sure there are. Good ones, too. But they cost a fortune. We can't afford that."

I take a long breath because now the time has come. "Hub, can we step out for a minute? I need to tell you something." Don Efrain and the brothers have been working during our conversation, their heads bent over their carvings, but I know they've been straining to understand what Hub and I are saying. Hub and I go to stand under a big tree that shades the yard.

"What's up?" Hub says, seemingly perplexed.

"You can afford a private hospital, Hub."

"Why do you say that?"

"Because Ma left you an inheritance. She left you the house on Holmes Avenue and all that's in it."

As if the news might topple him, Hub falls back against the tree. The apple in his neck bobbles as he gulps. "You've got to be kidding."

"No, I'm not. Your inheritance amounts to maybe three hundred thousand dollars. Property values in Uptown have gone through the roof. People are lining up to buy. Lots of times, they're paying more than the asking price."

"I can't believe it."

"So look, this is what we can do. If Luli has to go to the hospital, take her to a private one. Whatever it costs, I can cover it for now with my credit card. I have a substantial limit. Later on, we'll get squared up."

Hub shakes his head, as though to wake himself from a dream.

I think of all that Hub has endured. He lost a sister and a father, too. He had a mother who threw him out. A mother who refused any communication. I think of his tumbleweed life, of our long, and what seemed like a never-ending, separation. It all makes me so sad.

"Annie, I don't deserve this," Hub says.

"Oh, yes you do."

 We've had to bring Luli to the hospital, after all. She's been in labor all day and still no baby. It's almost eleven at night and we're all very tired. Luli most of all, of course. She, her mother, Hub and I arrived a while ago. The rest of the family stayed behind to care for sleeping grandchildren and to put the final touches on the radishes. Now, the hospital's paperwork is completed, my Visa card swiped, and Luli's in a private room being examined by a doctor, a tall, broad-shouldered woman named Doctora Buenavida. (In Spanish, her name adds up to Doctor Goodlife, and I take this as an omen.)

All of us are edgy. Hub said that when Uberto was born, Luli's labor was relatively quick and unremarkable. Why this birth is so different is anybody's guess. Maybe Licha is right, maybe the baby's in the breech position and Luli will need a cesarean section to bring her baby into the world. Whatever happens, I'm thankful that I'm here, that my Visa can make a difference. I can't imagine Luli in the Social Service hospital, the place churning with patients and visitors, the doctors most times out of reach, the beds set one after the other like a production line.

This hospital is a little jewel. Amazingly, it's in the heart of down-town Oaxaca, only five blocks from the casa and the same distance from the zócalo. The hospital had once been a colonial residence, and a grand one at that. It's two-storied, with an ample central patio circled by the patients' rooms. On the corridor outside each room are settees and chairs for visitors. Hub and I sit here now, waiting for Luli's door to open and for the doctor to come out to tell us what's going on. Doña Fausta has not wanted to join us, preferring to pace up and down the corridor, her long black rosary spilling from her hand.

The hospital is quiet, yet its high walls cannot keep out the raucous noise of a calenda happening nearby. Hub tells me these processions are a Christmas tradition. Streets are clotted with the faithful trailing behind the image of a saint being carried high, on a stand. Revelers in colorful costumes, some of them charmingly grotesque, some walking along on stilts, add to the drama and merriment. Firework spinners and sparklers frequently thicken the air with their smoke. When we drove in from Luli's parents' house, the streets around the hospital were so congested, we had to park two blocks away and walk in. Luli used her hands like a sling under her belly and held on to her baby all the way. Hub says that these festivities will go on practically all night. He says they'll continue until well into the new year, given that we're also cele-brating the millennium.

Hub's cell phone chimes and it's Rogelio, Luli's brother, wanting to know if there's any news. Hub tells him what we know. "I'll call the minute something happens," he says before signing off. Hub stretches and yawns. He props his head against the chair back and gives me a weak smile.

"What are you and Luli hoping for?" I say, surprised that, until now, I hadn't thought to ask the question. "Another boy or a girl this time? I know Luli's mother definitely wants a girl. That's all she talks about."

"I don't blame her. If we have a girl, she'll be the first one in the family besides Luli."

"What about you?"

Hub pulls himself up and leans toward me so that he's very close. "You know what I want? I want a little girl. If we have one, we're naming her Margarita. We plan to call her Maggie."

"Oh, Hub, I can't believe it." Inside me, the sweetest of joys commingles with grief, deep and newly felt.

"Yeah, Luli's all for it. So we've got to pray for a girl."

I blink back tears. "That'll be something, to have a Maggie again. It'll help make up for everything." I remember when Jack and Will were born, how each time I waited to hear the doctor say, "It's a girl." When a boy was announced, I think I was actually relieved. I guess I thought that, because of what I'd done, I didn't deserve to have a baby girl. I also thought that nothing I could ever do would bring my sister back again. But that was so many years ago. That was before this transformative time in Oaxaca, and now I think that having a new Maggie would be an amazing and wonderful thing. Despite the long distance between us, oh, the spoiling I will do!

Luli's door opens and the doctor steps out and Hub and I stand to meet her. Doña Fausta spots the new activity and hurries down the corridor, her rosary swinging like a pendulum. I study the doctor as she explains, in Spanish, what is happening to Luli. In spite of the late hour, la doctora is as fresh as if she just stepped from the shower. I listen carefully to her, understanding the words "dolor," "ultra-sonido," "aguas," "epidural." Hub asks a few questions and so does doña Fausta. Their heads nod almost in unison as the doctor responds. Then the doctor says, "Okay?"

"Okay," Hub says.

"Ey," doña Fausta echoes.

The doctor smiles at us, myself included, then turns and goes down the hall. I wonder what she thinks of me, standing there, blonde and as dumb as a clam. God, I wish I could speak Spanish. "What'd she say?" I ask Hub.

"They're taking Luli to delivery, that's upstairs. They'll break her water and start her on some kind of IV drip. The doctor says the drip should speed things up."

"What about the epidural? Didn't the doctor say something about an epidural?"

"She said it's too late for that."

"What about the ultrasound?"

"Oh yeah, right. There's an ultrasound in delivery. They'll hook her up there."

"Did you ask if she could tell if the baby was breech?"

"She said nothing about that," Hub says, and I feel a flare of irritation. What is it about men and their not asking all the right questions? I stifle myself from saying anything.

The three of us go into Luli's room. She sits back against the pillows. "They're taking me upstairs," she says, and even her voice is as limp as she looks. "I hope something happens up there."

"It will, it will," Hub says, while doña Fausta smooths out the sheet. She lays a palm on her daughter's belly, she kisses her hand. Soon, a nurse with a starched hat appears with a wheelchair. Hub and the nurse help Luli struggle out of bed.

"I can come too, right?" Hub asks.

"Papi, stay here," the nurse replies. She informs us that we're to wait on the veranda. She'll come down with any news. Before Luli's wheeled off, Hub kisses her. Doña Fausta does as well. I give her a little wave. "Don't worry," Luli says. We watch as she's wheeled out of sight around the corner.

To break up the tension, I say to doña Fausta, "Muy pronto una nieta." Very soon, a granddaughter.

Doña Fausta raises her rosary high and looks heavenward. Then, she tries out a smile on me. She tries out a smile on Hub.

It seems we've just settled down for what might be a long wait when the nurse comes back around the corner. This time she's hurrying. This time her face is lit up. "Felicidades, Papi," she says to Hub. "Tienes un varoncito." This is all happening so fast, I'm confused as to what she said. Did she say "niño"? or did she say "niña"? What's a "varoncito"? I guess all I need for an answer is to see the fleeting look of disappointment cross doña Fausta's face. Hub, on the other hand, looks thrilled, no matter what the sex. "¿Cómo está Luli? ¿Cómo está mi mujer?"

"La mámi está muy bien," the nurse says.

And then something extraordinary happens. Another nurse comes around the corner. She also is hurrying. A wide grin is spread across her face. "¡Hay más!" she exclaims. "¡Hay una niñita!"

Hub, doña Fausta and I, we all have to sit down or I think we'd fall over.

"¡Gemelos!" the grandmother says.

"Twins!" Hub says.

"Twins?" I say.

Hub says, "It's a boy and a girl. No wonder Luli was huge!"

Doña Fausta asks what time it is and Hub looks at his watch. "Twelve-thirty," he says. Hearing this, her face lights up for the very first time. "It's Night of the Radishes day!" she says. "What good luck to be born on such a day!"

This has been the very best day. This morning I held Maggie. But only for a moment, hospital procedures being different in Mexico than they are back home. I stood at the viewing window, looking in on the babies. I must have looked so forlorn, mouthing the words, "Soy la tía," I'm the aunt, my nose against the pane and pointing to her bassinet, to the name Margarita Fausta Hart Huerta, that the nurse brought the baby out and laid her in my arms. Seeing her there, so tightly swaddled, her little head in a pink, knitted cap, her black hair poking out around it, I thought my heart would melt right down into my shoes. "Hello there, Maggie," I whispered, and the tears ran when I voiced her name and she looked at me soberly, her dark eyes wide open and alert. I thought, Maggie, Maggie, wherever you are, look at this. Look.

Noting my tears, perhaps fearing they might douse the baby, the nurse gently pried her from me. Not wanting to be partial, I asked to hold Luis Eugenio. "Soy la tía," I said again, and the nurse brought him out. "Por un momentito," she said, making a gesture with two fingers, in case I didn't understand. Little Luis, named after his recently departed uncle, was as serious and watchful as Maggie had been. He, too, had lots of hair, judging from the locks spilling from under his little blue cap. The babies looked alike, but then so many do when they're only hours old.

Afterward, I went to see Luli, who'll be staying until the day after tomorrow. The babies are so healthy, they'll all be discharged on Christmas Day. Luli looked so fine when I came into her room. She was sitting up in a chair, in jeans and a sweatshirt, her hair a wild halo around her pretty face. Doña Fausta was with her. The rest of the family was at the zócalo, setting up the radish tableau in their booth— lucky number twenty-five. Luli thanked me once more for what I'd done to get her into the hospital, but I reminded her that it wasn't me, but my mother who had made it possible. Doña Fausta kept silent and lowered her eyes when the subject came up. It's what you do in these parts when you feel beholden. Perhaps to balance the scale, she let me know that she and don Efrain were planning a fiesta for the babies' baptism.

"You have to come," Luli said. "Your husband and sons, they have to come, too."

Doña Fausta added, "Ya sómos familia." We are family now. When she said this, she looked as somber as the babies had been.

Staying for the baptism is certainly something to consider. It's scheduled for the thirtieth, only a week away. I called Sam this morning before going back to the hospital, hoping to discuss all this, but he and the boys were out. When the machine answered, I left a message. I said, "It's me. Surprise, surprise, Hub and Luli had twins! A boy and a girl!

The girl's name is Maggie. The boy is Luis. They are healthy bouncing babies. There's going to be a party, and I want you all to come. So please hop on a plane. The boys have Christmas vacation, so you can do it. E-mail me saying that you will. Please, please. Okay. I love you. Bye."

It's after supper now, and Joe and I have strolled down to the zócalo to join the festivities for the Night of the Radishes. As usual, he's freshly scrubbed and smelling good. He's wearing a pair of chinos and a sunny yellow shirt. I'm in my raspberry slacks and matching shirt. We make quite a contrast: he, deeply tanned; me, still pink from a day in the sun.

"Will you look at this place," Joe says, when we come around the post office corner. The streets leading to the square are jammed with pedestrians. The restaurants are packed. Rousing music comes from an orchestra playing in the garden kiosk. Around its perimeter, the radish carvers sit in their booths, behind their tableaux. People have already formed a viewing line, and it creeps along from booth to booth. In about an hour, the judges will follow and make critiques. The award ceremony announcing the three prizewinners is scheduled for ten, in the patio of the town hall, the ayuntamiento, on the east side of the square.

Joe and I join the line of radish admirers. What the carvers have fashioned from radish flesh, from radish tops, from radish skins is astonishing. There are mariachis and dancers, merry-go-rounds and wedding scenes; there are bullfighters with bulls, saints with halos, holy Virgins in red, in pink, in white radish-skin robes. There's the Last Supper and the Crucifixion. And a multitude of Nativity scenes: the baby Jesus in his crèche. Joseph and Mary, the three kings, the holy angels, the cow, the sheep, the dove. As we go along, I study the artisans standing behind their creations. Eager expectation lights their faces. The top prize money is roughly the equivalent of one thousand dollars. Second prize is eight hundred, and six hundred goes to the third. In everyone's eyes shines the hope that they will win "el premio mayor."

Soon we arrive at booth twenty-five, and I introduce Joe to the Huerta family: don Efrain, Rogelio and Mauricio, their three sons and my nephew Uberto. Even doña Fausta is here tonight, and I'm careful to give her a special introduction: "This is the twins' grandmother," I say. "Little Margarita is also named for her." I can see doña Fausta puff up with pride. I save my brother for last. "And this is Hub," I say to Joe. To Hub, I add, "Without Joe, finding you might not have happened." With a tide of people following behind, it's impossible to linger at the booth, so our hellos are hasty and incomplete. But we do comment on the griffin, the winged horse, the dragon, the centaur, all minutely detailed and in startling contrast to the more common manger animals. We remark about the sweet baby Jesus, his body a blush of pink, his swaddling clothes in red; we note how contentedly he lies while surrounded by such a bizarre menagerie. The crowd pushes us on, but as before, Joe and I wish them all buena suerte, good luck.

"That's my new family," I say to Joe, looking back over my shoulder at them. Doña Fausta had voiced the thought earlier: Ya sómos familia. Until now, I hadn't grasped the importance of this, but tonight, under Oaxaca's big sky, I'm struck by the magnitude of my blessing: It's no longer just me and Sam and the kids. I have a new, extended family. I have a brother once again, and a sister-in-law. I have a pair of nephews, and little Maggie, too. As for Sam, he, too, can now claim them for his own, a compensation for his being an only child with parents long gone.

"Now you're like me," Joe says. "Now you're part Mexicana."

I slip my arm through Joe's and give his arm a squeeze. "Just think, that would make me a Minnesota Mexican." I chuckle. "That's a wild combination."

We stroll around the square waiting for the award ceremony to start. We stop at the atole booth and watch a woman throw a pottery bowl over her head and hear it smash on the paving behind her. "What in the world?" I say, and Joe explains the custom: Atole is a kind of corn drink. After you finish it, you toss the bowl over your head; it's so you'll have good luck. Judging from the piles of shards lying on the sidewalk, lots of good luck is being handed out. I consider trying my hand at this, but the line is so long, I'm dissuaded.

We go on, around the square again, then through the garden, and soon it's time for the prize ceremony. It's taking place in the patio of the town hall, an impressive stone building with grand interior arches and balconies. We sit halfway back, but in full view of the dais, a long table covered in green felt with a banner reading "1999 Noche de Rábanos, Ceremónia de Premiación" pinned to the skirt. The patio fills up quickly, and the balconies are soon jammed, too. I have not seen Hub or the Huertas since we visited their booth, and I wish now that I had invited Hub to join us afterward for a drink. In any case, Hub and I will visit tomorrow. We'll meet at the hospital, and then Hub will take me home for lunch. It will be just the two of us. I've decided to stay past Christmas, whether Sam and the kids come or not, a decision I made tonight, as Joe and I were strolling. The truth is I'm falling under a Mexican spell and I don't want to go home. Not for the time being, I don't.

A hush comes over the crowd as the city officials take their places at the table. "That's the mayor," Joe says, pointing to the small, round man in the middle. The mayor welcomes the crowd, then relates the history of the radish contest. I understand only bits and pieces, but I've read up on the tradition, so it's not hard to get the gist. It all began ninety-nine years ago. (I lean over to Joe and whisper in his ear for verification, and he nods that it is so.) The first radishes were carved by accident. Some farmer planted his radish crop in sandy soil and his radishes grew into long, distorted shapes that were inedible. So being a resourceful fellow and a wood-carver as well, he carved the radishes. These first carvings were simple, and most of them involved phallic symbols. Símbolos fálicos. The crowd laughs and then claps. We've come a long way since then, the mayor says, or words to that effect. Tonight, we have a brilliant variety of carvings. "Una variedad brillante de rábanos." The mayor thanks all the participants for their creations. He says he wishes that every one of them could win "el premio mayor," the big prize, but at least, he says, thanks to the municipal government, every participant will be fifty pesos richer after tonight. I make a quick calculation and find the amount to be five dollars and twenty-five cents.

The crowd starts clapping as the mayor gets ready to announce the winners. When he lifts his hands, the crowd quiets down.

"Premio número tres, premio de seis mil pesos, va a la familia Reyes y su retablo, El Vía Crucis." Prize number three, with a purse of six thousand pesos, goes to the Reyes family for their tableau of the Stations of the Cross.

The crowd cheers as the Reyes, all nine of them, come hurrying up to claim their prize.

"Premio número dos, premio de ocho mil pesos, va a la familia Santos y su retablo, Los Danzantes, The Dancers." Another round of cheering as the family comes up to collect a little over eight hundred dollars.

"Y finalmente," the mayor says, thrusting out his chest and turning up the volume on his announcement, "el premio mayor de diez mil pesos va a la familia . . ."

I'm so on edge, I reach for Joe's hand and hang on tightly.

"¡García! ¡A la familia García va el premio de diez mil pesos!"

The mayor goes on, but I stop listening. The crowd erupts into more wild applause, and I am stunned. I look at Joe. I think my lip is curling under in disappointment. "They didn't win," I say.

Joe shakes his head. "No," he says, "they didn't win."

I think about don Efrain and how sure he was of placing first. I think of how hard the family worked carving their bestiary, but then I think of the two miracles that will more than make up for the lost prize. Little Maggie and little Luis. And, as a bonus, Hub's windfall inheritance.

 After the ceremony, Joe and I find a table at the Portal de las Flores, next to the one where the man with the red umbrella and I had conducted business. Can it be that only eight days have passed since then? Time, place and circumstance have worked a kind of magic on me, and I find myself feeling reborn and vibrant. My life in Hopkins, Minnesota, my life with Sam and Jack and Will, seems now to belong to somebody else. At this moment, I'm here, with Joe Cruz, in a place thronging with Oaxacans and tourists, every man, woman and child under the spell of Christmas, the radish displays and the nearing millennium, all three celebrations rolled into one grand and perpetual fiesta. I ask myself, Is it permissible for a woman to sometimes want to belong entirely to herself? Is it permissible for a woman to surrender to a moment so set apart from everything she's known? My head pulls me in one direction, my body in another. My reason says, Watch yourself, Annie Rush, you're a wife and a mother, while my heart, my every

nerve says, Annie Rush, what you are, first of all, is a woman. I think of doña Clarita, who swept me clean with a rosemary branch, who jumped over me three times, and I feel myself wanting—no, needing—to fall into, to finally claim, my own womanly self.

We order margaritas. I want one in honor of Margarita Fausta. Joe chuckles when I mention it.

"I don't think I've ever been in a place where so many people are having so much fun," I say. "It must be like Mardi Gras, or the carnival in Brazil, but I've never been to those."

Our drinks arrive and the waitress sets them down, along with a bowl of peanuts. "Salud," I say to Joe, raising my glass to his. "To your health."

"May all your dreams come true, Annie Rush," Joe says.

We clink our glasses together. "They already have, Joe Cruz," I say.

"That's right. You found your brother, and now there's another Maggie. That's pretty amazing."

"I still can't believe it." My drink is tart and icy cold. I lick the salt from my lips with the tip of my tongue.

"So, did you find out if your family's coming down?"

"I still don't know. I checked my e-mail before we left, but no messages." I take another sip of my drink. "Maybe it's ridiculous to think they can make reservations at the very last minute. It's the holidays, after all."

"That might hold true for Christmas Eve, but for Christmas Day, I bet there's seats available."

I tilt a handful of peanuts into my mouth and lick their coating off my fingers. Soon, my mouth is on fire. "Whoa! Those things are hot!" I quickly take a gulp of margarita.

"Well, of course! That's chile powder on them."

I fan my open mouth. Take another big sip of my drink. "Boy, that was stupid." My eyes start to water and I lift a hand to them, but Joe stops me. "Don't get chile in your eyes! And stop chugging that drink! You'll get smashed."

I wipe my hands on my cocktail napkin. Then I use Joe's. "You're right." Already, there's that warm glow, that delicious percolation. "You know what, I think I'll get a Coke. Forget this margarita." I lift a hand for the waitress, who comes and takes my order. When she arrives with the Coke, I drink it down so fast, I have to hold a hand to my mouth in order to stifle a burp.

When Joe finishes his drink, we continue strolling around the square, my arm through his. We watch the radish carvers packing up. Hub's and the Huertas' spot is empty now. Live music starts up. A trio of guitarists serenade a couple at one of the tables set out on the side-walk. Joe and I stop to listen. They are playing a bolero, one of those mournful Latin songs filled with close harmonies that recount stories of love found and lost. A few couples are dancing to the music. On impulse, I lower Joe's arm and place his hand to the small of my back. "Let's dance," I say, and I give a half turn, and we are dancing. Dancing in the street. We dance slowly, more of a rocking back-and-forth motion than anything else. I feel the span of Joe's hand against my waist. I feel his chest pressed to mine. His warm hand wrapped around mine. When the song ends, we pull back, hold each other's gaze.

"Do you think we need some coffee?" I say.

"I can make some at the house. How's that?"

"Vámos."

We walk slowly up the hill. Halfway to the house, Joe takes my hand. I don't let go of him.

 Joe has fired up the Krups. We're sitting on his patio, some sad, sweet music coming from the player. "This has been the very best day," I say. Joe does not reply. He sits there, in the semidarkness, and I can feel his eyes on me. I can feel the lightness of his gaze falling on my face, my arms, my breasts. Before coming to Mexico, had this situation presented itself, I would've immediately stood, all businesslike, and pulled the plug from the outlet. But not tonight. Tonight, I'm surrendering to the situation, my pulse speeding up, my blood rushing in my head. It's late and the night is soft and it whispers to me.

I slip out of my chair, a slow, silky move. I've taken off my shoes and the patio tiles are faintly damp as I cross over to Joe and hunch down before him. "Joe," I say, and he lowers his head, cups my face in his hands, holds my face as if it's something precious.

"Oh, Joe." Again his name, but now against his mouth. I part his lips, shyly, with my tongue and soon we're kissing deeply, eagerly. We nibble on each other's tongues, lips, the world spinning.

"Let's dance," I say, and I'm pulling Joe up. We sway, sway in place to the sensuous music, our arms around each other's necks, my forehead set against his. As if it's the most natural thing, we slowly find our way through his door to the bed, where we lay ourselves down, one facing the other.

"What are we doing?" Joe whispers and I hush him, a moan of need and want burbling in my throat. I lay my mouth on Joe's cheeks, search for his lips. Joe wraps himself around me. He kisses me with the same yearning. His hands fumble with my blouse, and I quickly stand, undo the buttons and pull it off, unhook my bra, let them both drop. Joe has taken off his shirt, and now he stands beside me as we finish undressing. Looking into each other's eyes, we lie back down together. The night air comes through the open door, caressing our skin. "You're beautiful, Annie," Joe murmurs. "Oh," I whisper, straddling him, lowering myself gently upon him.

"Oh, sweetness," he says, and he reaches up to meet me, draws his tongue across my collarbone, across the dip in my throat, until my nipple fills his mouth. He pulls and tugs at me, his mouth, his teeth, his tongue, electric and vibrating. I'm on fire. He is thick and hard as my hips glide against him. Slowly, faster, and then, as suddenly as we began, I let out a small cry and it is over. Joe falls back. I collapse upon him, and we hold each other tight. Soon, we are lying side by side, our breathing slowing. There is a blanket at the foot of the bed, and I reach down and pull it over us. Joe has an arm thrown over his face. I can just make him out in the scant light coming in from the patio. I lie back down beside him, closing my eyes to everything beyond this place, this moment.

Sometime later, Joe stirs. He says, "You're so kind, Annie, and I'm grateful."

"I think that tonight we both needed that kind of tenderness."

Joe turns on his side, so that we lie face-to-face. "Do you think you can stand one more confession?" he asks.

"What?"

"Since Grace died, I haven't . . ." He stops, his voice catching.

I lay my lips on his forehead. "It's okay," I say, and I make a promise to myself. I promise to feel no guilt for allowing my own sweet body the lead tonight.

In spite of what I promised myself, I feel the guilt the moment I snap awake. The clock on my bed stand shows it's almost time for the breakfast bell, so I swing to the floor. I take a long, hot shower, letting the water pound my head and shoulders. I need to talk to Joe. I need to tell him . . . Tell him what?

I've finished showering and have dressed and I'm at the bathroom mirror, putting on my lipstick, when there's a rap on the door. "¿Sí?"

"Annie, it's me. Joe."

In the mirror, I think I see the blush blooming on my cheeks. I call out, "I'll be right there," trying to keep my voice steady, normal. I go to the door and Joe steps back as I swing wide the screen. When I'm on the veranda, next to him, I say, "About last night . . ."

Before I can go on, Joe says, "Look, the worst thing in the world would be for you to add last night to your list of things you think you need forgiveness for. You know what I mean?"

I nod, but add, "I think I'm a little ashamed of myself."

"Shame? That's heavy."

"I know."

"You know what? There's a quote I like. It's by Marcus Aurelius. It says, 'Remember the first rule: Keep an untroubled spirit.' "

"Keep an untroubled spirit. Is there a second rule?"

"Yes. It's 'Look things in the face and see them for what they are.' "

"Oh." It dawns on me what Joe is trying to tell me. "And last night . . ."

"Last night was just last night."

"Okay."

"Come on. Let's grab some breakfast."

We both eat, and periodically I look over at Joe, thinking of Sam, but Sam seems so far away. In fact, the Annie I am with Sam seems equally distant. I think that perhaps the Annie of last night was a different me than the Annie-the-best-daughter, Annie-the-guilty-survivor, Annie-the-perfect-person, Annie-the-perfect-wife. It is this thought that gives me comfort, that thanks to Joe Cruz and my own eager will, I have begun a transformation. That no matter what I've done, I can forgive myself and move on.

Ginny Powers walks in for breakfast; as usual she is her sparkling self. "There you are," she says, coming up to Joe and me. I look to see who she's talking to, then she says to me, "I just opened my e-mail. There's a message from your husband. It looks like he and your boys are coming to Oaxaca."

"What?"

"Tomorrow, on Christmas Day. They'll be coming in on the seven P.M. flight."

"Oh, my goodness." I look at Joe. At his face and how he's working hard not to look too disappointed.

"I'm so happy for you, Annie," he says.

"Yes," I say. "It's great, isn't it?"

After breakfast, I return to my room and take out my laptop and open the e-mail and there's Sam's message:

> Dear Annie, Your wish is my command. The kids and I are coming to Oaxaca to meet the family and see the babies! We'll be there on Christmas Day. At seven p.m. I know that's late, but these were the first and only reservations I could get. The kids and I are picking up some gifts at Target and Dayton's and Creative Kid Stuff. We'll bring them. We'll wait to open our own gifts to each other when we're all back home. I'll bring some cash, too. You might need it for your brother. I can't wait to see you. It's been too long since I held you in my arms. Love, Sam. P.S. I'm sending a second e-mail to Ginny Powers, so that she knows we'll be there. P.S.S. I found the wrapped presents for Milly. I'll take them over before we go.

I write an e-mail back: "Dear Sam. I'm so happy you all are coming. I can't wait to see you. Please hurry. Annie. P.S. If you get this in time, bring some cans of Spam for Hub." I pause. Take a breath. Realize how much I mean these words.

I click on the Send bar, and off the message goes, along with my heart.

 "Okay," Hub says to me. "Explain this one thing. When you said Ma left me the house, you meant she left me half of it, right?" We're sitting at Hub's kitchen table, having lunch. He's fixed chicken quesadillas, guacamole and pico de gallo salsa. We're drinking freshly squeezed limeade made with sparkling water. It's only the two of us today. Even Popeye is away. "Ma left both of us the house, right?"

I pour myself more limonada. Take a long drink. Set the glass down before I respond. "No, Hub. She left you *all* the house. All that's in it, too. And by the way, your room, Ma never touched it. It's still the same since the day you left."

"You got to be kidding."

"No. Your desk where you carved your initials, your bed, the spread with the bucking broncos. Your books, the pennants on the wall. Two paintings. One of the pond and one of the barn. All of it, still there."

"Holy God, I can't believe it. Maybe Ma missed me after all." Hub appears to turn inward for a moment, then he adds, "But how can it be that Ma left me all the house? What about you?"

"She left me everything else."

"But what else did Ma have besides the house and all her stuff? Life insurance. Is that it?"

"Yes, that. Also her investments." I know what comes next. I will tell my brother the extent of my inheritance and he will learn the vast discrepancy between his share and mine. He will be angry and resentful and jealous. One small part of me wants to scream the figure out, tell him it's only right that my loyalty and devotion should be so richly rewarded. But most of me feels guilty to be so clearly favored. Guilt. Try as I might, guilt is never far away. In my skirt pocket is doña Clarita's whole nutmeg seed. I pat the seed for courage.

"Ma had investments?"

"Yes. Look, what I'm going to tell you is what I found out after Ma died, when I was going through her papers. Turns out Ma was quite an investor. You'd never know it, of course. All those years and she never said a thing. And remember what I told you, Sam's a financial officer at an investment firm, but she never asked him for advice. Never. She just quietly bought Microsoft stock when it was low and kept buying it. Then the stock split, doubled, tripled. And, as they say, 'the rest is history.' "

"Microsoft? That's the Bill Gates stock, right?"

I nod. Cut to the chase. "Ma left me almost a million dollars, Hub." There. The news is out and I feel better for having said it.

"Holy shit!"

"Holy shit, indeed."

Hub pushes his chair back and it makes a scraping noise. He lifts his hands and lowers his head into them. For a long, long moment, he says nothing. Obviously, he's stunned. "You know what?" he says when he finally raises his head and looks at me. "I am so relieved." He draws the words out, like a sigh.

Now it's my turn to be incredulous. "You're relieved?"

"Yes. When you told me Ma had left me the house and all its contents, I couldn't believe it. I couldn't believe that Ma would leave me anything. She and I, Annie, she and I just didn't . . . it doesn't matter. The point is, you said she'd left me the house and told me what it was worth. Maybe three hundred thousand, you said. Since hearing it, that figure's swirled around and around in my head. I kept thinking I'd misheard you. I kept thinking whatever it was she left me, that's money I don't deserve. So when you said the house was mine, I assumed that was all she had to give, and that for some perverse reason, she'd left you with nothing. If that was true, there was no way I could accept it. I planned to take only what covered Luli's hospital stay. I planned to give you the rest."

"Oh, Hub."

"It's only right. I know Ma started it all. She threw me out, but I should've come back."

"Maybe you should've, but you didn't. And maybe Ma felt guilty for what she'd done. Maybe her leaving you the house was her way of making up. She threw you out of the house, now the house is yours. How's that for an ironic twist?"

Hub shakes his head. "Three hundred thousand, whatever thousand, you know what it means? To me, to Luli, to Luli's family? It means the world, Annie. Money like that sure takes the sting out of not winning a cent with the radishes this year."

"I'm happy for you, Hub." And I am. Hub has suffered his own kind of grief. Mine *with* Ma. His *without* her. In the end, it's all the same, grief being grief and not an avocado.

"You know what? You can take your time deciding what to do. You can sell the house, pay the taxes, then invest the rest, or maybe just hold on to the house and rent it out. The house is free and clear, but you'll have to pay the property taxes and the upkeep. We can find someone to manage all that for you. There are firms that handle that kind of thing. In any case, you have options."

"These days, what do you think a house like Ma's would bring in monthly rent?"

"Oh, I don't know. That's Uptown, so it's pretty trendy now. Maybe two thousand? Maybe more if you rent it furnished."

"God, Annie, that's a fortune down here."

"I know." We go on to finish our meal, continuing our conversation but turning it to less earthshaking matters. Hub tells me about meeting Luli. They were both working in San Diego: She was a housekeeper for a huge home in one of the ritzier suburbs, and he spent a month there, doing faux painting. Walls, stencils, murals, even text in some rooms. Each day he had a chance to study the dark-eyed housekeeper. After a month, he was in love. I talk about Sam. How we met at the university; he a business major, me in educational psychology. How we both were great library users. I tell Hub that every time I'd come into the reading room, my eyes would sweep the place for the guy who looked like De Niro. "A young De Niro, that is."

"That good, huh?" Hub asks.

"That good." I smile. Talking about Sam, bringing him so to mind, makes me realize how much I miss him. "I can't wait for tomorrow. I can hardly believe they'll all be here."

"Tomorrow Luli and the twins come home. Two days ago there were only three of us in this little house, now it'll be five. Pretty amazing, when you think of it."

"Well, maybe now you can build a bigger house."

"Wouldn't that be something," Hub says. "I know one of the first things I'm going to do. I'm going to see to it that Luli's father has his eyes fixed. He needs cataract surgery. Not too long ago, he almost sliced a finger off. We can't have that. A wood-carver with cataracts."

 After we finish lunch, Hub gives me a tour of his paintings. We start in the kitchen. As if in a gallery, we stand before each painting and he tells me its story. I notice there are birds in a number of his works. Big black birds. Birds poking their iridescent heads through the leaves of trees, their ebony eyes gleaming. Birds on roofs. Birds pecking at shiny objects on the ground. There's one stunning painting of a girl wearing a long, loose robe, one of those colorful serapes. She stands in mid-canvas, her head bowed, her arms lifted gracefully straight out from her sides. A wreath of marigolds rings her thick, dark hair. Five blackbirds perch along her arms, as if on telephone wires. "I love this painting," I say to Hub. There's an intensity to the colors and in the images that moves me. "She reminds me of Christ crucified. That marigold wreath, it's like the crown of thorns."

"Yes, that was the point."

"Why the blackbirds?"

"Those are ravens. As you can see, I have a thing for them. Ravens are very mythic birds. They mean a lot of things, depending on who you ask. For me, they have a lot to do with birth and death. With magic and rebirth. They're spooky to some people, but they fascinate me."

I study the painting and note that each bird is looking in a different direction. I ask Hub about this.

"I mean to show the four directions. You know, north, east, south and west. In mysticism, each direction represents something special."

"Like what?"

"Well, north is for the mind; east, the spirit; south, the emotions; and west, the body."

"But you've painted five birds. What's the fifth direction?"

"Ah," Hub says, his eyes lighting up with energy. "That's a personal thing. Everyone has to create their own personal direction."

"I love what you've done. I'm touched by the girl's stance, the way she piously bends her head."

"She's resigned," Hub says. "She's resigned to being her own cross."

There's something in me that understands what's represented here. "That's heavy, Hub. But you know what? I get it. I do."

We continue into the living room and walk around its perimeter, and soon we stand before the painting hanging above the sofa. I lay a hand on the nutmeg again. I've had to steel myself for this painting, and when I see the field, the trees, the tractor, I drop down onto the cushions. "I can't take looking at that painting."

Hub sits down beside me, taking my hand. "When Luli and I moved to Mexico, that was the first painting I did, even before the cactus hedge. I'd been carrying that image around with me for so long, I just had to get it down. It's one of the only paintings I've titled."

"It's titled?"

"Yeah. I wrote the title in the left lower corner. It's written small, but it's there."

"What does it say?" I want to stand up and look, but I can't.

"It says, 'oh, steady and perpetual serenity.' "

"That's the title?"

"It's from a quote. Something someone said ages ago. I found it in *Bartlett's Quotations.*"

"But why serenity? What that painting represents is anything but." I can't keep myself from standing, from facing the painting, from really, really looking at it. I see Hub's title, his writing in ocher, like a tiny rutted road. Also his name, Hubert Henry Hart.

"There's nothing *but* serenity in that painting, Annie. It's why I painted it. To reclaim serenity where chaos had been."

I stare at the painting. Taking it in. There is the rich dark earth, turned up and ready for seed. There is the feathery line of trees. A calm, impassive buttress over which a bright blue sky is spread. There is the blurred green tractor as it proceeds, riderless, across the land. In the top left corner, blackbirds, like kites, skitter lazily in the breeze.

Hub says, "You see? There's no chaos there. No tragedy."

"I see that now, but it's just that . . ." I sit back down, beside Hub.

"It's that you're carrying the chaos with you. You're overlaying present serenity with the old tragedy of the past." Hub reaches an arm around my shoulders. "I'm sorry I sound so preachy. It's the painter in me, we see symbols and meaning in everything. I can get tedious, I know."

"No, it's not that, it's just that that old tragedy is still real for me, Hub. For all these years, I haven't been able to put it to rest. It's because I feel responsible. It was all my fault that day. My fault when Pa killed himself . . ."

"What are you talking about? You think Pa's suicide was *your* fault? How in the world do you figure that?"

I look at Hub, at his brown eyes, the pale pale lashes. "Well, if I hadn't forced Maggie to ride on the tractor, Maggie would be alive. If Maggie were alive, Pa wouldn't have killed himself. See? It's as simple as that."

Hub's mouth opens and his jaw actually drops. "Is that what you think?"

"What?"

"That you forced Maggie to ride on the tractor?"

"Yes, I did. She was on her bed, content with doing her beadwork. An Indian initial bracelet, as I remember. She was finishing up the initials. She was so eager to wear it and here I come, all bossy and threatening. I told her that if she didn't come along with me on the tractor, I'd tell Ma she'd broken her vase. It was that tall green one, with the scalloped edges that Ma liked to put her peonies in. Maggie broke it and she glued it back together, hoping that when Ma used it, she wouldn't notice, and that worse, it wouldn't leak." The memories come fresh like they often do. It's as if I'm living the old tragedy again.

Hub stares at me for a long moment, then he unfolds himself from the couch. "Let me show you something," he says. And he goes out of the room. Soon he's back beside me. He sets an envelope on my lap. "Open it," he says.

I do as my brother says. Inside, there is something long and slender wrapped in tissue paper. Sky blue tissue paper. I lift it out. Fold back each corner.

"I've had it for all these years," Hub says. "I always meant to give it to you. That's why it's all wrapped up."

It's an Indian bracelet lying there. Green and yellow beads. The thread they're strung on is not taut, so that, here and there, the beads slip to and fro.

"That's the back side," Hub says. "Look at the front."

I turn the bracelet over. AMH. My initials, spelled with black beads.

I look up at Hub, a question in my eyes.

"That's your bracelet, Annie. It was you who was making it that day. Remember? I was in my room, sick with a sore throat. I heard everything."

"No." In my head, the scene comes alive again.

You put that bracelet down. I want to ride the tractor and you're going with me.

No, I'm not. I told you I'm not.

Yes you are. If you don't go, I'll tell Ma what you did to her vase.

You better not.

I most certainly will.

Hub shouting, *You both get on out of here. How can a sore throat get any rest with the likes of you two bickering?*

I take my brother's hand and give it a shake as if to knock some sense in him. "Hub! Do you realize what you're saying?"

"I sure do. I'm saying it was Maggie who pushed *you, she* who coerced you into riding on the tractor."

The revelation stupefies me into muteness. How can this be true? For most of my life I've built a very tall house of cards based on the belief that it was because of me that Maggie died. Because of me that Pa went on to kill himself. Now Hub's disclosure threatens to topple what I've so carefully built up. "But that's not how it was," I finally say. "I don't remember it like that at all."

"Maybe you don't, but I'm telling you the truth. Maggie bossed you into getting on the tractor. I swear to God, Annie, Maggie was like that. She was always bossing you around. She bossed everyone around."

"That can't be."

"Look, remember what I told you about the cigar box? That it was Maggie, not you who took it? You had that wrong, too."

"I'm confused."

"It's true. Maggie pulled that box out from under my bed. Mind you, I didn't see her do it, but I know it was her. I do, because she stole my sea horse before putting the box back. When I opened the box myself, the sea horse was gone. And you want to know *why* Maggie stole it?"

"Why?"

"Because I snitched her diary key, that's why."

"No! That was *my* diary key, Hub." I feel sick to my stomach.

"Annie, listen to me. You've got everything backward."

My head is a kaleidoscope in which objects float up and melt away: a tree house, a backpack, the cigar box, the sea horse, the diary key. "That little key wasn't mine?"

"No, it wasn't. But that bracelet is."

"Are you sure, Hub? Are you really sure?" How I wish that Ma were alive. That I could ask her about all these things.

"I'm positive." Hub lifts a hand, like an Eagle Scout. "I swear it, Annie."

"I can't believe it." I fall back against the sofa cushions. "All these years, I've had everything wrong. But why would I do that? Why would I turn things around like that?"

"I'm no therapist, but it seems to me that trauma can cause a person to think all sorts of things. It had you thinking you'd done things Maggie had done. It had you thinking you caused her death, and Pa's, too. But that's just plain wrong."

The kaleidoscope in my head abruptly presents me with a clear, uncomplicated picture: me at the mirror looking in the glass and seeing Maggie there. I sit straight up. I think I'm starting to understand.

"What's wrong?" Hub asks. "Why are you looking like that?"

"Remember when Maggie and I used to play the mirror game? 'I am Maggie,' I'd say. 'I am Annie,' Maggie'd echo back. 'We are we forever.' " I'm silent for a moment, remembering. "After Maggie died, I pitched a tent and lived in it. Remember that?"

"You bet I do. That was my tent you pitched under the tree house. I think you lived in it all summer. You also whacked off your hair. You looked pretty pathetic that summer. 'Course we were all pretty pathetic."

"You know why I did that? Why I lived in the tent? Why I cut off my hair?"

"Why?"

"Because there were no mirrors in the tent, that's why. I didn't want any mirrors, because if I looked in them, I'd see Maggie. That's why I whacked my hair off. To look different from her."

"I don't get it."

"I know, it's complicated. But I think it has something to do with my trying to protect myself. Looking in the mirror and seeing Maggie was just too painful, so I figured out a way to avoid it. Of course, I couldn't live in a tent forever. Sooner or later I had to go back into the house. Back to where the mirrors were. To this day, I never willingly look in them, you know. When I use them, I do what I have to do in a flash. It's beginning to dawn on me how hard that must have been for Ma. Every time she looked at me, she must have seen Maggie. Did you ever feel like that?"

"No, I didn't, but when you put it like you do, I can see your reason for it. But what about you getting things backward? What's that about?"

"Maybe it's about guilt and remorse, the twin emotions of my life. Anger, too, of course, but I keep that pretty much suppressed. Maybe I took on some of Maggie's characteristics in order to keep her alive. Sounds a little woowoo, doesn't it? And it's confusing, because on the one hand, I push her away by not looking in the mirror; on the other hand, I make her up inside myself so she won't be lost." I shake my head. "Even with a degree in psychology, I can't quite get my head around that one."

"Well, I hope you'll stop thinking you were responsible for Maggie's and Pa's deaths. You need to climb down from that cross you've nailed yourself to."

 Hub drops me off at the casa before going on to the hospital to spend Christmas Eve with his family. I've turned down his invitation to join them, because I need some time on my own to think about all the astonishing things Hub and I talked about. Tomorrow, when Luli and the twins leave the hospital, I expect I'll be more sociable. In the morning, I'll meet Hub there. I'll settle the bill, and then hold little Maggie as she takes her first ride home. Maybe I can lend a hand at the house when family and friends drop in on the twins' first Christmas Day.

This is a Christmas of firsts for me as well: the first without snow. First Christmas morning in years I won't wake up to Jack and Will clamoring for Sam and me to "Get up, get up! Santa's been downstairs!" And it's the first Christmas in twenty years I'll share with my brother. While it's true that Sam and the boys won't be getting in until Christmas night, it still will be Christmas, no matter how late.

Don Gustavo swings open the casa door. "Buenas, Señora." He greets me in his usual cheery way. He asks about the babies as I step into the reception area. I give him a quick report, before heading over to Joe's. I have so much to tell him.

I bounce over the springy grass, and pass through the opening in the jasmine hedge. I have a smile on my face. Joe will be on his patio, relaxing in his lounge chair under the trees, some cool CD on the player.

But this is not the way it is.

What I see is perplexing. Joe's door is closed, not a particularly surprising thing. He could be taking a nap, or a shower, and have closed his door for privacy. But his table. The charmingly dilapidated one that sits under the window. The table holding the CD player and disks, the Krups machine, the cups and saucers, the wine bottles and the blue-rimmed glasses. This table is stripped of all Joe's possessions.

"Joe?" I call, as I step onto the patio. I rap on his door. "Joe?" No answer.

I turn the doorknob and find the door unlocked. I slowly push the door open and poke my head in. The bed is neatly made, the room devoid of any signs of occupation: no books on the nightstand, no personal items on the dresser, no clothing lying over the backs of chairs. I go in and take a look in the bathroom. No damp towels on the racks. No toothbrush in the holder. I go back into the bedroom and open the closet door. A line of empty hangers rests on the rod. "Joe?" I say to the room. "Where have you gone?" A lump forms in my throat. Feeling suddenly bereft, I leave the room and close the door behind me. I cross back over the grass and find don Gustavo. I ask about Joe.

"El Señor se fué."

"He left?"

"Sí. Después de la comida."

Joe left after lunch. While Hub and I were having ours, Joe was packing up.

I ask if Joe is planning to return.

"Pues, no parece. El Señor pagó su cuenta y se fué."

Joe has paid his bill. He's gone. I smile weakly, hearing that it doesn't look like he'll be back again. I thank don Gustavo and head for my room. I open the door and step in. I see the envelope, white as milk, lying on the floor, directly in my way. The lump in my throat grows larger.

I sit on the bed, the envelope in my hand for a very long time. When I feel ready, I open it up. There are two pages.

Christmas Eve 1999 Oaxaca

Sweet Annie,

I hope you can forgive me for not saying good-bye. I'm off to Zipolite Beach. I'll spend Christmas there and welcome in the new millennium on Gloria's strip of sand. I hope you see that, all around, it's best that I leave. You have been an angel since the first time I saw you, coming around that jasmine hedge so late one night. I thank you for what you've given me. Thanks to you and your generous and open ways, I've been able to think about my own tragedies and grief, and I think I've turned a corner. Please know that I'll always carry you in a corner of my heart.

I leave you and your husband my room, that way your children can have yours. I've already talked to Ginny about this.

Maybe you didn't know, but there was no more room at the
inn, given it's the holidays. But that's not the reason I'm leav-
ing, to provide you with a room. I'm leaving, because it's sim-
ply time to go. I know you understand.

I'm attaching a copy of Mary Oliver's poem "Wild Geese." I
recited the start of it that one night, remember? Well, here's the
whole thing. Her words have meant so much to me. I hope
you'll feel the same.

Un fuerte abrazo,
Joe

Oh, Joe, I say, the tears streaming down my cheeks. I hug you back
as fiercely. I do understand. I understand that you were an angel in my
life as well. I understand that meeting you turned my life around. And
I also understand I'll never see you again. More than anything else, I
understand this.

I turn to the second page of Joe's letter. I read Mary Oliver's poem.
It is a gift.

WILD GEESE

You do not have to be good.
You do not have to walk on your knees
for a hundred miles through the desert, repenting.
You only have to let the soft animal of your body
*   love what it loves.*
Tell me about despair, yours, and I will tell you mine.
Meanwhile the world goes on.

Meanwhile the sun and the clear pebbles of the rain
are moving across the landscapes,
over the prairies and the deep trees,
the mountains and the rivers.
Meanwhile the wild geese, high in the clean blue air,
are heading home again.
Whoever you are, no matter how lonely,
the world offers itself to your imagination,
calls to you like the wild geese, harsh and exciting—
over and over announcing your place
in the family of things.

 I fall back against the pillows propped along the head-board. I long for a shoulder to cry on, for a hand to lift me up. I roll on my side, pull a pillow down and fold myself around it. I want Sam. Now, now, I want him now. My eyes fall on Ma's notebook, lying all these days untouched on the nightstand. I reach for it, but the anger I feel at her cruel disregard makes me hesitate. But then I think of the poem, of the wild geese calling, and I set Joe's note aside and prop myself against the headboard again and take up the notebook and start to read. I read as daylight leaks from the room. I switch on the lamp and turn page after page, my eyes soaking up every one of Ma's words. As I read her story, love and despair, pity and hate, anger and compassion collide and then converge inside me. The supper bell clangs, but I ignore it and read on. When I reach the last page, I find this there:

Well, I guess this is all I have to say. I hope I have the grit to leave this for Annie. I hope I dont just tear it up. Its what I want to do.

Tear it up and burn it in the fireplace. If I do leave it I want Annie to know the way it was. If she ever finds Hub I want him to know too. I want both of them to know how much I loved them even though my broken heart kept me all closed and clamed up. I know I was a hard customer. I did some things Im not proud of and I pray for forgiveness. Every person deserves a little of that, especially when its the end. Theres only one thing I can say thats good about this dying. Ill be seeing Maggie soon. I picture her up there waiting for me. I picture her arm stretched out to welcome me. Its what I hope and pray for anyway. I loved those girls. The two so identical, but so different in there ways. Maggie a niagara falls Annie a lake placid. Maggie bossy Annie meek. Maggie yelling you get over here right now! stamping her feet and going all red in the face. Annie saying okay okay Im coming. Never one to get all flustered. Oh boy the thought of them together makes my heart ache.

I gasp, looking up from the page. I can't believe it. There, in Ma's own hand, is confirmation of what Hub has been telling me. It's really, really true. It wasn't me who forced Maggie to ride that day. It wasn't me. It wasn't me. The significance of this is almost too huge to understand, so I turn back to Ma's notebook and read on.

The thought of my boy breaks my heart to. Who knows where Hub is what he looks like now. Probably like Elmer. Its what I regret most of all that I threw him out and now Ill soon be gone and will have to wait till forever to maybe see him again. My three darlings. All year round they smelled like summer like the smell on your arm when its been out in the sun. I hope and pray that Elmers up there too. I hope and pray God has forgiven him for what he did and let him come in. God knows I forgive him. Its taken me until now to

*understand what he did. I guess he had no choice. I guess he did
what he had to do. Okay enough of this. Theres nothing more to
say. Only that I was lucky to have such a family. When I take my
last breath Ill be thinking of them.*

Ma's writing ends. Only her signature follows, the writing shaky
and weak. I close the notebook. Oh, Ma, I say to the room. I'm sorry for
you. I want to cry, but I have no more tears to express my sorrow. I
need to leave the room. I grab a shawl and switch off the lamp. I go out
of the house.

I head up the street, climbing the steep hill away from the square.
Where I'm going, I couldn't say. I'm going to where my feet take me,
surrendering again to the cosmic will of Mexico. It's Christmas Eve and
the night is velvet against my arms. Now and again, the sky lights up
with the dazzling glare of fireworks. Now and again, there are long
hisses and startling bursts. Constantly, there is the sharp smell of their
propelling powder. I walk alone, though the way teems with humanity.
I try to keep to the sidewalk, but it's easy to be nudged off. A procession
lurches rowdily by. A baby Jesus is carried down the hill, high above the
crowd. He lies in his crèche, the angle of his descent in constant need
of releveling. I dodge costumed processionists and plain-dressed revelers. All of Oaxaca seems to be outside this night. The air pulses with the
sonorous beat of drums. Flutes provide a reedy counterpoint. Like the
sound of pure sorrow, I think to myself.

Up ahead, I see a simple whitewashed church, "Capilla Pentecostal," Pentecostal Chapel. Its name is lettered above the door. Under
that, on a large plaster medallion, is painted a triangle, God's all-seeing
eye painted within that. As Ma's notebook had beckoned me, so does
the chapel. I leave the crowd and go up three shallow steps and walk
into a room of song. A song of praise, judging from the jubilant beat,

from the sight of hands swaying above heads. I slip quietly into a pew. The chapel is unlike any church I've visited before. It's no larger than the space allotted to side altars in the city's grander churches. Along the window ledges there are a few wall lamps and many candles. These provide enough light for me to note that the chapel has no altar at all, no pulpit. Its only decoration is the painting on the front wall: a robed male figure (Jesus, perhaps?), arms lifted and outstretched. Rising from his head, a red and yellow flame. It dawns on me what this signifies. Pentecost. The descent of the Holy Spirit. Of course. I'm so engrossed in my thoughts, I don't notice the young woman tugging at my sleeve. "Venga, Señorita," she whispers. Come, Miss. She points across the aisle. "Véngase al lado de las mujeres." Come to the women's side. I realize, then, I've been sitting with the men. It's only men on the left side of the chapel. All the women sit on the right. I whisper an apology in my clumsy Spanish and follow her, down the aisle and into a pew. We sit side by side.

I feel so self-conscious. I would leave, but I think it would be an insult. I'm certain everyone is aware of me and my blond hair. I, in turn, am now aware that I'm the only woman without a head covering, so I pull the shawl from my bag and lay the cloth over my head. Out of the corner of my eye, I see the woman beside me give a slight nod. Her approval calms me. I decide to concentrate on the music, on the way it rises insistently, then falls in a lament. The more I hear, the more I begin to understand that it is not Spanish being sung. I pitch a keen ear and start to make out some phrases.

Shama sila ama tila oye oye ode oye node tiki mila taka nali shama shama sila.

I think I might be hearing an indigenous dialect. After all, Oaxaca is the land of sixteen tribes, but then the truth strikes like a sparkler going off: What I'm hearing is tongues! Pentecost. The people are singing in tongues! I let the music wash over me. I feel it collect in the center of my chest. A strange kind of peace settles over me. It is Christmas Eve, like no other Christmas Eve I've ever known. I can't speak in tongues. Were the song in Spanish, I wouldn't know the words. But I can hum, and so I do. I close my eyes and hum, the vibration inside me incandescently mesmerizing.

When the singing dies away, it does so slowly, gently and with reverence. The congregation settles itself comfortably into silence. After a while, a man leaves a pew and shuffles up to the front. He turns and faces all of us. He is middle-aged, rail thin. He works his jaw as if to bring up words that might be caught in his throat. From the looks of his mouth, he appears to have few teeth.

"Hermanos," he says, "hermanas." His brothers and sisters greet him with soft amens. He begins to speak and this time it's Spanish I hear. Though the man's pronunciation is somewhat garbled, I recognize the Spanish cadence, the vowel sounds, the shifts. I understand a few words: enfermedad, fiebre, trabajo, dinero. Sickness, fever, work, money. Simple words, but weighty ones. From the pews, amens in affirmation. As the man tells his story, his shoulders slump, his mouth collapses, he wrings his hands. I understand a few more words: gracia, Jesucristo, el Espiritú. Grace, Jesus Christ, the Spirit. His fellow believers clap encouragingly. They shout out alleluias. There's a general rumble of appreciation when he heads, visibly renewed, back to his pew.

Over the next hour, the scenario repeats itself. An old woman. Two young girls, each sobbing heartbreakingly. An old man who, as he speaks, turns his hat slowly through his big, gnarled hands. Mouths open and stories come, in Spanish, in Indian dialect, in tongues. No matter what the language, stories rise from the heart and are released. The chapel air is thick with stories, it is thick with shouts of exaltation, with joyous amens and alleluias. The more I hear, the more I understand I don't need to know the words. We are saved by the mere act of telling. Doña Clarita had said this very thing to me. By emptying ourselves, we are saved. A whirlwind of deep emotion takes my breath, makes me suddenly lightheaded. I lower my head to help myself. My own story clamors to be told. I think of something else doña Clarita said: Important things must be done in threes. I have told Joe my story. And to doña Clarita, too. Now it's time for a third and final retelling. I keep my head down and begin to whisper my own story to myself.

There is a tug at my sleeve. I lift my face to the woman beside me. She smiles shyly, points with a finger at what I might do. If I wanted. If I could. Out the pew, down the aisle, up to the front. Like the others. "Vaya, vaya." Go. Go.

And I do. I do because I can't help myself.

"Brothers and sisters," I say when I face them. "I am Annie Rush. I miss my mother. Her name was Flo. She had a hard life because my sister died. Then my father died, too. My mother wrote everything down in a notebook and I just read what she wrote and I didn't know how lonely she was. I didn't know she was holding so many things inside herself. My mother smoked cigarettes and she smoked herself to death. We kept saying it was bad for her but she didn't seem to care. It was like she wanted to die and then she got her wish."

Though I speak in English, I see people nodding. I see one woman raise a hand. Give her hand a little shake.

"I forgive my mother for all she did and didn't do. She did her best with what she had, so I forgive her." I glance quickly upward. "Do you hear me, Ma? Well, I forgive you. I do, Ma." My voice has risen and it prompts some to shout out their amens.

"And I forgive you, too, Pa. I forgive you because I know the guilt you felt. I know how bad it feels to be pressed down by the guilt. But it wasn't our fault. It wasn't our fault! Accidents happen and there's nothing we can do. It wasn't my fault that Maggie got on the tractor. It wasn't your fault you hit a pipe in the field. It wasn't our fault Maggie fell off. It wasn't our fault we couldn't reach out to save her. So I forgive you, Pa. And I forgive myself, too." I raise a hand for affirmation. "I forgive myself for everything."

Tears come and I lower my hand and poke it into my skirt pocket to retrieve a tissue, but there's no tissue there, only my nutmeg seed. I give it a squeeze for added courage. I'm about to use the edge of my shawl to soak up the tears when a woman in the front pew lifts a roll of toilet paper from under her shawl and winds a goodly length of paper around her wrist, then snaps the paper off. She half rises to hand the gift to me. I thank her in Spanish and dab at my cheeks.

"And thank you, God, for my brother, Hub. Thank you for his revelations. Thank you, God, for Sam and Jack and Will. And thank you, Joe Cruz, on Zipolite Beach."

There. Rambling or not, I've run out of steam and have come to the end. "Gracias hermanos. Gracias hermanas." The congregation thanks me back with allelulias. I walk back to my pew, my eye down the aisle and on the night framed so plainly by the open chapel door. The Mexican night, now gone silent. The holy night.

I slip into the pew beside my companion. She gives my arm a little pat.

I smile, feeling released.

Christmas Eve. All is calm. All is bright.

EPILOGUE

I ask you, what is happiness, but what I'm feeling now? It has been five days since Sam and the boys arrived, and we've been going like a house afire. At the moment, there are sixteen of us on the Huerta family's porch; all of us in various stages of giddy exhaustion. We've been on our feet since morning. The babies' baptism was at eleven, in the San Antonino church, its altar decorated with pyramids and garlands of fruit growing abundantly in the village: bananas, limes, tangerines and oranges. The priest—tall and lean, and goateed like a Spanish grandee—celebrated mass and then baptized the babies. Rogelio, Luli's brother, was Luis Eugenio's godfather, and I, miracle of miracles, was Margarita Fausta's madrina, her godmother. I held her in my arms, steadying her halfway over the baptismal font, as el Padre dripped a stream of water over her sweet head. She was brave and didn't fuss, though her eyes went wide when she felt the water. As if she understood the importance of the occasion, she listened solemnly to el Padre's prayers.

My boys watched the proceedings from the second pew, alert and rapt by all the strange and wonderful new things they'd experienced since arriving. High on the list, the hot, sun-filled days, their own room at the casa, their new male cousins (they count Uberto's cousins as theirs), their uncle Hub and his paintings, don Efrain's wiggly mustache, plus his "way cool" carvings. That's Will's expression. Add to that the usual tourist pleasures, like climbing a pyramid, coming upon the mummy in the museum, and, especially, the way they've been allowed to stay up late and amble down to the zócalo with Sam and me each night. "Gol, it's practically midnight!" That's Jack's expression.

Rogelio laid Luis Eugenio in his mother's arms after the baptism, while I delivered Maggie into the arms of her grandmother. Both Luli and doña Fausta looked appropriately elegant. The grandmother in her dark satin shift with the lace collar, and Luli in her pantsuit with the easy-open, easy-close top, just the thing for a nursing mother. The babies' little bodies were lost in their long, embroidered dresses. Only their heads poked out. The dresses came with embroidered caps, but both twins cried and squirmed when Luli tried tying the caps' ribbons under their chins. So, needless to say, that was it for the caps. Luli and I found the baptism outfits at a religious store in downtown Oaxaca. They are Sam's and my gift to the babies. As will also be the photographs that Sam's been taking with his heavy, clunky Nikon. Today, Sam shot rolls and rolls of film to mark the festivities: the babies being held at the baptismal font, before the altar with the priest, under the old tree in the churchyard. And then lots of photos during the fiesta.

After the service, we all trooped over to the Huertas' house. Don Efrain and the uncles, following doña Fausta's explicit instructions, had tidied up the area around the carving shed. They'd brought out every chair from both the house and the shed, and set them in the yard, under trees festooned with tissue-paper cutouts called papel picado.

Doña Fausta had cooked for three days to prepare for the fiesta. When we arrived from church, she put on her best apron, and I, along with Uberto's aunties, helped her parade the food out of the kitchen and into the yard. There were pots of tamales, both salty and sweet. Deep ollas filled with rice and beans and plantains. Stacks and stacks of tortillas. A platter of quezo manchego, a tart, crumbly cheese. And the pièce de résistance, the yellow mole made with azafran. The Coca-Cola cooler did double duty for the fiesta. In its icy water floated bottles of Dos Equis and soda. For dessert, there was three-layer coconut cake with vanilla cream icing and roasted coconut shavings.

The family dogs feasted all day along with us, hustling from chair to chair, begging and getting handouts. Jack has fallen in love with Popeye. He's been persistently trying to convince us that Elvis needs a puppy named Popeye for a companion. In response to his pleas, Sam and I just smile at him sweetly. "You guys are sure no fun," Jack says to our obvious condescension.

Now, all the food is gone, all the partying done. Even the radio has been turned off because Luli is resting. The remainder of us are bunched on the front porch, the grown-ups in chairs, the cousins stacked up and down the porch steps. We're watching the sun set over the farthest hills, hoping that evening will bring some coolness. Hub's rocking his new son and little Maggie is lying straight-out on my lap. Sam's beside me on the bench. He's leaning over the baby, who's wrapped her tiny fingers around his thumb. Her eyelids droop, and soon she's asleep.

I'm like a newlywed since Sam arrived. Everywhere we go, I want to be next to him. Sometimes, I glance at him out of the corner of my eye. When I catch his eyes on me, my heart gives a little jump. Today, while he was taking pictures, I loved the way he bent, squatted and turned to make the shots. I loved the way he'd rolled the sleeves of his white shirt up to his elbows. I love the look of his arms. The way his arms enfold me.

"What do you think?" Sam keeps his voice low. He nods down at little Maggie. "Think you might want one of those?"

"You're kidding."

"No, I'm not. When we get home, we could start trying."

We're leaving tomorrow. We have to be at the airport at eight in the morning. If we don't run into bad weather, we should be home by seven. On New Year's Eve. On the brink of the new millennium. And a new era for me personally. I feel I've cleaned the slate, and now, who knows what's in the future.

Sam adds, "Think about it, okay?"

I'm totally nonplussed. It's not as if I'm against it. It's just that, for some reason, I thought that after Jack and Will, our family was complete. But there's no question that having another baby is entirely possible. All I have to do is go off the pill. I'm only thirty-four. With the security of Ma's inheritance, I don't really need to work. And we have plenty of space. There's even the extra room downstairs that we've been using as a storage place. We could move Jack into that and use Jack's room for a nursery . . . I shake my head, catching myself in all this planning.

"What?" Sam says.

"I can't believe it. I'm actually *thinking* about it."

"Good. It'll be fun trying." Sam gives me a little poke with an elbow. "Maybe we'll have to try and try and try."

"Wouldn't that be fun."

A while later, Luli gets up and comes out onto the porch. The radio's switched back on. As if someone's called "Time!" the babies, both awake now, are delivered into new laps. A cha-cha-cha plays on the radio and the cousins put on a show. Six boys lined up on the path at the foot of the steps. Six boys shaking their little booties. Doña Fausta stands up from her chair and regales us all with a shake of her own. We all clap her on; at our encouragement, her face lights up and she throws back her head and laughs heartily. When the merriment dies down, Hub motions for Sam and me to follow him around the corner of the house. We go into don Efrain's shed and Hub turns on the light.

"I have something for you," Hub says. "But first this." He hands me Ma's notebook. "It's the most amazing thing. I've read it once, but I'd like to again. Do you think I could keep it for now? I can bring it to Minnesota when I come." Hub will make the trip in the spring. After talking it over with Sam, he's decided to sell Ma's house and haul back to Oaxaca whatever furniture or household items he and Luli or the Huertas can use. After the sale, Sam will help Hub invest his money.

"Keep it as long as you need to," I say.

"Reading it, it was like I could hear Ma's voice."

"I know."

"But here, there's something else." Hub pulls out a long mailing tube from one of the shelves. He takes the top off the tube and pulls out a thick roll. "I painted this for you." Hub lays the roll on the table and unfurls it.

I set Ma's notebook down and hold my breath.

It's a painting of me.

That's my long blond hair with the marigold crown. Those are my green eyes. That's my round face. My chubby cheeks.

I'm in a long peach-colored robe. Above my left breast, there's a small heart pierced by an arrow. My arms are lifted and straight out from my sides. Along my arms, ravens. Four of them, their heads pointed in four directions. A fifth raven sits on my head, its shiny eyes looking out, as if peering eagerly into the future.

In the painting, I appear to be floating. Floating off the canvas. Floating away from the shadow my own floating body is leaving behind. The shadow of a cross.

The painting is titled. In the lower left corner is written, in burnt umber, like a little rutted road: "and she is freed . . ." In the right corner, "Hubert Henry Hart, Oaxaca. 1999."

"Lord," Sam says.

I lift a hand to my mouth. I try to speak, but nothing comes. I lurch over to my brother, feel him take me in his arms.

Behind me, my husband. Ready to catch me, should I fall.